THE MIDWIFE'S
IN TOWN
A Novel

Kate Jessica Raphael

author of
Murder Under the Bridge, a Palestine Mystery

Salted Rose Press
Berkeley, California

Salted Rose Press
Berkeley, California
www.saltedrosepress.com

Publisher's Note: This is a work of fiction. Names, characters, places, and incidents are a product of the author's imagination. Locales and public names are sometimes used for atmospheric purposes. Any resemblance to actual people, living or dead, or to businesses, companies, events, institutions, or locales is completely coincidental.

Publisher's Cataloging-in-Publication data

Names: Raphael, Kate Jessica, author.
Title: The midwife's in town : a novel / Kate Jessica Raphael.
Description: Berkeley, CA: Salted Rose Press, 2022.
Identifiers: LCCN: 2022900849 | ISBN: 978-0-9864263-3-9 (paperback) | 978-0-9864263-4-6 (epub) | 978-0-9864263-5-3 (Kindle)
Subjects: LCSH Abortion--Fiction. | Abortion--Law and legislation--Fiction. | Midwives--Fiction. | Nurses--Fiction. | Women's rights--Fiction. | Southern States--Fiction. | Thriller fiction. | BISAC FICTION / Thrillers / General | FICTION / Women
Classification: LCC PS3618.A7254 M87 2022 | DDC 813.6--dc23

Book Layout © 2017 BookDesignTemplates.com
Cover image Susan Greene
Cover Layout free download by https://usedtotech.com

The Midwife's In Town/ Kate Jessica Raphael . -- 1st ed.
ISBN 9780986426339

In Grateful Memory of
Patricia Maginnis
Jean Pauline
Rose May Dance
Sarah Weddington
Dr. George Tiller
Jane

Foreword

I began this novel in 2013, during National Novel Writing Month, which happens annually in November. Governor Jerry Brown had just signed a new California law enabling nurse practitioners, physician assistants and nurse midwives to perform early abortions using a procedure known as aspiration. The aspiration method is effective throughout the first trimester of pregnancy, up to about fourteen weeks since the person's last menstrual period.

This expansion of abortion access in the nation's largest state came amidst a record number of laws restricting abortion access in other parts of the country. Walking home on October 31, 2013, with no idea about what to write a novel about, I imagined a retired nurse midwife from California being recruited, at some time in the near future, to come use her abortion skills in an area of the country where abortion had become illegal, after the Supreme Court reversed *Roe v. Wade*.

I don't write science fiction, so I planted my story in a time not so distant that I would need to conceive of brand new technologies or social conditions. The year I haphazardly assigned to the world of the novel was 2021. I wanted to write about a place I knew, but not the San Francisco Bay Area or Palestine, the only places I had lived in the last thirty years. It might have been wiser to choose a fictional town in a fictional state, or even a fictional country very similar to our own, but that kind of world building is not my forte. I settled on Richmond, Virginia, where I spent my first seventeen years and where my mother still lived.

During the eight years over which I have periodically revisited this book, some things I envisioned have come eerily true, others have turned out worse than my fantasy, and a lot has happened to transform the social environment. For a while, I attempted to play catch-up but given the cases sitting on the Supreme Court's docket, I decided to release this book in early 2022, in a political moment when I feel it can have impact, and not sweat the details. If imagining masks in every scene helps you immerse yourself in the story, please do so. This story could be taking place in a few months or a few years; in many ways, it already is.

While everything about OWLS and the fictional clinic is dreamed up by me, I have learned that there are already groups much like OWLS, doing very similar things. That is not surprising, since I've spent much of my life in queer and feminist direct action movements, and I know how women and queers organize to care for ourselves and our communities.

This is not a handbook. I'm not a medical provider, though I did have some among my early readers, and I have tried to be as accurate as possible. Abortion options, especially medication options, are constantly improving and some of what is imagined here would probably not be the best way to approach a real unplanned pregnancy. So please do not read this as a "How-To" but as a "How-Might" for addressing the one fact that has not changed since 2013 or 1913 and will still be true in 4013: it is up to freedom-loving people to meet every crisis with creativity, collective strength and humor.

Enjoy the ride!

KJR December 31, 2021

CONTENTS

CHAPTER ONE

Landing

I woke with a start, and tried to figure out where I was. Weird yellow lighting, the body odor of too many people who'd been in close quarters for too long, and the fact that I couldn't move my arms clued me in. It could only be an airplane.

The flight attendants, with their shellacked bobs and Pepsodent smiles, wove up and down the aisles, offering us warm washcloths. I suppose a cup of coffee would have been redolent of the decadent 1980s. I took the terry cloth square, placed it over my nose and mouth and tried to breathe normally. If I'd flown direct from Oakland, I would have at least rated a packet of Lorna Doones, but you can't fly direct from Oakland to Richmond, Virginia. Instead I had shuffled off a plane in Atlanta at ten pm, expecting to be in Richmond by midnight. But after four hours on the tarmac with scant information, we blearily trooped off one plane and onto another, where we proceeded to wait two more hours for the guys to show up to transfer our luggage. I considered offering to go do it myself, but I'd been a union member my whole adult life. I was not going to launch my retirement by becoming a scab. So I ate the paltry snacks I'd brought for the trip—a hard-boiled egg, some trail mix and a few stale organic cheese puffs—and then tried to doze.

Instead of sleep, what came were a steady barrage of images from the bad movie I'd been living in for most of a week: me dragging my heavy wheeled suitcase into the house, stumbling over the cat, half-eaten French toast on the breakfast nook table, Jen emerging from the bathroom dripping on my prized Turkish rug, her mouth opening slowly like a flower as she stared at me, Sidney yanking the sheet up to cover one breast, as if that might make me unsee the classic scene of betrayal.

I'd called my first girlfriend, Nell. She could solve any problem, and she solved mine.

"Your timing is perfect," she said, as if being dumped while I was out of the country was a career choice. "We're starting a new project, and you're just the person we need."

She'd made all the arrangements. All I had to do was get on the plane. A Josie Miyamoto would meet me at the airport.

I hoped Josie was waiting at baggage claim with a sign reading "Mollie O'Shay." I didn't have her phone number and didn't fancy going up to every Asian woman waiting for relatives and asking if they were Josie. Though, come to think of it, the flight had gotten a lot less Asian since arriving in Atlanta.

I needn't have worried. Richmond International Airport could pass for an ice rink in San Francisco. It wouldn't have taken me long to go up to every person in the building, but I didn't need to, because the six-foot tall Asian chick with a modified shag buried in a copy of Jane Austen's *Emma* was unmissable.

And yes, she had a sign.

She didn't look up from her book until I stood in front of her with a rollaway in each hand, my combination laptop bag and granny purse pressed to my right side.

"Emma?" I said.

"No, Josie," she said, looking up. I pointed to the book.

"I'm Mollie," I said. "How do you like Emma?"

"I like it," she said. "It's not my favorite. Northanger Abbey is. But it's better than Pride."

She was already striding out the door. I huffed to keep up. "Are you in a Jane Austen book club?" I asked.

She hadn't even offered to carry one of my bags. Whatever she was getting out of her Jane Austen fixation, it wasn't etiquette lessons.

"I'm writing a dissertation," she said.

"Women's Studies?" I could have left off the question mark.

"Gender Studies," she said, stretching out the *gen.* "Austen's subversion of the binary through the introspection of subaltern consciousness."

I didn't understand a word she said. She was definitely going to get honors on her degree.

After I'd crammed my bags into the trunk of Josie's red Ford Focus, we hit the highway. I tried to soak in my first sights in the Old South, but she was going at least 80. The road was as deserted as the airport had been. I started to wonder if it was the apocalypse that had delayed my plane.

"Can we stop somewhere for breakfast?" I asked. "I need a hefty dose of protein, followed by a hot shower and a long nap."

"Sorry," she said. "You'll have to make do with a Starbucks latte and scone. You're late and the first two patients are already at the clinic. Two more are coming this afternoon."

"You scheduled them for today?" I groused. "I thought I'd have a day to settle in."

"The clock's ticking," Josie said.

That yanked me out of my self-pity party. After twenty-eight years as a nurse-midwife, I knew what a ticking clock meant. Since the Supreme Court overturned *Roe v. Wade*, the southern states had been toppling like sand castles in an earthquake. Six weeks ago, Virginia's newly Republican legislature had voted to make abortion a crime, except in a few rare circumstances. The expected court ruling staying the implementation had not come; or rather it had, but had been overturned by the court of appeals. The two existing clinics in Richmond that performed abortions had shut their doors abruptly. The patients waiting for me probably had appointments scheduled for weeks. I was their last hope for a chance to go back and make the same mistakes again.

* * *

"I had an IUD," Vanessa kept repeating, over and over.

"It isn't your fault," I said, as if it was a call and response prayer. "Contraception fails."

The exam table she lay on looked like a reclining chair. The head could be tilted up or made to lie flat, and there was a clever drop-panel that enabled me to position myself between her legs without having to use stirrups. Josie told me it cost a lot more than a normal exam table, but the group felt it would make the clients more at ease.

The kind gesture was lost on Vanessa. She was so tense, I was afraid I wouldn't get the speculum in without damaging her vaginal wall.

"I'm going to need you to relax a little," I said. "Let's take a few deep breaths. Iiiinnnn," I modeled a good, deep belly breath. She half-heartedly sucked some air through her nose, her chest barely rising.

"I want Danny," she said, half-wail, half-sulk.

"I know but he can't come here. It's for his own protection, and yours." Out of the corner of my eye I saw, or sensed, Josie nodding. That's what she had told me to say. I was not sure it was the best approach, but we'd discuss it later. Josie and the rest of her group were taking most of the risk. They had rented the office, bought the equipment, posted the ads on social media, fliers in church basements and stickers in school bathrooms, even made the medical waste connection. I owed it to them to follow their rules.

Though, of course, I was the one with my hands inside a young woman's vagina.

I cocked my head toward the iPad on the desk, and Josie fiddled with it until some vaguely New Agey music filtered out.

Vanessa's muscles softened slightly. I held out my hand and Josie passed me the slim forceps called tenaculum. Vanessa only cringed a little as I brought her cervix forward and injected the anesthetic. I gave her a couple minutes to get numb, before threading the dilators into her os. I heard rustling as Josie unwrapped the cannula. When the cervix was open enough, I inserted it and nodded to Josie, who switched on the aspirator. I had questioned the decision to go with an electric aspirator; a handheld pump would have been cheaper and quieter, but Josie said the group had agreed we needed the speed and accuracy of the electric vacuum.

I removed the cannula and cleaned Vanessa's vagina with an alcohol wipe. That simple, I thought, just like wiping my face on the airplane. That had only been a couple hours ago. It felt like much more. Vanessa's cervix was contracting properly, cutting off the blood supply. She would be right as rain before lunch time.

"We're nearly done. I'll be back in one minute," I told her.

Josie had already removed the cup containing the waste. We moved to a corner of the room to examine it.

"Have you done this before?" I asked.

She shook her head, which was a little too small for her body. Leaning forward, she resembled a question mark. Keeping my voice low, I showed her how to count tiny body parts to make sure the pregnancy had been completely removed. By the time we were satisfied that it had, Vanessa was already trying to sit up.

"Is it over?" she asked.

"Yes, it is." A mere "yes" would have sufficed, but seemed too curt. Extra words needed to mark the moment of an event her body would not remember in twenty-four hours. An event dozens of women experience every hour, the lucky and the unlucky indiscriminately. Too bad we couldn't bank unwanted miscarriages, transfer them seamlessly to women like Vanessa. I escorted her into the recovery room, festooned with a Georgia O'Keefe print and a red and yellow wedding ring quilt draped over the reclining chair. I settled Vanessa in the chair, covering her feet with the quilt (she didn't want it on her torso, said she was warm). I checked her temperature – 98.2, and asked if she wanted tea or orange juice. She chose the juice.

I brought the juice and handed her the instructions for aftercare, a small bottle of Tylenol and another with fourteen doxycycline pills and a small package of sanitary pads. I warned her not to have sex or use a tampon for two weeks.

"How long are you and Danny together?" I asked.

"Six months," she said. "Really, five and a half."

"Do you love him?"

"I don't know. I think so." Her dark blue eyes were wet.

"Are you in college?" I didn't know if I should be asking such questions. Maybe I should have as little information about our clients as possible. But I wanted Vanessa to remember who she was, why she had chosen to end her pregnancy.

"High school," she said. "I'm going to Reynolds next year." I didn't know what she meant. The Richmond FAQs I'd found online had told me that the Reynolds tin foil company was headquartered in town, but I doubted that was what she was referring to. I'd have to read up on local schools.

"What do you want to be?" I asked.

"I'm not sure – maybe a librarian?" A tear made its way out of the corner of her eye and down an alabaster cheek. Another followed rapidly, threatening a rainstorm. I squelched my panic reaction to people crying, recognizing it as nothing more than pent-up anxiety mixed with relief.

"You didn't do anything wrong," I said once more. She probably didn't remember hearing that, even though it had only been about ten minutes ago. This was Bible country. I doubted anyone in her family would agree with my assessment. Good that Vanessa liked books.

I pointed to the top of the instruction sheet, where "Dr. Mary" was written in next to a phone number. The last tenant in this office was a psychologist named Mary Jenkins. There was also an orthopedist named Mary Jenkins in town, so the group decided all its practitioners would function under that name. It was suitably nondescript and a cursory internet search, should anyone have reason to initiate one, would not raise red flags. I worried that representing myself as a doctor would add to the risk, but Josie insisted that Richmond's women wouldn't trust someone who wasn't a doctor to remove the contents of their wombs.

I said goodbye to Vanessa, after reminding her to call if she ran a fever or had excessive bleeding. How would she know what was excessive? I wondered. If women started calling us every time they spotted, I would refine my spiel. I ducked back into the makeshift operating room where Tanisha was already positioned with her legs up. I hadn't even seen who had brought her. Vanessa would be escorted out the back door, which exited into the parking lot. The direct door to the lot was a major reason the group had chosen this office. Josie had mentioned they bought a used Lexis with tinted windows so that clients would not need to be blindfolded. They didn't want to add to their tension, or risk someone witnessing what looked like a kidnapping.

Another big plus of this building was the apartment upstairs where I had only had time to drop my bags and check out the bathroom. I thought longingly of the queen-size bed which, if my spatial memory was accurate, stood directly above where I was now washing my hands with antiseptic soap.

I performed eight abortions that day, in just under six hours, with a half hour for a pesto, cheese and olive sandwich and a cup of the Mexican dark roast I'd brought back from Chiapas. By the time Josie and I popped the last set of instruments into the autoclave, I felt like someone had put me through one of those old fashioned washing machines with a wringer.

"Hurry," Josie said, as we stripped the bed for the last time. "It's time to go meet the others."

"Others?" I put the linens in the hamper.

"The organizing group," she said. "They're waiting upstairs." I clamped my teeth shut and counted to ten.

"No rest for the wicked," I said.

Josie packed all the instruments into a big toolbox she stashed in the supply closet, which locked with a code punched into a metal keypad. Thankfully I came up with an easy mnemonic for the code. She picked up the two Sharps containers full of biological waste and headed for the back door. I awkwardly got my arms around the hamper and followed. I made a mental note to invest in one of those rollaway kinds.

Josie looked around carefully before placing the two Sharps in the trunk of her VW.

"Wouldn't it be easier to use paper sheets?" I asked, huffing up the steep wooden staircase with my load of laundry.

"We decided it would be cheaper and greener to use real ones," she said. Cheaper sure, because no doubt I'd be expected to do the laundry in the apartment size washer-dryer upstairs.

"This would be the same 'we' that thought it was a good idea to have a meeting after my first day of surgery?" I couldn't resist saying. "After flying all night?"

"Well you were supposed to get in last night," Josie said. I thought she sounded more accusatory than apologetic, but maybe that was just my nerves.

CHAPTER TWO

The OWLS Hoot at Night

Ten women sat in a circle in my living room: two on a faded brown couch, one in a faux leather recliner facing the thirty-inch TV on the wall (be still my heart), the rest on assorted wooden and folding chairs crammed among the book cases. I felt all twenty eyes evaluating my movements as I entered with my arms full of laundry. I concentrated hard on not dropping anything. After I ditched my burden in the kitchen, the Black woman standing under the television set pointed to an empty chair beside her. She apparently planned to stand for the entire meeting.

Josie perched on one wide arm of the couch, next to Nell, who wore her clerical collar with a black button-down shirt. I met her eyes and mimed falling asleep. "You'll be so busy, you won't have time to mourn," she'd assured me on the phone. She had undersold it. Next to Nell was Rabbit, whom Josie had introduced as her partner. Rabbit was either trans or genderqueer, but used 'they' so it didn't matter. Their delicate features made them look very young, but I guessed they were a few years older than Josie, early thirties.

The leader cleared her throat. She had intricate braids coiled into an elongated knot on top of her head. I couldn't tell if they were natural or a weave. She wore a knee-length yellow dress and black patent leather heels.

"Let's get started," she said. "I'm Evelyn Grandis, local president of the National Organization for Women, and one of the founders of Options for Women Life Situations, which we call OWLS."

Two women young enough to have grown up reading Harry Potter laughed. The dyke with the graying crew cut and snake tattoo looked at them in baffled annoyance. Obviously she had not contributed to the lesbian baby boom.

Evelyn had a commanding presence. I nicknamed her Evelyn Grandiose right away. She explained – probably for my benefit, since everyone else must already know how OWLS had formed – that the idea had been hatched at an emergency meeting after the legislature passed HB7, making abortion illegal in the state. She and several others from NOW – she pointed to them as she said their names – Yvette, Maureen and Shawn – had gotten together with Sandy, director of the women's health center at Virginia Commonwealth University. Sandy sat to Evelyn's left. She looked like a softer version of a Fox News anchor. Yvette was the only other African American woman in the room. I suspected she was the butch to Evelyn's femme, but I couldn't be sure. Yvette wore black jeans and a starched short-sleeved blue plaid shirt, tucked in. Her hair was cut very short, with a flat top. She sat directly opposite Evelyn, maybe so they could maintain eye contact. I hadn't picked Richmond as the place that would have a Black lesbian running their local NOW chapter, but what did I really know about the New South?

Maureen and Shawn were white women in their sixties. I'd bet anything they were ex-nuns. Both wore slacks, not jeans, and sensible dark shoes. I doubted I would be able to remember who was who. I'd be lucky if I remembered anyone's names at all.

Josie was the only Asian present. I'd done enough cursory research online to know that Richmond had a small Latino community, but I hadn't heard any Spanish when I came in, and no one in the room was identifiably Latinx. Nell had volunteered at a migrant worker center in

Alabama for a while, but that probably wasn't enough to bridge the Catholic-Protestant divide on abortion.

"Officially, all we do is counseling," said Evelyn. "We help women understand the law and their options. All of that will take place over at the safe house."

I noted that she didn't say anything to suggest where that was. Either everyone else knew, or she didn't trust everyone in this room.

"Our plan is to change abortion providers every six months," Evelyn continued. "That will hopefully make it harder for the right wing to target them and build a criminal case against them."

I noted her strategic use of the word "hopefully". I had thought about the risks, of course, but they hadn't been at the top of my worries in the flurry of getting ready to leave home just days after returning from Mexico. I'd had more immediate concerns, like avoiding my lying, cheating girlfriend in the house we'd owned together for fifteen years. I'd jumped at the chance to get three thousand miles away from her and all the so-called friends I imagined snickering behind my back. It would serve them all right if I ended up rotting in a Southern prison.

"Mollie here," Evelyn acknowledged me with a sweeping gesture worthy of her name, "stepped in on very short notice as the first. I'm going to ask her to say a few words now."

No one had told me I would have to make a speech. Public speaking is not my favorite thing, and I usually rely heavily on index cards and PowerPoint slides. If I'd known about this meeting, I would have spent time on the plane writing my remarks and practicing under my breath. But now all these rapt eyes were pasted to my face, so I would just have to muddle through. I sucked in air.

"About ten years ago, it became legal in California for nurse practitioners, nurse midwives and physicians' assistants to do first-trimester abortions. I'm certified as both a nurse midwife and women's health nurse practitioner. My practice specialized in home births, so we didn't generally get abortion requests, but I recognized that fewer and fewer doctors were willing to do abortions, and it seemed like a good idea to gain the skills. So I volunteered at a grassroots women's clinic in San Francisco. The only procedure I was allowed to do by myself was what's known as a vacuum aspiration abortion."

I had no idea if this was the type of information they wanted. I was just babbling. But I didn't see anyone checking their phones, so I figured I wasn't boring them yet.

"But I also assisted doctors – which means doing everything while they watched – in what's known as dilation and extraction, or D&E. In a D&E, you basically scrape the fetal tissue out of the uterus."

The Harry Potter aficionados were looking like they had eaten vomit-flavored jelly beans. But really, what did they think they were doing here?

"Sorry to be so graphic," I said. "The point is, women need these procedures and I am very well trained in doing them. These are very safe procedures. Many women don't even know they are pregnant until they are past the time when aspiration abortion is possible, which is about thirteen weeks from the start of the last menstrual period. Our clients will have to arrange time off of work and childcare and transportation. We don't want to tell them we can't help them."

Good, a hand was up. That meant I could stop talking and catch my breath.

"Why here?" The questioner was blonde and femme, in skinny jeans and a hot-pink blouse stretched tight over ample – possibly artificial – tits. "Why not help women go to Maryland, where abortion is still legal?"

"Still" was the operative word. There were bills pending in seven states replicating the one that Virginia had passed, and Maryland was one. But the Maryland House was still Democratic controlled, so for the moment, abortion remained legal there.

"The clinics in Maryland already have more clients than they can handle," Josie said. "Setting up a legal clinic takes a lot of time and money, and we don't have either. But there's more to it than that. If you're trying to do everything legally, you can be stopped easily. If you start out illegal, you set up your systems to prevent people from finding out who you are and it's harder for them to stop you. It's not to say it's safe, but it's eyes open. That's the mistake that the early abortion rights activists made after *Roe v. Wade*. They dismantled the grassroots, underground networks that had worked really well for so many women for so many years. You can't blame them. Who would want to keep running an underground clinic when you could be aboveground and get paid for it and advertise openly? It seemed like a great plan. But that gave the right wing a target and it added layers and layers of expense and political pressure that, honestly, got us to where we are. The Planned Parenthoods and the Women's Options organizations, they forgot how to fight."

The two women opposite me were knitting, their needles clicking in syncopation like nineteenth century suffragettes – if the suffragettes had had silver buzz cuts and tattoos. The clicking rose to a furious tempo. These knitters had probably helped build those First Gen women's clinics.

"Look, I'm not attacking anybody," Josie said. I thought some of the assembled would disagree, but gave her A for Amelioration. "But what we're doing here is a different approach altogether. We are going back to the old self-help model, the Jane model." Several women nodded. The Jane collective operated in Chicago from the mid-sixties until abortion became legal in 1972. Lay health workers provided safe abortions to tens of thousands of women. It had been the subject of a few recent books and movies, so the reference did not leave the younger women completely in the dark.

Maybe I'd start knitting again too. It had helped get me through those boring nursing school classes on The Role of the Nurse, which meant following doctors' orders without question. Nursing school back then didn't have a Social Justice track like the ones my young colleagues had gone through at Cal State East Bay.

"This is an all-volunteer project," Josie went on. "None of us is getting paid to run it. Mollie isn't getting a salary. We're paying her

expenses, but she's donating her time. That's our plan – to recruit retired nurses, maybe even doctors, to come spend half a year here.
We –" she swirled her head around the room, trying to catch each person's eye and bring them into her orbit, "will provide the administrative
support, security, counsel the clients and assist the practitioners. We'll
raise money to cover the rent and the transportation for women who
can't afford to get here on their own."

I listened for Bunny, tucked away in the bedroom. I'd insisted on
bringing her, even though Sidney protested that cats hated change.
"She'll adapt," I said. "And anyway, female cats aren't as territorial as
males."

I didn't hear any mewing or rustling. I assumed that meant Bunny
was curled up, sleeping, on top of the new quilt Josie said her grandmother had made special for me. I'd have to make sure it wasn't totally
shredded before the next practitioner arrived.

I pulled my mind back to the meeting. Evelyn was talking about
working groups. Fundraising was the most important, she said. They
needed two thousand dollars a month for the rent, equipment, medical
waste disposal, transportation stipends and insurance.

"Insurance?" I burst out without thinking. "How can an underground
clinic get insurance?"

"We bought renter's insurance," Nell explained, "in case of a fire or
something."

A fire or something. My home and workplace could be the target of
arson, *or something*.

Volunteers was another big need. Josie was heading up that group.
We needed to recruit people for medical assisting, publicity, and security.

Security. My lone experience on a security team had been on May
4, 1970, at Kent State University, where I was a freshman. With twenty
other kids, I had put on a red armband. We had somehow thought that
made us capable of protecting the people who came to protest the bombing of Cambodia. The National Guard had not paid any attention to our

armbands when they aimed their rifles at the students chanting "Pigs Off Campus."

A harsh sound interrupted my journey into the past. The landline was ringing. Josie had shown me the phone when we put my luggage away. She said it was more secure than cell phones. *Secure*, that word again.

I automatically ran to the kitchen to answer the phone, even though as far as I knew, no one had the number yet.

"Hello?"

"Renata Kellam?"

"Who is this?"

"Is this Renata Kellam?" It was a man's voice, raspy and low. I didn't recognize it.

"No, you've got the wrong number." I hung up, but not before I heard him say, "I know where you are."

CHAPTER THREE

Bring on the Baingan

The next night I drove to the North Side to have dinner in Nell's painstakingly restored two-and-a-half story Victorian. She declined my repeated offers of help, so I nestled into the breakfast nook, sipping the Merlot I'd brought and watching my first great love slice red onions for Baingan Bharta.

"So what do you think of Richmond?" she asked. The string of a bright red apron rode in a loose bow above her sturdy glutes, while her half-blonde, half-gray head bent toward the cutting board. Her presence was still irresistible, after all these years.

"I haven't seen much of it," I said. "Just driving over here, and that was in the dark. But it seems – quaint."

"That's one word for it." She piled the onions on a gently curved plate and started peeling the eggplant in one long coil. "It's changed a lot in the last few years. Did you come up Monument Avenue?"

I nodded, then realized she couldn't see me. "Uh huh."

"Did you notice all those empty pedestals? Every one of them used to have a statue of a Confederate general on it. They all came down in a minute back in 'twenty."

"I remember." Richmond, I recalled, had more Confederate statues than any other city in the country, and the city had decided to take them all down in the frenzied days after George Floyd's murder in Minneapolis. That might have been the first time I'd ever read three words about the city where I was now living. If I'd had a crystal ball then, I would have paid more attention to news that could have been from another country – and nearly was.

"You've owned this place a long time, right?" I was pretty sure I'd had this address in my book, in the days when I had a book.

"More than thirty-five years," she said. "It's all paid off. When I bought it, this was one of the few integrated neighborhoods in the city. By the time I'd gotten it painted, I was one of three white homeowners in four blocks. I think a lot of my neighbors would have just as soon I'd moved too, but I didn't see any reason why I should. I loved the house when I bought it, and I still do."

"It's perfect for you," I said. It suited a priest's needs, with a large living room and dining room on the main floor, a guest room and study along with the master bedroom upstairs, and a small den off the entrance downstairs. The exterior was off-white – a concession to the neighbors, no doubt – but she'd trimmed the gabled windows in exquisite deep blue. The generous front yard boasted azaleas and lilacs, as well as the ubiquitous dogwood tree, which was just sprouting pinkish buds.

"The neighborhood's seen better days and worse days," Nell said, tossing the onions into a pan of sizzling spices. The air was filling up with the heavenly aromas of toasted cumin and coriander. My stomach growled, and I realized I hadn't eaten since breakfast. Nell heard it and turned around, laughing.

"You and your appetites," she said. "One of the things I always loved about you." She shook some nuts into a bowl and set them in front of me. "Just don't fill up so much you can't eat my food."

"I don't see a problem," I said. I counted six almonds and eleven peanuts or cashews in the little dish. That didn't even make an appetizer where I came from. Nell grew up in International Falls, Minnesota, "on the Swedish side of town," she had told me many times. Thrift ran in her blood.

I popped three peanuts in my mouth in a row, then made myself nibble on an almond. "Tell me about the OWLs," I said. "How'd you get involved with them?"

"Evelyn lives just up the street," Nell said. "I've known her forever. I'm the one who got her involved in NOW. She was working at the Boys' and Girls' Club, which back then was just the Boys' Club. That was when her sons were little. She didn't want anything to do with feminism. But I just kept inviting her to things – lectures, parties – and eventually she ran out of excuses. And the rest is history."

"She seems like a powerhouse," I said. "What about Shawn and Maureen? They're ex-nuns, right?"

She chuckled. "You picked that up, huh? More than thirty years ago, but still carrying the scent."

"The scent of the convent," I said, smiling at the unintended rhyme. "Sounds like a really bad movie."

"The Sound of Music, Part II," Nell said. "A sense series. The next one could be 'The Sight in the Apse'."

"Or in the Alps," I said. Riffing with Nell was like settling into an old armchair that knew the slant of your shoulder blades. I wasn't drinking as fast as I had been a few minutes ago. I was losing the jittery, disoriented feeling I'd had since the plane landed.

"They were in El Salvador," Nell said.

"Who were?" I asked. "Oh, you mean Maureen and Shawn?"

"Yeah." She swirled the pale green eggplant cubes around in the pan with a wooden spoon. "They were in the same order as those nuns that got killed by the death squad."

"Oh. Wow." I vaguely remembered the incident in the 1980s. A Salvadoran government death squad killed four American missionaries they thought were sympathetic to Communist rebels, and our own government tried to cover it up.

"Is that why they left the order?" I asked. I couldn't blame them if it were.

"No, they left sometime in the nineties. I think it had more to do with the sexism. Remember JP II, and the fight over women's ordination?"

"Vaguely," I said. "I never followed religious news the way you do."

"Professional hazard," she said lightly. When Nell told me she was going to divinity school in the late eighties, I'd thought she was joking. She had the foulest mouth of any woman I knew, and her sexual taste ran to the kinky. When I'd tried to probe her motivation, she'd mumbled something about a vision and a calling.

"Ex-nuns helping to start an underground abortion clinic," I said. "There's some justice."

"They're doers," she said. "Shawn was a nurse, and Maureen was a middle school principal. They know how to make stuff happen."

"So you think you all can really make this thing work? Sounds like it came together very fast."

"We had no choice about that. We miscalculated," Nell said. "We couldn't do anything until the new laws took effect, but we had the ACLU and the National Women's Law Center all lined up to file suits as soon as they did. The lawyers assured us the courts would grant a restraining order, keep the clinics open while the cases wound their way through the system. We figured we'd have a year, even two, to get backup plans in place. But this is a different world. Things change on a dime. Sometimes for the better, and a lot of times for the worse."

With the eggplant simmering in the cast-iron skillet, she transferred a large ball of dough from a metal bowl onto her butcher block counter and began rolling out naan. I got up and went to the stove.

"Hand them to me as you roll them, and I'll bake them," I said. She shrugged, her shoulders making that fluid rolling motion I recognized. She squatted in front of a cabinet, passed me a long-handled iron griddle. I turned on the flame, and when the griddle was hot enough for a drop of water to dance across it, I took the first round bread from the counter top, waited 'til little bubbles formed on top, then flipped it, pressed gently with a spatula and watched the satisfying air pockets appear. When it was nicely speckled on both sides, I moved it to a plate and smeared it with butter before reaching for the next one.

"So how are you doing, with Sidney and Jen and everything?" Nell asked.

It would have been the perfect moment to tell her about the phone call. She was the only person I could have told, one of the only people on earth who knew the story of Renata. Instead I said, "Well, I'm still heartbroken."

"Of course you are," Nell said. "It's only been a week. But I have to tell you, I never liked Sidney. I thought she was smug."

"She's not smug," I said. "She's opinionated."

Why was I standing up for Sidney? I should have been glad to hear someone trash her. But I'd loved her for sixteen years. If Nell thought she was smug, what did that say about me?

"You're opinionated," Nell said. "She's smug." She put a spoonful of eggplant to my lips. I opened my mouth and let her slide the spoon in, even though I could tell it was too hot. I hoped that wasn't a metaphor for this whole enterprise.

CHAPTER FOUR

The Fundraiser

I had been in Richmond for six days. I'd done more than forty abortions, all of which had gone perfectly, and provided another dozen women with abortion pills they could take at home. Two women had jumped off the table at the last minute, and I'd sent them off for counseling with volunteers who hooked them up with prenatal care and a list of places that offered gently used baby gear. I'd gotten over my jet lag and was starting to be able to understand people's accents, except for the oldest white people, whose words all ran into each other like molasses spreading on a plate. That cost me five bucks at the grocery store, when the cashier's "Need help out?" sounded like "Is that all?"

OWLS' first benefit was being held at an upscale Black church in what Nell told me was called the Museum District. Officially, the money was to help women from the South travel to states where abortion was legal. Evelyn Grandiose had organized it, of course, with help from Yvette. Yvette, I'd learned, had been Richmond's first Black female firefighter. Now retired, she was heading up the OWLS security committee. She had come over a few times during the week to check that everything was working right with the clinic alarm system. She was efficient and a little gruff with me, but surprisingly gentle when she encountered the clients.

Tonight she sported a green and gold embroidered shirt over black slacks, while Evelyn clacked around in her three-inch stilettos, showing off Michelle Obama shoulders in a below-the-knee black silk dress. I still hadn't absolutely confirmed that they were lovers, but they had arrived at the church together. I would have to ask Nell. I spotted her near the makeshift bar and threaded my way through the already sizable crowd.

At least this was a Methodist church, and the Southern Methodists, unlike their Baptist cousins, tolerate alcohol in moderation. Another thing I'd learned from Nell, my coach for all things Southern.

By the time I made it over to the bar, Nell was walking away with two bottles of beer. I followed her with my eyes, wondering who she was with. She'd recently broken up with a schoolteacher called Hillary. Hillary was, at this moment, schmoozing by the food tables with Shawn and Maureen, who appeared as inseparable as Evelyn and Yvette.

Nell handed one of the drinks to a glamorous redhead with a dancer's long legs stretching out from under a red chiffon dress. Nell wasn't one to stay single for long. In five decades, the longest period I could remember her not having a girlfriend was two months. I would have to ask her about Evelyn and Yvette another time. But what was I going to do with myself tonight? I hardly knew anyone, only the women who volunteered at the clinic, and they were all busy with tasks. Josie was taking money at the door. Yvette, of course, was running security.

Maybe I should hit on Hillary. She and Nell had stayed with me and Sidney once, and I'd enjoyed her company. She wasn't really my type – my ideal woman was tall, butch-of-center and not so WASPy looking. But beggars couldn't necessarily be choosers. I'd been no beauty even in my heyday and eye bags and gnarled hands didn't make you a hot commodity, even among other women with sagging necks. Hillary's soft brown hair was only flecked with gray, and her curvy body looked like it would be fun to snuggle up with. Plus she was smart, even if her favorite authors were Beverly Cleary and Jacqueline Woodson, while my tastes ran to Elizabeth George and Octavia Butler. I headed over to where she stood with Shawn and Maureen.

Hillary greeted me with a kiss on each cheek, an affectation I'd never acquired. My effort to reciprocate landed somewhere east of her ears.

"How've you been?" I asked.

"Oh, pretty well, you know…" Her lips smiled but her green eyes didn't. In fact, they were a little damp. "I miss Nell," she said, scrunching her mouth slightly.

"I can relate," I said. I wished I hadn't said it. I didn't want to talk about Sidney. Not at a party. The last thing I needed was to end up in a quivering ball on the floor at an event where everyone was sure to be surreptitiously watching to see if I was sane and competent.

"I need a drink," I said to Hillary and the others. "I'll be right back."

I wandered over to the bar. Two women I didn't recognize were moving fast to keep up with the demand for beer and wine. They both wore white shirts with black bow ties, like real bartenders.

"What can I get you?" asked the tall one. Everyone looks tall to me because I'm only five-four, but she was what my parents had called a green bean.

"Red wine, please?" – Why did I make it sound like a question?

"Coming up." She uncorked a middling New York table wine and poured a generous amount into a plastic cup. This was a cash bar. I squinted at the sign with the prices, and dug in my purse for seven bucks.

"It's on the house," said the bartender. She had deep-set black eyes, with dark brown hair in kind of a pixie cut. I put her age around fifty-five. "It's the least we can do."

"So you're an OWL?" I asked. I didn't know if they used the singular, but she half-smiled.

"More of a hanger-on," she said. "I'm a friend of Yvette's. I saw you talking to Hillary. She's my ex-ex," she added with a grin. "I'm Toni." She stuck out her hand, and we shook. I picked up the wine and sipped. It was marginally drinkable.

"Small world," I said. "Nell's my ex-ex. Ex," I added. "I guess that makes us ex-ex in-laws."

"An army of ex-ex-lovers," Toni said. Her teeth shone like mirrors, lighting up the dimness for a second. "Everyone here is tight with their exes. Hell, we're even tight with our enemies. The scene's too small not to be."

"The Bay Area's not that different," I said. "There are lots of lesbian cliques, but people rarely move from one to another. You just try to find someone you haven't already slept with."

"I heard Oakland has the highest proportion of lesbians in the world," Toni said.

"I'm not sure how scientific that is," I said. "There are definitely a lot, but everyone basically hangs out with their own crowd. The political dykes, the clean-and-sober crowd, the women of color, the softballers. Within each, it's very incestuous."

"Incest comes naturally to lesbians," Toni said. "It's a cultural adaptation. There's no biological imperative for lesbians to avoid having sex with siblings or other close relatives. So our culture has evolved knowing that."

"Let me guess, you're an anthropologist."

"Guilty as charged. I teach at UofR."

"If I'd had *you* for freshman anthro, I might not have gotten a D." I was absolutely lying, I'd never gotten a D in college. But lying was an old habit. It had stood me well over the years, and was likely to come in very handy now. Especially if someone in town knew about Renata Kellam. I put that thought aside. This wasn't the time for it.

"Maybe I can fill in some of the gaps in your knowledge," Toni said. She walked around the bar and stood so close to me, her shoulder grazed my earlobe. I felt a familiar tingling in the back of my neck. That was always the first place attraction made itself known in my body. Nell had called it my "weird wiring."

Toni put a hand on my bare arm. Her hand felt hot, though I was pretty sure it wasn't.

"You seem uncomfortable," she said. "Am I moving too fast?"

I thought about how to answer. Was she moving too fast? It had been such a long time since I'd had anyone move on me at all, since I'd even been open to anyone's moves.

"Aren't you supposed to be tending bar?" I said.

Toni shrugged, glancing behind her. "It's not that busy right now. Dre can handle it."

Out of the corner of my eye, I saw the other bartender handing over beers.

"I feel like people are watching me," I said. "It's a bit of a fishbowl."

"I really doubt anyone is," Toni soothed. Involuntarily, I swept the room with my eyes. People were dancing, chatting, eating, drinking. I didn't see anyone who appeared to be studying me.

"And if they were, what would you be doing wrong?" Toni persisted.

"I'm not ready," I said. "Two weeks ago, I was in Mexico. I came home to find my lover of sixteen years in bed with my best friend. Now here I am, thousands of miles away from anywhere I've ever lived. New town, new job, new people, new rules. I can't just dive into a new relationship. That's not who I am."

"Okay." Toni removed her hand from my arm and strode back behind the bar. A minute later, she was pouring out wine for a woman with blonde curls. I saw her eyes crinkle as she laughed, and she flashed her mirror grin.

I felt a second of triumph and then a long moment of disappointment. What had I expected? That Toni was going to grab me in her arms and whisk me off somewhere? I thought of Josie and her Jane Austen complex. Toni wasn't going to be Mr. Darcy to my Elizabeth. She had plenty of other fish to fry. But what I had told her was true. I wasn't ready to risk getting hurt again.

My glass was nearly empty, but I was not going back to the bar for another. I slipped through the crowd, out the door and into my car. I could still stop at the grocery store for a bottle of wine and drink it alone in my apartment. Tomorrow, Sunday, was the one day I didn't have to work in the clinic. I might as well celebrate.

I poured myself a glass of California red – a little taste of home – and logged into Netflix on the TV. Ridiculously, the first suggestion in my queue was the new season of Call the Midwife. If ever there was an algorithm fail, that was it.

I flipped through the crime dramas, rejecting the Blue Murder episodes with heavily pregnant Janine Lewis, the Prime Suspect where Jane Tennison has an abortion, Hunter where Janet McTeer tries to intercept radical anti-abortionists bent on mayhem.

I decided a music documentary would be safe. I clicked on "Twenty Feet from Stardom" and settled back in the reclining chair. It felt like the first time I'd relaxed in two weeks. Before long, my eyes were closing, the film providing a powerful soundtrack to some crazy dream where I was trying to climb over a mountain of cannulas while being chased by faceless men in bowler hats who kept popping up to say "Renata."

From my deep occupation with the dream reality, it took me a while to realize that someone was really knocking on my front door. The knocking was tentative, more Morse Code than Gestapo raid, but it still sent my pulse into a percussive staccato. My legs seemed pinned to the chair; I couldn't get up if I wanted to. Which I didn't. I tried to hold perfectly still so whoever it was – and it had to be a wrong address – would give up and go away.

They didn't. A few minutes passed, and then the tap-tap-rapping started up again. Finally, I ventured to slide off the chair and skitter off into the bedroom. From there, I could peek discreetly through the shade and just make out the figure on the front porch.

Toni saw me, and waved a hand clutching something I couldn't make out.

I considered putting the shade back down, turning off the light and playing possum. But she had given every indication of being willing to stand out there for an hour. Though the block was mostly medical office buildings, there were some others like this one, with residential units attached. I couldn't afford to draw attention.

By the time I got to the door, she was scribbling a note on a gum wrapper. I saw her mouth moving rhythmically. She must be chewing the gum so she could use it to stick the note to the bottle in her hand.

Apparently I had overestimated her determination. When she saw me, she spat the gum out into the wrapper, folded it neatly and shoved it into the pocket of her jeans. She was still wearing the black bowtie.

"I felt bad that I chased you out of the party," she said, holding out the bottle. "We had some leftover booze, so I brought you a nightcap."

I took the bottle from her hand. It was a decent California cabernet. I doubted it was what they were serving at the party.

"Come on in," I said, and she did.

CHAPTER FIVE

Dykes Go Home

Monday was insane at the clinic. It seemed like every didn't-wan-nabe mom in Virginia and its environs had scheduled her procedure for that day. By noon, I had done five aspirations and inserted laminaria for two D&Es. One grateful client had left a persimmon and a nickel bag of walnuts on the reception desk. Sandy, who was on reception duty for the morning, had kindly left them for me. It didn't seem like that satis-fying of a lunch, but I had no real food in the apartment, just cereal and the semi-stale bread I'd toasted for breakfast. I had planned to shop on Sunday, but then Toni had happened, and I didn't leave the house on Sunday.

I didn't regret it for a second.

I took the fruit and nuts, set the clinic alarm and headed around the building to the apartment steps. Just as I stepped onto the bottom stair, I thought I saw someone walking toward the clinic, but when I turned back, there was no one nearby. I mounted the stairs and paused on the landing, a good vantage point to survey the street. It was silent, as it so often was: only a few cars in the lot of the pocket mall across the street, no one out walking at all. People didn't walk much in Richmond, just from the door to their cars. Since I'd been here, I had been constantly repeating that line from "Annie Hall": "We can walk to the curb from here."

The newspaper was on the doorstep. The delivery person assigned to my route seemed to think 10:30 was when people wanted to read their morning paper, so I usually read it at lunch. I picked it up and unlocked the door. As I pushed open the door, something fell out of the newspaper onto the ground.

It was a white return envelope, the $2.50 for a hundred kind you can almost see through. In fact, I could see that what was inside looked like a ransom note, pasted up from magazine articles. Did people really do that?

My vision blurred. I thought I might be having a stroke. I nearly fell into the apartment, double bolted the door behind me and leaned against it.

"Calm down," I told myself. "Whatever it says, it's just a piece of paper. It can't hurt you. You'll read it and then figure out who to tell and what to do."

I set the newspaper on the kitchen table, along with the persimmon and the nuts. Bunny crept out of the bedroom, looking for lunch and petting. I shook some dry cat food into her bowl and scruffed her fuzzy head with my fingertips.

My hands shook as I picked up the envelope by its corners. Better not to get fingerprints on it. Then I thought about how absurd that was. First of all, my fingerprints were probably all over it already, and second, I couldn't call the police. Even if the letter had nothing to do with the clinic, they would want to know why someone might want to threaten me, and I certainly couldn't tell them. Deliberately, I ran my hands all over the envelope, as if to strip it of its magic power.

I put the kettle on and fished out a brown paper filter from the box on top of the refrigerator. I plucked the coffee cone from the sink, where I had placed it after breakfast, and set it on top of the same cup I'd used in the morning. Maybe I should drink mint tea now instead. Coffee would just make me more anxious. But no, I was going to need to be alert this afternoon, no matter what, and I really couldn't stand tea. The only reason I kept it around was in case someone came over.

Standing square to the table, leaning on my hands, I stared at the paper's headlines, trying to understand what they meant. Something about the race for school board, which was still being contested. Progressive groups were claiming that the Republican Secretary of State had improperly disqualified some ballots. Another kid had been shot downtown. Americans For Prosperity was funding a lawsuit to bring prayer back to high school football games.

A piercing squeal sent me reeling backwards. I stumbled and sat down hard on the straight backed chair, bruising my sitbone. The squealing continued, even louder now, it seemed. Finally I realized it was just the water boiling. Jeez. I turned off the stove and used a potholder to bring the kettle back to the table, poured the water over the coffee grounds, holding one hand with the other to keep from shaking and spilling. I watched the deep brown liquid fill the cup, got the milk, splashed some in. At once, the milk bloomed into a roiling flower, turning the coffee a lovely caramel color. At least the milk wasn't sour, as I half expected it to be. I lifted the cup to my lips, blew and took a tiny sip. Then I sat down, cautiously this time, took the envelope in my hands, turned it around and over. It bore no return address, and no address either for that matter. No stamp, and it wasn't sealed. I untucked the flap and slowly pulled out the scrap of manila paper, no bigger than my hand.

"dyKeS Go hOMe," was all it said, in blocky black letters cut from a glossy white magazine.

Part of me wanted to dance a jig because it didn't have a picture of a bloody fetus, or any reference to Renata Kellam. But this message was far from comforting. It could, of course, just be random homophobia, but from whom, and toward whom? It said "dykes," not "dyke," so it must be aimed at the clinic, but then why did whoever sent it put it on my doorstep and not downstairs? How did the letter composer – couldn't say writer – know we were dykes? Had someone seen Toni arriving last night, or leaving this morning? It's not like we were making out on the street. Then I realized it was a ridiculous question. There were a million ways to identify us. Not least was the number of dogs in the parking lot all the time.

And what did "go home" signify? I was the only one of the "dykes" who wasn't at home in Richmond. Did the sender know that, or did they assume Lesbians came from Lesbos or some distant planet? Had I nearly seen the person sneaking away, or had that really been my imagination? And why in the newspaper and not under the door? Maybe it was the newspaper delivery person. Maybe they weren't just delivering my paper so late out of laziness.

I heard the chime of the downstairs bell. Yvette had rigged it up so it would ring in both units. I looked at the clock. It was still quarter to one. Josie was supposed to be on reception duty this afternoon, but she was evidently not there yet. The doorbell rang again. I couldn't imagine who it was. Clients arrived at the back door with escorts from the safe house. Clinic volunteers were supposed to have the key.

I quickly cut the persimmon into eighths and shoved two into my mouth. It was not ripe enough, but I chewed it until it was soft enough to swallow. I wondered where in the world persimmons grew in March. I tore open the bag of nuts and grabbed a handful. I balanced the poison letter on my palm, wondering what to do with it. After a long moment, I stuffed it into my pocket and headed out the front door, locking it securely behind me.

From the balcony, I could see a tall figure at the clinic door, one hand on the knob while the other rested on the molding at the top, as if feeling for a hidden key. I was pretty sure there was none, but maybe there was something I didn't know.

"What are you doing?" I called, as I bounded down the steps. Better be careful, I told myself, or you'll end up in a heap on the asphalt. Bones were brittle at my age, even if you did yoga twice a week like I tried to.

Toni turned as I approached. I felt the familiar flutter in my throat and knees, but annoyance welled up too.

"You scared me!" I half shouted. "What are you doing here?"

Toni still had her left hand on the doorknob, a leather purse slung over her right shoulder. I didn't see anything in her right hand, so if she'd been looking for something on top, she hadn't found it.

"I'm working with you this afternoon," Toni said. "Didn't you know?"

"I thought Josie was."

"Josie? No, she had to work."

"At the health food store? I was sure she said she only works there Thursday through Saturday."

"Maybe someone called in sick." Taking an extra work shift when she was supposed to be at the clinic didn't sound like Josie, from my limited experience. She was nothing if not reliable.

I had gotten the door open and disarmed the alarm. Toni followed me as I headed to the little storage closet by the bathroom to stow my purse and gather supplies for the afternoon.

"I'll be right back," I said. I exited through the back door and dashed up the fire escape to my apartment. I always left the back door unlocked. Maybe I should change that, but I didn't have time to think about it now. I ran to the bedroom, slamming the door as if Toni would hear – and who knew, she might, given the porousness of the walls – and picked up the house phone. Receiver in hand, I realized I had no idea what the name of the health food store was, let alone the number. And my cell phone was downstairs in the supply closet.

I ran back down, the wasted five minutes intensifying my frenzied state. I ducked into the supply closet, ignoring Toni, who was doing something in the Procedure Room – PR, we called it. Shit, I should not have left her here alone, this woman I didn't know anything about. I dug in my purse for my phone, finally found it. My hands were shaking so hard I could barely hit the right keys, but I managed to send Josie a text – "U at work? What's up?"

"Mollie," Toni said from the other side of the door.

"What?"

"I'm sorry. I lied to you." I tossed the phone into my purse and opened the door.

"Lied? About what?" I couldn't take any more bad news today. If Toni was about to say she had a lover, I needed to stop her right now. "Actually, I don't care about what," I said.

"Well, I'm going to tell you anyway." Toni advanced on me, placing my hands on either side of my neck. Was she a serial strangler? Was I about to be Victim #8?

"I got Josie to switch with me," Toni said, her voice a caress. "I was supposed to come on Thursday, but I couldn't wait that long." She was still wearing her leather jacket, too warm for the day. The only time I'd seen her without it was when she was naked in my bedroom.

She bent and touched my lips lightly with her own. Against my better judgment, I leaned in. She smelled slightly of honeysuckle, which was blooming everywhere in Richmond. My left hand reached down and cupped her right buttock. She moved in closer, pushing her pelvis into mine.

"Hey, we can't do this. We have patients coming." I put my right hand on her left hip, pushing her lightly away.

I was pretty sure that was a gun I felt in her jacket pocket.

CHAPTER SIX

Are You Just Glad to See Me?

I tried to tell myself I really hadn't had time to ask Toni about the gun.

A moment after I felt it, I heard the car pull up and a Black woman in her late thirties was escorted in by Josie's partner Rabbit and the Designated Driver for the day. Toni showed the client into the PR, and in a tone of soothing normality, gave her a gown to change into and explained the basics of what would happen. I waited outside the door and when Toni emerged, I yanked her into the reception area.

"You weren't at the training last weekend," I said. "Do you even know the first thing about health care?"

"I was a paramedic for years," Toni assured me. "You can ask Yvette. We used to work together."

Yvette was one of my favorites among the OWLS volunteers I'd gotten to know. She was solid and quick with a wry remark; her years of dealing with racist misogyny had taught her to shake off the small stuff. If Toni was a friend of hers, I could trust her. I made a mental note to corner Yvette next chance I got and get the low-down on Toni.

Toni did seem to know her way around a medical facility. While I scrubbed and gloved, she pulled the correct instruments from inside their sterile envelopes and placed them in the right order on the silver tray. She held the door open for me so I didn't have to touch anything, and set the tray into its groove at the foot of the table, where Collette lay covered with the light purple blanket. Toni introduced me to Collette and asked if she was doing okay. When Collette nodded, Toni moved to stand near the door as I took my spot on the little stool between Collette's legs.

Collette's abortion went off without a hitch. Toni gave Collette her right hand to squeeze, and handed me the instruments at the right time with her left hand. Ten minutes later, she settled Collette in the recovery room while I degloved and got everything ready for the next patient. When I finished that task, I went into the kitchen for some water. Toni was there, making chamomile tea with lemon for Collette.

"You're good," I said, smiling at her back. "I'm glad you're here." She turned and put an arm around my shoulder, which only came up to her armpit.

"I'm glad you're here too," she said.

I snaked an arm around her waist and leaned in. There was that bulge again.

"Um..."

"What?"

She had her tray loaded with the tea, along with crackers and hummus and cheese.

"Nothing," I said. "Go on and take care of Collette."

Pretty soon, the doorbell chimed: Rabbit arriving with the next patient. We had agreed that the drivers would ring so we could make sure the patients didn't see each other. I grabbed the follow-up instructions and precautionary meds and went to speak to Collette as Toni headed for the back door.

Collette was already up and putting her jacket on. I saw that a few of the crackers had been eaten, and a little cheese (but no hummus). She must be doing okay. I handed her the instruction sheet and explained about the meds. Toni popped her head into the open door.

"Ready?" I asked. If she said yes, that would mean the next patient was ensconced in the PR, and the coast was clear for Collette to go out.

"Not quite," she said. "Can you come here for a minute?"

I gestured to Collette to sit back down. "Sorry, we'll just be a minute," I said.

"What's going on?" I whispered to Toni in the hall.

"Just come with me."

She led the way down the hall, to where Yvette was standing with a young white woman, just inside the back door. At the young woman's left foot was a goose, long neck craning. Its orange beak opened and a strained half-cry squeaked out.

"Shhhh," I said reflexively. Then to Toni, "What the hell is that?"

The young woman petted the goose's head. Its neck shrank and its mouth closed. "This is Tia," she said primly. "She's my support goose."

I saw Rabbit behind her, shaking their head.

"Okay. What's your name?" I asked the goose's person.

"Danielle."

"Danielle, let's go over here."

I led her and the unsanitary goose across our nice clean linoleum floor to the door separating the clinic area from the small carpeted reception room. We didn't use the reception room much, since clients were escorted in through the back, but it was furnished with a loveseat and two vinyl-covered armchairs. I settled Danielle and Tia in there, with the three-year-old People magazines left by the original Dr. Jenkins.

"Why didn't you call?" I asked Rabbit.

"I did," they shrugged. "No one answered."

"The suction must've been on," I said. They collected Collette and left through the back door.

"You're going to have to look after the goose," I told Toni. "We can't have it in the PR and I'm not leaving it alone to wreak havoc in the office."

"I'm not a goose sitter!" she said. "What if it shits all over me?"

"I don't know – put on a gown," I said.

"Good idea," she said, to my surprise.

Danielle cried when we told her she couldn't have the goose in the PR. But I was firm: no goose, or no abortion. We assured her Toni would take good care of Tia.

"Just as if she was my own kid," Toni said. I wondered how Toni was going to entertain a goose. I had seen lots of geese while walking around Lake Merritt in Oakland. They never seemed to be doing much.

I managed the abortion okay without assistance, and didn't hear any big crashes or cries for help from woman or goose. After I settled Danielle in the recovery room, I decided it might be okay for her to have Tia with her. Recovery wasn't a sterile space, and how much risk could one goose pose? Probably less than a patient with a preschooler at home. We could spray Airborne when they were gone.

I went out to reception to tell Toni she was done with goose duty, but as it turned out, she was definitely not. I found her down on her knees with a bottle of bleach and a wad of paper towels. I didn't need to ask what happened. Tia was cowering under one of the chairs.

"I guess things didn't go so well," I said.

She scowled up at me, crossing her eyes. *Don't laugh*, I told myself sternly.

"I'm sorry," I said. "I'm going to reunite her with her person."

That sounded easier than it turned out to be. Tia was as traumatized as Toni by her little accident, and it isn't a piece of cake to coax a goose out from under a chair. I didn't want to grab her because I know geese can bite. I was on the verge of deciding we'd have to wait for Danielle, when I heard the phone ringing on the other side of the door.

I ran to get it. Maybe the next patient had a support llama.

"Is everything okay?" Josie said. She sounded hoarse and nasal.

"We're fine here," I said. "But it doesn't sound like you are. What's wrong?"

"I just have a cold," she said. "That's why I got Toni to switch with me. Didn't she tell you?"

"First she said you were working. Then she said she was the one who asked you to switch."

"Why would I be working on a clinic day? I texted you back, but you didn't answer so I was afraid something had happened."

"Sorry, I must have misunderstood. Didn't mean to scare you. Feel better." I hung up the phone, grabbed my head and dug my fingernails into my scalp. What the hell was going on here? If Josie asked Toni to switch with her because she was sick, why didn't Toni just say that? Either way, she ended up here, so what possible difference could it make? I couldn't ask Toni now, while she was cleaning goose shit off the carpet. I'd worry about it later.

We got the next patient into the PR, and when Danielle came into reception, Tia waddled right up to her. I thought Danielle looked mildly triumphant at how much trouble the separation had caused.

Three more abortions later, I finished my charts while Toni cleaned the instruments and stuffed the soiled linens in the hamper. I copied the files to an encrypted flash drive and deleted everything before turning off the computer, then went to the storage room to get the broom.

"I'll do that." Toni tried to take the broom from my hands.

"That's okay. I like it – it's kind of my end-of-the-day meditation." I needed to ask her about the gun and why she lied about Josie. But I couldn't just blurt it out.

"You must be exhausted," I said. "Why don't you go upstairs and rest while I finish cleaning up? Then we could go get some dinner. "

Her mouth turned down a little, and she glanced down at her wrist, where there was no watch. Then she looked up at the big round clock on the wall, its hands splayed at five and ten.

"I'm sorry, I have plans tonight."

I couldn't have misread her signals. She had been trying to get with me all day, right? And suddenly she was too busy? This woman might be more trouble than she was worth – except I was really starting to fall for her. Seeing her with her hands in goose shit had sealed the deal. Had my less than compassionate reaction turned her off?

"How about tomorrow night?" she said. "There's a chamber concert at the museum."

"You like chamber music?" I hadn't picked her for a classical music aficionado.

"I do, yeah. Plus my friend Lee is playing."

"A friend? Or an ex-lover?" I couldn't help asking.

"Both, since you asked." Probably a cellist. There were a lot of lesbian cellists.

"Sounds fun," I said.

"Okay, great, I'll pick you up here at six."

"Perfect." I opened the door for her, expecting a kiss goodbye. But she just waved her left hand, fumbling for her keys with her right.

I listened for the start of Toni's engine while I put the instruments away. I didn't hear it. I grabbed my purse from the desk and kept one eye on Toni's Mini Cooper while I set the alarm. She was sitting in the front seat, looking at her phone. Maybe checking email or reading a text. I crossed the street to the mini mall, where a convenience store was still open. I entered, greeted the clerk, and walked to the magazine aisle, which faced the window. I perused the offerings: *Mademoiselle* and *Marie Claire*, *Home and Garden* and *Rod and Gun*. Was Toni really carrying a gun? Would she have been crouching on the floor cleaning goose shit with a gun in her pocket? It seemed so unlikely. Maybe I'd imagined it. Back to the magazine rack. *Sports Illustrated*. Not a copy of *The Nation* or *The New Yorker* in sight. I crouched down on my haunches, fingering the smut mags. Perfect. I picked up a copy of *Boobs!*, held it in front of my face and peered over it. A tall swiveling rack of Hallmark cards provided additional cover. I had a clear view of Toni's car, bifurcated by the words "Joe's Fine Food and Beverage Service" painted on the window in foot-high red letters. I didn't actually think baked beans, Pillsbury slice and bake cookies and beef jerky qualified as fine food, but hey, what did I know? Around here, maybe it did.

Toni put the phone to her ear. Her lips moved for a few seconds, then she lowered it. She got out of the car, thrusting the phone into her pocket as she walked back toward the clinic. She carried a green canvas backpack, the old kind soldiers used to use. She hadn't had it when she showed up at the clinic. I hovered. Should I run out and confront her, or wait to see what she was going to do? I fished in my purse for my own phone. Maybe I should call Josie or Yvette to come. But really, I had no idea what Toni was up to. I didn't want to seem like a drama queen. Josie was sick and Yvette was Toni's friend – according to Toni, anyway.

Toni didn't walk up to the clinic door or up the stairs to my place. She walked around to the other side of the building, where the garbage and recycling cans were kept. I could no longer see her. It was mostly dark now, but there were two bright street lights on either side of the mall parking lot. If I went outside, Toni would certainly see me watching. Well, what's wrong with that? I asked myself. I live here. She's the one who's snooping around.

I put the *Boobs!* back in its place and walked out of the shop. Incredibly loud bells jangled as I did. My throat tightened. Toni had to have heard it. She didn't reappear, though. Why would she? People came and went from stores all the time. Besides, she might not be doing anything but throwing away detritus from her pack. My own periodic purse cleansings were often motivated by noticing a garbage can hanging around when I was getting out of my car. Probably Toni had been looking for a phone number or something in her pack, brushed her hand against a wad of gum or an unrecognizable food item and realized it was time for a purge. Of course, this garbage can wasn't next to Toni's car, wasn't even visible from where she'd been sitting, but that was a small point.

I stood in the shadows by the closed coffee shop. Between here and the other side of the building there was no cover, only open sidewalk and bright street lights. If Toni saw me walking past my own building, what would I say I was doing? Out for a walk, I decided. Perfectly natural after a long day of work.

I walked out to the street, just in time to see Toni come back around and get into her car. This time she started the engine and took off right away. I let her get nearly to the stop sign at the corner before climbing into my leased Volvo and pulling out. This sleepy area was going to be tough for following someone without being seen. Especially since I'd never tried to tail anyone before and had no idea how it worked. I stayed a couple cars behind her as she drove up Libbie to Broad Street, Richmond's main drag. She headed west, toward the booming suburb of Short Pump. One of the clients had told me that thirty years ago, Short Pump had nothing in it but a gas station. Now it was big box store haven, but I doubted Toni was meeting someone at Best Buy at seven thirty at night.

Following a car was a lot harder than it looked in the movies. The extra traffic on Broad gave me more cover, but made it harder to keep track of Toni's car. It seemed like every fourth car on the road was a beige Mini Cooper – something I'd never noticed before. After ten nerve-wracking minutes and two near-collisions, Toni swerved into the Olive Garden parking lot. Great, I had just put my life in danger, not to mention my fledgling relationship, to watch what was no doubt going to be a tryst with someone's blue-haired mother or aunt. Who knew, maybe this was where the AA dykes or the bowling set gathered for drinks and salad bar on Monday nights. Toni parked and got out right away, whoop whooping her alarm with the key fob. There was nothing surreptitious about her movements. I doubted people doing some kind of secret agent business would set their car alarms.

I drove around to the other side, parked and entered from the back. If Toni was hanging out with a group of women, maybe I'd ask to join them. I was very hungry, having eaten nothing except those few nuts and bites of persimmon since breakfast. I'd never eaten in an Olive Garden, and at home I wouldn't consider it, especially since they had been known to discriminate against queers and Black people. But, when in Richmond, I was learning to do as Richmonders do.

There was a big line at the front, and I didn't see Toni in it. With Toni's height, she could not be missed. I peeked into the dining room, using the throng of families and book groups as camouflage. I still didn't see Toni, so there must be a second room off the first. Only way to get there would be to visit the bathroom. I threaded my way through the crowd and got directions from a frazzled waitress. I hugged the wall all the way to the back corner of the massive back room where the little raised blue-skirted stick figure indicated I had found the right spot to relieve myself. I half turned, as if about to enter, and scanned the massive dining room with one eye. Toni was standing by a table populated by a forty-something white man and two children, one in a high chair. The older kid was copiously coloring on her placemat, brow furrowed in concentration. The man looked out of place, wearing a navy blue suit complete with burgundy and black striped tie. He said something that brought a concerned look to Toni's face. She walked around to where the little girl was, put a hand on her shoulder and bent to scrutinize the drawing. Her face brightened and she spoke to the kid, who threw her head back and chortled. Toni tousled her wispy blonde curls, then moved back to stand next to the man.

What was she doing? Was she joining them or not? Maybe she was meeting some other people and just happened to see someone she knew. This certainly seemed to be the happening spot.

After a few more exchanges of what appeared to be pleasantries, Toni pulled an envelope from the green pack and handed it to the guy. From where I stood, it looked just like the envelope I'd found in my newspaper, but of course, every person who still frequented a mailbox had a stash of those envelopes. The man put his fork and spoon down and tucked the envelope into the inside pocket of his jacket. Toni bent double to touch her lips to the cheek of the little girl, who tilted her head up and smiled, then dove back into her macaroni and cheese. Toni moved on to the high chair, where a bald little person in a bumblebee onesie was moving bits of breadstick around on the tray, occasionally popping one into its toothless mouth. Toni cupped the round head in her hand for a few seconds and then strode away. I thought she wiped a tear from her eye, but it could have been a bug. She didn't look furtive, just sad.

I went into the bathroom and splashed some water on my feverish face. I decided I would eat after all, as long as I didn't have to wait an hour for a table. The pasta smelled great, and my stomach was rumbling. I gave my name to the hostess and settled onto the red vinyl bench to wait for a table. Toni really had not done anything untoward, I concluded. There was no law against making phone calls in your car, or even opening someone else's trash bins.

The waitress showed me to a small table by the kitchen, the type family restaurants always had tucked away for single diners. I had to pull my arm into my body every time someone came barreling through the swinging doors with a tray heaped with pasta. I finished two helpings of the unlimited salad and eight breadsticks before my fettuccini ala quattro formaggio arrived, but I ate all the pasta anyway. It tasted wonderful. I tried to read Walter Mosely's latest mystery, but my thoughts kept drifting to Toni. Seeing her brief interaction with the children had made my suspicions recede. Gun or no gun, I wished I were with her now and looked forward to the next night's concert.

I was on my second glass of wine, perusing the Mosely book if not exactly reading it, when the man and his kids emerged from the back room. He carried the baby on his shoulders; a woman with stylish, brassy hair clutched the hand of the girl. Where had she come from? But of course, I hadn't been watching who walked to the back room, and wouldn't have paid any special attention to her if I had been. There was nothing otherworldly about them. So much for surveillance. I ordered a cappuccino to sober me up for the drive back home, and succumbed to the lure of cheesecake, which was complementary on Mondays. Replete and spacey, I climbed behind the wheel of the Volvo.

I backed out carefully, waiting extra long for the mom with the stroller to pass behind me. I turned right out of the lot and made it through the light at the corner just before it turned red. An SUV sped around the corner, barreling straight toward me. I started to swerve, but there was another car to my left. I had no option except to let the other car hit me. It did, swiping my passenger's side door with a sickening crunch. People were honking all around me. I flicked my left turn signal and slowly extricated my car from the SUV. At least I could drive it. I knew so little about cars, I had no idea what damage a crash like that could do to the engine. Shit, I hoped the leasing company would trade it for another one. I couldn't remember what the agreement said, but there was surely some kind of insurance involved. I pulled through the intersection, signaled and pulled over to the right. The SUV – dark blue, I couldn't tell what make – finished the turn, but the driver didn't pull in behind me. The car tore off, provoking another cacophony of horns.

I rested my hands on the steering wheel and rested my head on my hands. I bobbed my head gently up and down a few times, just to get the blood moving. What the hell had just happened? Nothing that dramatic, really; hit and runs like this happened all the time, but why did it have to be tonight, of all nights? Why on earth had I gone off on this harebrained adventure anyway? I should have stayed home and eaten cereal with unripe persimmon.

A knock on the window made me start and twist, nearly braining myself on the side of the car. I looked up to see a man; it was too dark to see what he looked like, even what race he was. Just for good measure, I clicked the automatic locks before rolling down the window a crack.

"Are you okay?" the guy asked. He had a husky voice, maybe a slight accent. In the flood of light from a passing car, I saw that he had pale skin and a scruffy beard above the collar of a brown leather jacket.

"Yes, I think so." I turned my head back and forth. I felt stiff. Maybe I had whiplash. "It was just so weird."

"Yeah, that guy was going a hundred miles an hour."

"That guy? You saw the driver?"

"Well, no … I guess I just assumed it was a guy."

Why was I harping on that? I would normally assume it was a guy too. But what if it wasn't? What if …? I was not going to go there. Toni was driving a Mini Cooper, not an SUV. This was a random accident, a coincidence.

"I'll testify it wasn't your fault," the guy at the window said. He was trying to pass something through the crack in the window. I reached up and took it, a business card.

"Josh Good – that's you?" According to the card, he was a handyman.

"That's me. My number's there. Tell your insurance company they can call me."

"Thanks – you deserve your name."

He inclined his head a little. "Huh?"

"Good," I said. "You're a good person."

"Oh. Thanks." He looked uncomfortable now. Did he think I was coming on to him? That would be ludicrous; he was half my age, if that. But of course, he could probably barely see me, just like I could barely see him.

"I'll be okay," I said. "Thanks a lot for your help. I expect the insurance company will be in touch."

"See you," he said with a wave. I doubted it.

I parked in the lot behind my apartment, which was of course deserted. When I gathered my nerve to exit the car, I saw that the damage wasn't as bad as I'd expected. Really, it was just a shallow dent in the back passenger's side door. The door even opened and closed.

Going up the narrow steps, I used the hand rail, which I usually didn't need to. I felt slightly unsteady, likely because of the wine and the long day, rather than the accident. My neck and shoulder were stiff, but that was hardly uncommon. Nonetheless I took two Advil prophylactically. My joints didn't bounce back as fast as they used to.

I knew I should call Josie or Nell, but there would be too many un-comfortable questions if I did. I propped myself up with a pillow against the armrest of the sofa and made a list. I eschewed the laptop, rustling up paper and pen for this exercise.

Reasons to Call Someone	Reasons to Call No One
Phone call first night	Don't want to discuss Renata Kellam
dyKeS Go hOMe (almost forgot about that with everything else that happened!)	
Someone crashed into car	It was a stupid accident
	You've been drinking and now you took pills on top of that
Never said you didn't drink or take over the counter medication	
Toni carries a gun	Relationship with Toni is none of their business (but they might think it is)
	Don't want Toni to find out you spied on her
	Too tired
	Shouldn't bother Josie if she's sick

The nays won by two. The Advil, mixed with the alcohol, was start-ing to make me groggy. I dragged myself off the couch and crawled into bed, promising that if one more weird thing happened, I would *def-initely* tell someone.

CHAPTER SEVEN

Death and the Maiden

Classical music tended to have a narcotic effect on me at any time. Tonight, after a full day of abortions and a steady diet of Advil, I started to drift off with the first thrums of the viola. I pinched my thigh to wake myself up. Toni's friend Lee turned out to be a slightly built man – in his early fifties, by my reckoning. His fingers flew over the strings, and he bobbed his head a little to the beat. The violinists were two young women who looked like twins – sleek black ponytails, high cheekbones, slender figures with long legs. All the musicians wore the traditional black bottom and white shirt, the two men in bow ties, the twins in be-low-the-knee skirts. The audience was a mix of university people and silver-haired museum patrons. Lee and the violist both taught in the University of Richmond music department, Toni had explained, and the women were students. She had met Lee at the gym and now they played racquetball twice a week. I imagined that the games must be pretty lop-sided; Toni had at least six inches on the poor guy, and she was a lot more buff. Still, Lee manhandled his cello pretty convincingly, and car-rying it around must take some upper body strength too.

After the intermission, the quartet was joined by a second violist for Schubert's "Death and the Maiden," my absolute favorite piece of mu-sic. I no longer felt exhausted. The music had such driving energy, it made me feel more alive than I had in weeks. I turned to Toni, wanting to take her hand and share the feeling, but she was gazing at the players with such rapt attention, I felt like I was intruding just by glancing at her.

I sank back into the plush seat and let my mind drift. Who was the maiden, and how did she die? Maybe she died of a botched abortion, or a birth she couldn't handle. Maybe she committed suicide because she was pregnant. Maybe she had been raped or maybe her lover had killed her. So many tragic stories flooded into my mind as the notes climbed to their crescendo and slowly sank again, like the maiden sinking into the sea.

The music ended and the crowd leapt to its feet. I usually refuse to participate in standing ovations; they have become too routine. But this time I joined in. My cheeks were wet and I saw other people mopping theirs. Toni put an arm around me, and I snuggled against her.

"Italian?" Toni asked, as we walked briskly to her car. The weather had taken a wintery turn. I was glad for her fake leather jacket.

I almost wondered if Toni had seen me in the Olive Garden. But I was not going to get paranoid. There was nothing sinister about suggesting Italian. I ate Italian all the time, and Richmond did not have the Bay Area's wealth of ethnic restaurants.

"Sure," I said. "But not Olive Garden."

Toni turned to me open-mouthed, her teeth glowing in the dark.

"Why on earth would you say that?" she asked.

"No reason," I said. "I've just passed it a few times and it seems really popular."

"Well not with me," Toni said.

She opened the door of the Mini Cooper and actually held out a hand to help me in. I briefly thought of ignoring it, demonstrating that I was perfectly capable of getting into a car without help. I decided to take the gesture as gallantry, not condescension. Toni was probably in her late fifties, not more than fifteen years younger than me.

She chose a hole in the wall on the edge of the Fan with plastic checkered tablecloths and candles stuck in wax-dripped Chianti bottles. It reminded me of the pizza joints in Portland, where I'd grown up. We ordered calzones and a bottle of house red, which turned out to be a serviceable Burgundy, despite the Chianti decor. I didn't feel that much like drinking; but if I didn't, I would need to explain why, so I sipped at the wine. After the first few sips, I stopped minding and started drinking faster.

"So, did you grow up here in Richmond?" I asked.

"No," Toni shook her head vigorously. "I'm a Navy brat. Grew up a million places, or no place really. We lived in Germany, Japan, Cuba and Puerto Rico, but when we were in the States, we lived in Portsmouth. It's on the coast, a little more than an hour southeast of here," she added, before I had a chance to ask.

"Did you like moving around so much?"

"It was okay. It gave me a good excuse for not having any friends."

"I can't imagine you without friends," I said. Toni seemed so at ease socially, not like me.

"I don't know if anyone really has friends in high school," Toni said. She removed the napkin from the basket of bread, releasing a wisp of steam. She took a roll and I did the same. Bread as an appetizer for bread. She slathered the roll with butter from an icy foil packet. At home, Italian restaurants served bread with olive oil and balsamic vinegar. There was something to be said for the boonies. I was a big butter fan.

"I don't think teenagers are really capable of friendship," Toni continued. "Their libidos are too strong, their amygdalae still developing. They might think they have friends, if they are good at tribal behaviors, but I don't think you can consider those real relationships."

"I don't know," I mused. The waiter delivered our salads – iceberg lettuce with one slice each of pale pink tomato and cucumber with the skin left on, swimming in gloppy Italian dressing. It didn't hold a candle to the Olive Garden salad. "I feel like my friendships in high school were some of the deepest I've ever had. We talked about everything, how our parents didn't understand us, what we wanted to do with our lives, how we saw the world." Everything but my attraction to my girl-friends, that is.

"Are you still friends with any of them?" Toni asked. She took a forkful of lettuce, held it over the bowl to let most of the dressing drip off before popping it into her mouth.

"Well, no," I said. "But we don't live in the same place. I went to a public school, where kids from different worlds were thrown together. It was a temporary existence. My nieces and nephew grew up in a very insular, religious Jewish community, and they have a lot of the same friends they've had since kindergarten."

Too late, I realized what I had said. Toni leaned forward.

"You're Jewish?" The wine had made me careless. Mollie O'Shay was clearly not a Jew.

"Their mother is," I said. "It was a huge scandal when my brother married a Jew." My brother had, in fact, intermarried. His wife had con-verted from Lutheran. It was her idea to send the kids to Jewish schools.

Toni accepted my answer easily. She tapped her fork against her lower lip, back to thinking like an anthropologist.

"Maybe being in a small minority creates a kind of solidarity that transcends the self-absorption characteristic of youth. But I think the principle still holds. Children and adolescents don't know who they are yet, so they can't build true relationships. It's all based on posturing."

"So are a lot of adult relationships," I protested. "I'm not sure I've known who I was for most of my life."

"You know what's important to you, right?"

"Sure, politics, activism. That's always been core. Providing quality health care to people who need it. Being a lesbian and a feminist. What about you?"

"Family. Feminism. Being a teacher, having something to impart to younger people. Producing good scholarship, thinking deeply about things."

"You didn't mention sexuality," I said.

"It's not that central to who I am," Toni said. "I've been a lesbian for fifteen years, but I was heterosexual for thirty or more."

"Heterosexual? Or confined by compulsory heterosexuality?" I held my breath. I had never been with a bisexual. Every one of my lovers had come out by the time they were twenty. Doing the math, Toni hadn't crossed over until her forties. But based on who she was now, I couldn't believe she had ever really been straight.

Toni didn't answer right away. She looked down at the table, as if she had never considered the question before.

"It's complicated," she said finally. She lifted her glass, took a big swill of wine. I followed, matching her swig for swig. "I had crushes on women in college, but then I met my husband, and I loved being married to him and being a mom. For most of that time, I never had any feeling that it wasn't what I was meant to be doing. So I would say I was heterosexual then."

"You had a husband?" I practically hissed the first syllable of "husband." I hadn't meant to sound so harsh.

"For twenty-four years," Toni said. "I met him my first day of college."

"And then what happened?" There were so many things I wanted to know about Toni's married life. I wondered why I had started at the end and if I would be able to get back.

"He died," Toni said.

I gulped, and my wine went down the wrong way. I coughed, spluttering drops of red on my blouse. When I could breathe again, I took a sip of tepid water.

"Sorry," I said. "I wasn't expecting that."

"I know," Toni said. "It's okay."

"What did he die of?"

Toni drank some more wine, ate half her tomato slice. I almost thought she wasn't going to answer.

"He committed suicide," Toni said. Great. This was going to be one fun dinner. "Gassed himself in our garage. One week after I told him I was gay."

At that inopportune moment, the waiter brought our calzones. I could feel the heat rising off of the perfectly browned dough. It smelled heavenly, I was quite hungry, and I could definitely not eat right now.

"I'm confused," I said. "I thought you said you weren't gay when you were married."

"I don't think I was gay when I *got* married. But I had started to notice other women, and wonder. I was working as a paramedic then, I told you that. I'd answered an ad recruiting women. There were five of us in my unit. I was the only straight woman."

"And you weren't that straight," I said. I didn't know if it was right, but it didn't seem like such a bad idea to inject some levity into the conversation. Toni smiled, a small, sad smile.

"No, not that straight. One night Ken and I were watching a documentary on television about Billie Jean King. You remember, when her relationship with Marilyn Barnett became public, her husband Larry stood by her. They didn't break up right away. They showed a clip of her saying she was taking some time off to work on her marriage. And Ken said, 'Boy, that guy was a wuss. If my wife was gay, I'd be out of there so fast.'"

"What an asshole," I wanted to say. I was starting to be glad this Ken was dead. I held my tongue, nodding in what I hoped was a sympathetic way.

"What did you say?" I asked.

"I didn't say anything right away. I wasn't even sure I needed to say anything. I didn't want my marriage to break up. I loved Ken, maybe not sexually at that point, but he was familiar. I didn't want to break up our family. But after the movie was over, I said, 'I need to tell you something.'"

"He turned and looked at me, and he was smiling. He looked exactly like he'd looked when he asked me to the movies for the first time. We saw 'E.T.'"

"E.T. phone home," I said, though I was in no mood to reminisce about old movies. "What then?"

"I started crying. He put his arms around me, asked what was wrong. I was crying on his shoulder and I blubbered, 'I think I'm gay.' He didn't understand, or he acted like he didn't. He pulled away a little, still had his arm around me, and he looked down at me – he was even taller than me. That's one of the reasons I fell for him."

Tears were welling up in her eyes as she remembered. I wondered if I should stop her, tell her she didn't have to talk about it if it was too painful. But I felt like I needed to know this part of her.

"He wasn't smiling anymore," she said. "He was gritting his teeth. 'Don't be ridiculous,' he said. 'You're not gay.' That made me mad, and I said, 'How do you know?' And he shoved me away. Just pushed me with the flat of his hand, and I fell and hit my head on the corner of a glass table. I was lying on the floor, bleeding and screaming, and he just said, 'Don't say that again,' and walked out of the room, into the bedroom. I lay there for a while, and then managed to get up and find a bandage to stop the bleeding."

Homophobic and violent. I definitely wasn't feeling Ken's pain. But Toni had loved him and even now she looked distraught, remembering. She took a deep breath and followed it with a slug from her nearly empty wine glass.

"I cursed myself for saying anything," she said. "I had just been having these thoughts and feelings for so long, and I wanted to share them with someone, and Ken was my best friend. I don't think I really even thought about what it might do to him."

"It wasn't your fault," I said. It was a cliché, but it was the best I could do.

"I know it wasn't," Toni said. "But I hadn't thought it out. I went into our bedroom. He was lying on his back, eyes wide open. He wouldn't talk to me. I slept on the couch that night, and every night after that. And then a week later I came home and saw the garage door closed and heard the engine, and I knew what he had done. He didn't leave a note. He didn't need to."

"How awful for you," I said. I reached across the table, but Toni didn't put out her hand. Instead she cupped them around the stem of her wine glass.

"Yes, it was."

"What about your kids? How many do you have?"

Toni's head moved very slowly from side to side.

"Two. Two girls. I lost them. They never forgave me."

"How did they know?"

"I don't know. Ken must have told them. They weren't living with us then. Caroline was in college and Joanna had already graduated. When they came back for the funeral, they stayed with Ken's mother. I sent them birthday and Christmas cards, but they always came back unopened. I called Jo every day for a year and a half. Caroline too, until she graduated and her number was disconnected. And then I just had to give up."

Toni picked up her knife and fork and started hacking at her calzone as if it were her husband's body. I watched her in a kind of horrified fascination. She speared an asymmetrical piece of dough-covered meat and crammed it into her mouth. She repeated that ritual over and over, occasionally taking a gulp from her wine glass. Only once did she reach up and swipe at her eyes with her forearm.

When Toni was halfway through her dinner, I turned to my own meal, dipping the spinach and mozzarella pie into the rich marinara sauce. Even lukewarm, it was delicious. We finished in silence and split the check on matching debit cards. Toni drove to her house, without even asking where I wanted to go. We went straight to the bedroom and made furious love for much of the night.

CHAPTER EIGHT

Manning the Phone

After six weeks, OWLS was running a well-oiled machine, albeit a machine that was always a bit short on cash. Mondays and Tuesdays I worked from eight in the morning until six at night, Wednesdays and Thursdays from noon 'til nine or so, to accommodate clients who worked days. Fridays were our longest day, eight am to eight pm, but on Saturdays we tried to be finished with everything at the clinic by three, in case there was a fundraiser at night that people needed to prepare for. Sundays, of course, were for church or softball. Or in some cases, both. Since I didn't play softball or go to church, I had a day free for shopping, sleeping, laundry and email.

Most of the work happened at the comfortably furnished one-story safe house on a residential street about a mile from the clinic. The OWLS didn't want it too close. If someone snitched, a wide radius would make finding the clinic itself harder for the cops. But it also meant our timing had to be excellent, because we didn't want clients to see one another. At the safe house, a woman could be counseled in one room when another showed up to be driven to the clinic, but one of them would need to be gone by the time the next person arrived.

We had taken a lot of our operating model from the stories we had read and heard about how Jane operated in the early nineteen seventies, but updated for the current technological climate. Clients reached Jane by leaving a message on a telephone answering machine. We did that too, with an encrypted voicemail, but we could also be reached through text, the Signal app, or a secure web form. If the client had internet, the initial consult was on Jitsi. If not, it was a phone call. The volunteers then arranged to meet the clients in neutral public spaces like cafes or parks. It was kind of like the medical version of Tinder.

The volunteer would chat with the client in the public place for long enough to ascertain that they were on the up-and-up and no one was watching them, and then the volunteer would drive them to the safe house.

There'd been a couple of no-shows and one woman had shown up with a boyfriend in tow. The no-shows didn't worry me, because I'd learned years ago that a certain percentage of people who call about abortions never follow up. The man was another story. The woman had been told to come alone, and had violated our trust. The volunteer called Josie, who had come up with a procedure on the spot. The volunteer called the woman on her cell phone and told her she couldn't meet with her because she'd broken the agreement. She was given another time and place and told if she screwed that one up, that would be it.

Volunteers asked the clients for their phones as soon as they met up, turned them off, and removed the batteries to prevent any surreptitious recordings. But we stopped short of frisking clients. The group had been split on that question – Yvette had argued in favor, Josie had vehemently opposed – and since we ran on consensus, the idea was scotched.

At the safe house, the volunteer would take vital signs and medical history, explain the options and answer questions. This was all encompassed in the job description we called "counseling." If the client opted for medication abortion, theoretically she could get the pills right then and there, but we were not doing it that way. Since the safe house was the most vulnerable to police raids, the OWLS didn't want anything illegal on the premises. We didn't even have any brochures about abortion, though there were a few copies of *Our Bodies Our Selves* and other women's health books that described the procedures. That meant even abortion pills had to be dispensed at the clinic. Right now, I was taking all those appointments, but I was training volunteers so they would soon be able to dispense prescriptions in the clinic's front office, while surgical clients came in through the back.

As word got around, we were getting more and more clients. Yvette and Josie, thankfully, were geniuses of scheduling.

OWLS couldn't afford an ultrasound machine. Clients were supposed to go get sonograms as part of routine pregnancy care from a doctor or clinic. It was risky, because then the doctors would want to know what had happened to the babies, but with the state of medical care these days, no one was likely to call and check on them. If anyone did, the clients were told to say they decided to go to another doctor. If a woman didn't already have a doctor, we sent her to Planned Parenthood, which offered prenatal care as well as contraception and other services. PP couldn't officially know about OWLS, but they could be trusted not to ask too many questions.

My first patient on this particular Wednesday was Caitlin, whose chart said she was twenty-one. She had told Josie she worked at the Denny's off Highway 64, and needed to be done early enough to make her shift at five in the afternoon. I would have preferred for her to take the day off, but I understood why that wasn't going to happen. Her three-year-old son, Jeremy, was in the apartment upstairs, being cared for by Sylvia. Since being down here, I had learned a lot about integrated medical care. No clinic I'd worked at in the Bay Area offered childcare. But after one woman cancelled her appointment because she couldn't find anyone to watch her kids, Yvette and Evelyn had been adamant: women should not be having more children just because they couldn't find care for the ones they had.

Caitlin said her last period was twelve weeks ago, but she didn't have a sonogram to show me. According to Josie's notes, Caitlin insisted she didn't have time to go to another clinic. With a full-time job and a three-year-old, that was easy to believe. Since she was pushing the deadline for a simple vacuum aspiration, Josie had scheduled her for the next open appointment.

As soon as I felt inside Caitlin's pelvis, I could tell the fetus was at least fifteen weeks in gestation. I resisted the urge to scream at the young woman. Anyone desperate enough to lie about how pregnant she was had a good reason to do it. I made a mental note to tell the volunteers to make it clear to the clients that they couldn't fake it.

"Caitlin?" Hopefully I didn't sound as frustrated as I felt.

"Hmm?"

"When did you really have your last period?"

"I can't remember," the young woman said. She curled her feet under her and sat up. "Are you going to send me home?"

I walked around to put a hand on her shoulder, easing her back down on the bed.

"No, I'm not. But I really need to know how far along you are. See, I would guess you are between sixteen and seventeen weeks, by what I can see. But without a sonogram, I can't be sure exactly how big the fetal head is."

When I was first doing abortions, I had to learn not to say "your baby's head." Women choosing abortion didn't need any reminders that the clump of tissue being evacuated from their womb was any relative of a baby. It was the exact opposite of what I had done as a midwife, which was to encourage women to start bonding with their babies as soon as the pregnancy was viable.

"Caitlin," I said. "The thing is this. Sixteen weeks is the absolute cutoff for the simplest type of abortion, where I use this," I gripped the handle of the vacuum aspirator, "to suction out the tissue from your uterus. After that, I need to use a procedure that is more complicated and takes longer, and can hurt a little."

I didn't know if I should say that, but I hoped that it might motivate Caitlin to tell me what was going on.

"So if there's anything you can remember that might help us to figure out just how far along you are, now is the time to tell me."

Caitlin drew her right arm across her eyes. Great, Mollie. You made the client cry. That's really gonna help move this thing along. I stroked her other arm ineffectually.

She said something, but it was too soft for me to hear. I wheeled the little stool around from the foot of the bed so I could sit close to her.

"I'm sorry, I missed that," I said, realizing I sounded like Siri.

"I got raped," she whispered.

Oh my God. This was not just terrible for the young woman before me. It was terrible for everyone scheduled for an abortion that day, because what should have been a half hour procedure was already heading for the fifteen minute mark and this was not the moment to hurry things along. I stripped off the latex gloves and took one of Caitlin's hands, giving it a little squeeze. Then I swiveled slightly toward Yvette, who stood near the door waiting to assist with the abortion. I only needed to tilt my head and she was out the door to call Rabbit and tell them to stall the next client.

I turned back to Caitlin. Good thing I'd been a rape counselor early in my career as a Second Wave Feminist.

"I'm so sorry," I said. "Do you want to tell me about it?"

She shook her head, tears filling her pale blue eyes. "I can't," she whispered.

"That's okay," I said. "Here's what we're going to do."

Caitlin angled her arm up so that she could look at me out of one eye, the other still covered – a compromise between despair and hope.

"I'm going to put something inside you to help you dilate quicker, and then we'll have you hang out upstairs with Jeremy for a while. Then in a couple hours, we can finish the procedure. How does that sound?"

"A couple hours? I'll be late to work."

"Um, Caitlin, you'd better call in sick today."

"I can't. They'll fire me."

"Come on. Just for being out one day? You work at Denny's, right?" It occurred to me that if Caitlin lied about how pregnant she was, she could have lied about other things too.

"Yes," she said.

"Denny's is a big company. You must get some sick days."

I wasn't totally clueless. I knew big fast food chains exploited their workers terribly, but it wasn't in their interest to fire every worker who took a sick day now and then. They'd constantly be training new people.

"It's not just one day." The arm came back down across the left eye. "I was out three days last week because Jeremy had the flu. That's all the time I had – more, even. He's always getting sick."

Caitlin's upper body was starting to quiver.

"Caitlin, would it be okay if I have a little chat with your manager?"

"I don't know." Her voice was still faint but her arm came off of both eyes now. I read a glimmer of hope in the watery eyes.

"I'll be polite, I promise," I said. I might have been polite twice in my life. "I just want to explain to him that you're really too sick to come in. I'm a doctor, he'll believe me." I still cringed when I claimed to be a doctor. But that was the rule and in this case, I had to agree with the group's reasoning. Caitlin's boss would be less likely to argue with a doctor than with a nurse midwife.

"Maybe so."

"Can you give me your boss's number?"

Caitlin got up, scrunching the back of her paper gown closed with one hand. She rummaged through her purse, came up with her cell phone, and read me a seven digit number.

"Okay, try to relax," I said. "I'll be right back?"

I went into the office, where Yvette was working on the computer.

"What did Rabbit say?" I asked.

"The house is full, so they're keeping the next client in the car."

"Oh, that's not good. I better hurry. I need to make a phone call."

Yvette logged out of Gmail before relinquishing her seat. She took her cup and headed to the kitchen. She was a nonstop tea drinker. I liked working with Yvette, was glad she had the most time to assist in the clinic. She supplemented her firefighter's pension as a professional pet-sitter. When she worked at the clinic, she often left two or three dogs hanging out in her VW van, dashing out to let them pee and refresh their water.

I waited until I was sure Yvette was out of earshot to dial the number Caitlin had given me.

"Hello, is this Paul Manning?" The voice on the other end was deep and scratchy, suggesting a several pack a day smoking habit.

"Yeah, who's this?"

"This is Dr. Jenkins. One of your employees, Caitlin, is under my care. She's very sick."

"Sick how?"

I wracked my brain for something Caitlin could miraculously recover from tomorrow.

"We're not sure yet. She's having severe stomach pain." That would be true soon enough. "It might be just a virus and she'll be better tomorrow, but we are sending her for some tests. There's no way she can work today."

"Hmmph."

"Mr. Manning, Caitlin's very worried about losing her job. She doesn't want to go for the tests, because she thinks you'll fire her if she doesn't go to work. But that's not true, is it? You wouldn't fire someone just for being sick."

"She's always sick. Or her kid is."

"You don't mean always, do you? How many times has she been out this year?"

"Well, maybe six or seven. But she was just out nearly all last week."

I pantomimed stamping on the guy's foot. It felt good, even if he was ten miles away. "Jeremy was ill then. Caitlin probably picked up a bug from him. Do you have children, Mr. Manning? Can I call you Paul?"

"Sure, I got kids. Three of 'em."

"And what do you do when they're sick?"

"Well, my wife don't work."

"Well, Caitlin doesn't have a wife. She only has herself. And Jeremy only has her. You wouldn't want her to leave him alone when he's sick, would you?"

"She told me her mom takes care of him when she's at work."

"Well, maybe her mom was sick too. I can tell you, Caitlin's not taking days off for fun. She works hard when she's there, right?"

"When she's here, yeah."

"Okay, so you don't want to lose a good worker and you certainly don't want to have a sick person serving food to your customers, right? I don't think the health department would like that, any more than the Department of Fair Employment and Housing would want to hear that you're discriminating against female employees with kids."

"You don't need to threaten me, lady. I said I won't fire the b– the girl."

"Good, that's good," I tried to summon my bright voice. "And I prefer 'doc' to lady."

"No problem, doc. Hey, what'd you say your name was? Jenkins? What's your first name, eh?"

"Thanks a lot, Paul. Have a great day."

I hung up. Josie, in her infinite wisdom, had blocked our number from callbacks as well as caller ID. Chuckling a little, I went to the kitchen to tell Yvette what I'd done.

"Can you let Rabbit know we're going to be a bit longer?" I asked. "Tell them to take the other client on the scenic route."

I went to give Caitlin the good news. She'd fallen asleep in the exam chair, her blonde hair matted on one cheek. I wished I could just let her sleep. Being a single mom with a tough job was no picnic, that was for sure. I would have loved to see Paul Manning try it for two days.

CHAPTER NINE

Luther Burger

I had to keep Caitlin waiting upstairs until all the other scheduled clients were done, and that meant Sylvia had to stay with Jeremy until nearly seven. Yvette stayed too, although I told her I could handle the D&E by myself. When Rabbit finally drove off with Jeremy tucked into our borrowed car seat and Caitlin dozing under an afghan crocheted by Josie's grandmother, I felt like I deserved a drink. I had a bottle of Chardonnay in the fridge, but I didn't relish drinking it alone in my apartment with only the TV for company.

"Are you in the mood for a drink?" I asked the other two women.

"Sorry, not tonight," Sylvia said. "Got to get home. Toni's cooking for Mah Jongg." She was already edging out the door.

"Toni plays Mah Jongg?" Why did hearing that make me feel cheated? I didn't play, had never even seen a Mah Jongg set except on my computer. There was no reason Toni would have told me, but I still felt like she should have.

"We've been doing it for nearly fifteen years. Same four couples. Except most of us aren't couples anymore."

"You and Toni were together?" I hoped I managed to sound just curious.

"Oh, yeah. We bought the duplex together. After we broke up, I moved upstairs."

I visualized Toni's flat, where I'd spent the last few Saturday nights. I had never thought to ask who lived upstairs and Toni hadn't volunteered the information. Had Sylvia been her first lover after Ken? She'd mentioned being attracted to some of the other EMT trainees.

"Were you an EMT too?" I asked.

"Me? No, I work nights at the blood bank." That explained why Sylvia had so much time to volunteer at the clinic. Also likely how she had met Toni, but I'd have to ask about that some other time because she was out the door. Hillary was Toni's ex. Sylvia was another. She'd called Yvette a friend, but what if she'd omitted a critical aspect of that friendship? This whole setup was starting to feel like a bad lesbian episode of *Dynasty*.

"What about it, buy you a drink?" I asked Yvette. I didn't remember if I'd ever seen Yvette drink alcohol. I knew Evelyn was Methodist, so Yvette probably was too, but she could be in AA, like so many of the other dykes in this town and every town.

"I'm supposed to have Bible study," Yvette said.

"Oh, that's fine then." Disappointment mingled with relief. As much as I liked her, I was nervous around Yvette. Her competence was a little intimidating, and I felt like I might easily offend her. I didn't usually socialize with people who went to Bible study and took care of dogs.

"But I'd rather drink," she said, laughing. She had a nice rough laugh, like someone with deeply buried secrets to share. "And eat," she added.

"Great, then!" I shrugged into my jacket and picked up my purse. I should probably go up and change, but I was afraid Yvette might change her mind in that time. Especially knowing that Toni was playing Mah Jongg with her ex ex, I didn't want to be abandoned.

"I have one thing to do, then I'll meet you outside," I said. I felt terribly rude, but Josie and Nell had told me not to let anyone else see me lock the supply room. Only they knew the combination. As head of security, Yvette might even have helped make the plan. Her eyebrows arched a tad, but she didn't protest.

"Unless you want to meet… where are we going, anyway?" I said, before Yvette could get out the door. If Yvette said Babe's — the city's only lesbian bar, which doubled as a steakhouse — that would settle the question once and for all.

"Sweet Sally's?" she suggested.

"Perfect, I've been wanting to try it."

"I'll drive," Yvette said. "My van's right out front."

"No dogs today?" I held my breath. I wasn't riding in a van with four smelly dogs.

"No, ma'am, not today."

I was left to wonder, as I put away the instruments and set the alarm. Maybe Yvette just had a hankering for Cajun barbecue? Then again, Babe's, the times I'd been in there, was very white. Maybe Black lesbians had their own secret places.

We ordered microbrews and parmesan fries with garlic aioli. I chose the veggie cheeseburger with mushrooms and onions. Yvette vacillated between buffalo wings and something called a Luther Burger, finally opting for the latter. I scanned the description before handing back my menu to the server. "named after Luther Vandross, the Luther Burger consists of two 1/4 lb. bacon cheeseburgers, served on a Krispy Kreme donut!" I read.

Yvette and I were definitely going to be friends.

We picked at the seemingly endless cone of fries and I delicately grilled Yvette about her background. She had grown up in Richmond — "born and bred and never want to leave." She went to Virginia Union University, a historically Black college — HBC, she called it — just a few blocks from here.

"What'd you major in?"

"Black Studies," she answered. "Would have liked to do Women's Studies, but they didn't have it. I wrote my honors thesis on the work of Angela Y. Davis. That was very risky back then. They nearly didn't graduate me."

"Really? Why? I mean, Davis was long out of jail by then, right? She was a professor and a scholar."

"She was a Communist," Yvette said, drawling out the o. "See, VUU – well, it wasn't VUU then, it was still just Virginia Union College – was a very conservative place, even for an HBC. They wanted us to be ladies, join our mamas' sororities, wear white gloves on Sunday. We weren't supposed to be studying rabble-rousers, especially not ones that wrote about stuff like race and gender."

Our food came. I liked the look of my veggie burger, but couldn't help being awed by the Luther Burger. I thought of asking if I could trade my bun for a donut, but I had the feeling they might call the food police on me. I took advantage of the waiter's fleeting presence to order another beer. Yvette debated, then asked for a second also. She seemed to be someone who took decisions about food and drink very seriously.

"Did you always know you were a feminist?" I asked.

"From the day I was born," Yvette said. "You couldn't grow up in my family and not be."

The look that crossed her face then could only be called ferocious. She opened her mouth wide, stuffed a corner of the burger in and chomped down. I thought she would continue. She had brought up her family, so she must want to talk about it. But Yvette quickly switched gears.

"What about you?" she asked. "You a California girl from the start?"

"Not even close," I shook my head. "I was born in Montana, then my folks moved to Oregon. Not enough … Catholics … in Montana." I had been this close to saying "Jews," had actually gotten a little bit of the "J" out before I remembered. Yvette didn't seem to have noticed. "Not so many in Oregon either, but we lived in Portland. My dad taught at OSU. It wasn't so bad."

"What'd he teach?" Yvette wanted to know.

"Forestry," I lied. "That's how he ended up in Montana. Good place for trees, bad place for Catholics."

"Yeah, Blacks too," said Yvette, bobbing her head. She had eaten half her sandwich, but was losing some steam.

"Definitely," I said. "KKK all the way."

"So y'all moved to Oregon, and then how'd you end up in Frisco?"

I cringed. San Franciscans hate that nickname for our city. But I didn't even live in the City anymore, so I didn't need to be so snobbish. The tech boom had brought more than enough snobbery to the Bay.

"Actually, I live in Oakland," I said. "Where the Warriors used to play."

Why had I said that? I am not a sports fan. I was nervous, and when I'm nervous, I babble. The J slip had reminded me that I couldn't afford to relax.

"I went to college in San Diego," I went on. Another lie. I had started at Kent and eventually finished at UCLA. Long ago, I'd adopted the motto, "Lie all the time, and you'll never be tempted to tell the truth."

"So you and Evelyn, how did you meet?" Seemed like an innocuous enough question, didn't necessarily imply anything, but might get the answer I was looking for. "Did she go to VU too?"

"Ms. Grander than Grand Grandis? Oh, no, dear." Yvette laughed that strong, husky laugh. "No, Ev went to Spelman, like her mama and her mama's mama. She's old Georgia money. Her people never were even slaves. I think they were slaveholders, though she'd never admit to it. Got some Seminole blood in her too."

"I can see that," I said. I called up an image of Evelyn's regal countenance and blue-black skin. "But you two are friends, right?"

"Me and Ev? We're lots more than friends." Aha! I felt a flush of satisfaction.

Why was I so interested in Evelyn and Yvette's relationship? I didn't have enough of a social life, I decided. I was still bereft over Sidney, and Yvette was my first new friend besides Toni. If I could even call Toni a friend.

"We're thicker than thieves," Yvette went on. What did that mean? "I'd do anything for Ev, and she's helped me out of plenty of close calls.

Been knowing each other more than thirty-five years now. She came up here right after college, with her husband. He went to Morehouse, natch."

"Are they still married?"

Yvette shook her head so violently I thought it might come off her neck. "No, ma'am! That man didn't stick around ten years. Evelyn put him through med school, then he took up with his receptionist – can you believe that? She was white."

She literally spat out "white," a little spray just missing my cheek. I didn't take it personally. I'd seen "Jungle Fever." Getting dumped is bad, but for a Black woman to get dumped for a white woman is a trope. As a loyal friend, Yvette was rightly outraged.

"All that money he makes and he didn't send those boys one cent. Then suddenly, when they're fifteen, he comes riding in, wants to take them to the ball game, to Williamsburg, to get a private tour of the White House. Ev was shaking mad."

"Did she let them go with him?" My head was spinning with all this information – Evelyn had twin boys, her ex was a doctor, and obviously a well-connected one. Why were we talking about Evelyn, when I had wanted to get to know Yvette? But we were, and I couldn't think how to change the subject without being rude.

"Yeah, she didn't want to but in the end she did. Figured maybe he'd pay for the boys to go to Morehouse too."

"Did he?"

"Those boys wouldn't go. Derrick went and joined the Marines. And Albert, he had to go to Harvard. Got himself a scholarship. You'd never think they were from the same egg, different as night and day."

"Sounds like she raised them well. Is Derrick still in the Marines?"

"Got his leg blown off in Kuwait." Yvette said it so matter-of-factly, I stared at her. Every time I went out to dinner with someone, they laid some tragedy on me. But Yvette didn't even seem to think it was a tragedy. She was actually smiling a little, maybe at how shocked I was.

"Is he... okay?" I asked. What an idiotic question. How could you be okay after losing a leg in war?

"He's fine," Yvette said. "He takes amputee kids on wilderness treks. Couldn't be happier. Albert's the one with the drug habit. In and out of rehab, mostly out, but he's doing better now. Got a job down at Walmart. Maybe not what Ev had hoped for when he went off to Harvard, but it just proves you never know where God's going to take you."

"You sound like you care about them a lot," I tried one more time.

"Oh, yeah, those boys are like my own kids," Yvette said.

I was going to have to be content with that. I grabbed the check when the waiter brought it, whisked out my credit card. Yvette offered once to pay her share, but didn't insist. I was glad. I might not have gotten the answers to all my questions, but I had learned a lot about the people I was working with. I had four more months with these folks. I didn't need to rush.

"I'm glad we got this chance to talk outside of the clinic," I said, as she started up the van.

"Yeah, me too." Yvette sounded like she meant it. Of course, she had gotten to eat a Luther Burger, so who could be unhappy?

CHAPTER TEN

America's Pastime

I'd wanted to ask Yvette about Toni, but the subject hadn't come up and I didn't want it to seem like I had an agenda. Toni hadn't volunteered at the clinic since the day she'd covered for Josie. She'd switched over to driving, maybe not wanting to end up on Animal Control duty again.

Since the night of the concert, we'd had a simple routine. Saturday evenings we got together, watched a movie or went to a concert or something, then went to her flat and had sex. Sunday mornings we had sex again, took a shower together, read the *New York Times* book review and made a decadent brunch of blintzes or Danish pastry, which took hours to make and seconds to devour. After that we sometimes went for a bike ride or a walk. Then I'd go home to do laundry – eighty percent the clinic's, twenty percent mine – and Toni went to shop for food provisions for the week. Sometimes we talked on the phone for ten minutes, maybe texted back and forth about possible things to do on our date night. It suited me fine. A perfect vacation romance, if this could be called a vacation.

It was a rude shock, then, when on the third Sunday in May, Toni's phone played a Sousa march and she bounded out of bed.

She dove into a plastic bin in her closet while I fumbled for my phone and strained to read the little numbers. Nine o'clock sharp. Much too early to be energetically rummaging like a chipmunk in an acorn factory.

"Hey," I protested, still trying to figure out how my vocal cords worked. "Come back. It's early."

"Found it," she said, thrusting a swollen right fist into the air. She brought the overgrown hand down and smacked her left fist into what I now understood was a softball glove.

"A little tight," she said. "But it'll loosen up."

"What's going on?" I asked. "You play softball?" I knew Nell had been practicing with her team for weeks.

("How can a priest play softball on Sundays?" I had asked.

"I couldn't when I was full-time," Nell said. "But now I'm Emerita, I'm only doing pastoral care. The new priest wouldn't want me coming to services anyway, cramping her style.")

"My father said I was born with a softball in my hand," Toni said. "He was disappointed at first that he didn't have a son, but once I learned to pitch, he got over it. I wasn't going to play this year, but Nell's team lost their pitcher – she had a baby. So I'm gonna save the day."

"But this is our time," I protested. Toni was already dressed, clad in sweatpants and a pink "Nasty Woman" t-shirt. I snaked an arm out from under the blanket and caught her hand. "Tell them you're sick," I pleaded, trying to look winsome. It's not really that easy to look winsome in your seventies. It's easier to look wizened.

"We'll make up for it," she said, dropping a light kiss on my forehead, like a mom checking my temperature. "It's just a couple hours. Go back to sleep, and I'll wake you when I get back."

I tried to obey, but sleep was gone. I showered and changed into the extra clothes tucked in my oversized purse. I'd forgotten to bring a hairbrush. I glanced around the bathroom and bedroom, didn't see one in any of the obvious places. I'd never seen Toni use a brush or a comb, just run her fingers through her hair. Short and straight, it didn't require much styling, unlike mine, which was thick and unruly. Still, no woman could have made it to her late fifties through five decades and not have even a comb in her house. After checking the medicine closet to no avail, I started tentatively opening drawers in the bedroom. Underwear on the left, socks on the right, t-shirts below, pants and sweaters below that. It made no sense for someone to tuck a comb into a bottom drawer. I ran my hand around the edges of the underwear drawer and when I touched paper, moved the collection of boxers and sports bras aside. Naturally, Toni would keep her important papers in her underwear drawer like everyone else.

A manila envelope was taped into the bottom of the drawer. I started to peel off the tape, but when I touched a corner, it started to crumble in my hand. Clearly this was a fixture. If I didn't want Toni to know I was snooping, I'd have to do it without dislodging anything. I reached into the envelope and pulled out a passport and two folded sheets of paper. The passport had been issued four years previously, at Richmond, Virginia, to Antonia Anders Griffin. There was only one stamp in it, a one-week stay in Italy two years ago. She had mentioned a vacation in Venice with Lee and his partner. I unfolded the first sheet of paper. The thick white bond had faded to a light yellow. It declared in the old fashioned typeface of an electric typewriter that Antonia Alexandria Anders had married Kenneth Oliver Griffin on December 4, 1985 at Grace Church, Richmond, Virginia. It was signed by the bride and groom, two witnesses, and the officiating priest, Eleanor Iverson.

I'd talked to Nell a little about my relationship with Toni. She'd been mildly encouraging. She'd never mentioned knowing her when she was married to Ken, let alone that she had performed their wedding. I wondered why not.

The other piece of paper was a permit to carry a concealed handgun, issued by the state of Virginia thirteen years ago to Antonia A. Anders. Under "Reason concealed carry is requested," the box next to "business or professional use" was checked. Thirteen years ago, I assumed Toni was an EMT. Did EMTs carry guns? Recently, during the debates over defunding police departments, people had argued that EMTs and other medical professionals were better trained than police to handle people having mental health crises. I had assumed those professionals would not be armed, but maybe that assumption was naïve, or valid only in hippie-crunchy California.

Why had Toni applied for the gun permit under her maiden name? Maiden – stupid word that didn't seem like it would ever have applied to Toni.

The permit verified that what I had thought I felt the first day Toni came to the clinic really was a gun. Or did it? If she was carrying the gun, wouldn't she have the permit with it?

Where was the gun? I didn't imagine she'd be wearing it under her softball outfit. Was it hidden in the glove box of her car? A cursory sweep of the apartment didn't reveal a safe, lockbox or any other obvious place to hide a weapon. It wasn't in the desk drawer or file cabinet in the office. I went back to the bedroom. When we slept together, Toni always insisted I sleep next to the wall, she on the outside. There were matching night tables on each side, each with a lamp on top and a drawer underneath. I jiggled the drawer on Toni's side. It didn't budge.

Thrusting guns and concealed carry permits resolutely out of my mind, I decided to make a special brunch. Toni had just grabbed an apple to eat on her way to practice; she would certainly be hungry when she returned. I padded into the living room to consult her extensive cookbook collection for ideas. Maybe something with Hollandaise, but not poached eggs. I can't stand runny yolks. I grabbed *The Vegetarian Epicure*, Volumes I and II, and settled down at the dining room table. Rummaging through the well-thumbed Veggie Epicure, crusted with little bits of petrified wheat germ and stained with olive oil, was like looking into a reel viewer of my own youth. 1972, the year this first vegetarian cookbook aspiring to gourmet was published, would have found me in L.A. with Nell, recovering from my tumultuous years at Kent State and then in Portland. I smiled at the memories prompted by Pizza Rustica and marinated cauliflower "à la grecque".

Matching the recipes to the contents of Toni's fridge was a little like crossing a jigsaw puzzle with a scavenger hunt, but I concluded I could make cream scones and little vegetable tarts with Hollandaise if I substituted half and half for cream, broccoli for cauliflower, and left out the peas. After lining up the ingredients on the kitchen counter, I retrieved the cookbook from the dining room table, marking each of the recipes I wanted to use with a finger. As I carried the book to the kitchen, an envelope fluttered to the ground.

I put the book on the counter and went back to retrieve the envelope. It was small, almost square, cream colored with no stamp or return address. The only writing on the front said "Mom" in curly, teenage cursive. It wasn't sealed, so I figured I wasn't violating any confidences when I pulled out the red rectangle from within. Inside a heart-shaped frame cut from a paper doily, two girls, maybe ten and twelve, smiled up at me. Flipping the red card over, I read in more felt-tipped cursive, "Happy Valentine's Day to the BEST Mom Ever."

I stared at the picture of Joanna and Caroline – I assumed. The colors in the matte photo had faded, making their features a little indistinct. Both had bold, eager expressions on wide faces, cascading curls and high foreheads slightly inclined toward one another, so that they seemed to be sharing a secret. Straight, even teeth, the younger, Caroline, I thought, with just a trace of an overbite, which I was sure had been corrected with braces a few years after this photo was snapped in the drug store. I could read in the picture the serenity of growing up with love and comfort, incapable of imagining the tragedy that would rock their world before too long.

How, I wondered, had the valentine ended up in the pages of *The Vegetarian Epicure*? Had the kids given their mother the cookbook as a Valentine's Day present, or had they slipped it in between the pages of the German Apple Pancake recipe where they knew she would turn to make her signature Valentine's Day breakfast? I wished I could go back to the time when this little missive was penned and placed, to glimpse this family before its rupture.

I looked around the neat apartment, with the gabled windows I admired, realizing that there were no pictures from Toni's previous incarnation. None of the shadowy Ken, or of the kids in high school graduation caps and gowns. On the mantle, I saw scattered shots of Toni with Hillary, Toni with Sylvia, Toni grinning in the middle of a group of women in matching blue polo shirts, a softball extended toward the camera. Toni and two young men leaning on an ambulance, all three in white uniform shirts. A few pictures featured people I didn't recognize, women at demonstrations with signs and pussy hats, hiking in the mountains, sitting on beaches, even playing in the snow. There was one, on an end table near the door, of a man in a parking lot, holding the hand of a small girl with blonde curly hair. Could that be Ken with Joanna? No, in the background a slightly-out-of-focus person was talking on a cellphone. This was not the mid-eighties. In fact – I picked up the photo and held it just an inch from my nose. This *could* be the man and the little girl from the Olive Garden. A brother and niece, maybe? But Toni had just said her father didn't have a son, which presumably meant she didn't have a brother, and anyway, this guy would be too young.

I popped a Chicks CD into the CD player. The outdated equipment made me smile. Toni's anthropologist side imparted a fondness for antiquated cultural artifacts. Singing along with Natalie Maines, I cut butter into flour and separated eggs for Hollandaise. Magically, everything came out of the oven moments before Toni's key turned in the lock. The scones were light and buttery, the Hollandaise rich and creamy, the vegetables tender but not mushy. The sex after was worth waiting for.

We snacked on the brunch leftovers over a last cup of coffee before I headed out to face the crowded grocery store and piles of laundry at home. Lingering near the door, I casually picked up the photo from the end table, as if I'd just noticed it.

"Who is this?" I asked, showing it to her.

"Oh, that? That's my cousin, Eric, and his kid. What's her name? Samantha?"

How on earth should I know if Eric's daughter's name was Samantha? I'd never heard of them before.

"Do they live here?" I asked.

"No, in Wisconsin," she said.

"You have family in Wisconsin?" She'd never mentioned that, but why would she? "I thought all your family was from the south."

"God, no. Midwestern to the core. My family moved to Virginia because my dad was in the Navy."

Okay, she had said her family moved around a lot, that she was a Navy brat. So maybe this really was Eric from Wisconsin with his daughter who might or might not be named Samantha. Just because I was a habitual liar, didn't mean everyone else was. I leaned in for one last long kiss before making my exit.

CHAPTER ELEVEN

Slurpees

Six girls, aged fifteen to seventeen, sat in a circle in my living room. Three held specula, and three had their legs spread wide, with sofa cushions wedged against their butts to help with the angle.

Initially, I had squawked about spending my evenings teaching menstrual extraction when I wanted to be vegging out to Rachel Maddow or curling up with the latest Maisie Dobbs book.

"Don't I work hard enough downstairs?" I whined to Josie.

Josie and Evelyn had been adamant.

"We've got to train the next generation," Josie had said.

"You're the next generation," I growled. "You and Rabbit."

"I meant the next, next," Josie said. "Even we aren't going to be here forever."

So I had agreed, as long as Evelyn brought snacks. My kitchen table was heaped with garlic mashed potatoes, mac and cheese and peach cobbler.

One of the girls was Evelyn's granddaughter, India, a bright and fearless sixteen-year-old. She'd brought along her best friends, Sarita and Ming. Sarita was prim and completely inappropriately dressed for this activity, in ultratight skinny jeans, and pointy heels she refused to remove. I liked visitors to remove their shoes; I did enough vacuuming all day in the clinic.

Ming was the easygoing third member of the trio, up for whatever her friends wanted her to do. That's why she was now wriggling as India tried mightily to position the speculum inside her vagina. Sarita was doing the same to Josie's niece, one of the two Kaylas in the room. Sarita sat with her legs splayed in an incredibly uncomfortable-looking position to keep from spiking her bottom with one of her heels. She kept grimacing and I could make out the word "yuck" on her lips frequently. She was better at placing her speculum than any of the others, though.

Josie was conducting the class, reading aloud from "A New View of a Woman's Body." I was just there to answer advanced questions. So far, no one had had any. Later on, the girls would be learning to use a hand-held suction device to remove the contents of their uterus when they were bleeding. Eventually, they would be able to teach their friends to do early abortions in their own homes without having to risk exposure by going to a clinic. That, at least, was the theory.

I was skeptical. I'd known several women who had had menstrual extraction, or Manual Vacuum Aspiration, abortions decades ago, and several of them had ended up having to have another procedure at a clinic. Those self-help groups, though, had been using manual suction – basically a big syringe connected to a straw. (They had called it "making Slurpees.") Our group would use a bicycle pump, which could generate much more pressure. It should work as well as what I did in the clinic, if the girls could learn to position everything correctly.

Right now, medication abortion – misoprostol and mifepristone – was a much easier option, but the supply of those drugs could always dry up. The government could hardly outlaw bicycle pumps.

I went into the kitchen. I berated myself for not waiting for the others, but then grabbed a plate and scooped a healthy portion of mac and cheese onto it, decorating it with a little salad. I rearranged the rest of the macaroni in its foil pan so it wouldn't be obvious that it had been touched. I took a beer out of the fridge, popped the top and drank a few swigs, then put it back. Wouldn't want to set a bad example for the little dears.

The doorbell rang. I jumped. Evelyn wasn't supposed to come back for India and her friends for another hour. I thought about the hate letter I'd gotten months ago. I'd almost forgotten about it, tucked away in my underwear drawer, gathering dust. I went out to the living room. Everyone was frozen in their last position, as if playing freeze tag.

"Sarita?" a deep male voice boomed. "Sarita, come here."

Sarita flushed bright red beneath her brown velvet skin.

"It's my dad," she whispered.

"How did he find you?" Josie whispered back.

"GPS on my phone." Sarita was trembling a little. I knelt and encircled her thin shoulders in a one-armed hug.

"Where did you tell him you were going?" I asked.

"Bible study." The girl choked out a sound that was half laugh, half sob. I felt like laugh-crying myself.

"Shit, I do not even have a Bible here. Anyone?" I asked half-heartedly to the tight circle of girls and women clustered around them. Six heads shook in unison. Where was Evelyn when you needed her?

Sarita's dad had given up on the bell and was pounding on the door with his fist, periodically shouting, "Sarita! I know you're in there!"

"Get rid of the tools," I whispered to Josie. "You girls get dressed!"

I opened the door a crack and slipped through it, pushing it closed with my backside. Sarita's father was about five foot ten and compact. He wore black slacks and a button down white shirt, open at the neck, reminiscent of an usher or a waiter in an upscale Italian restaurant. His face was round and dominated by a full but manicured mustache, which made it impossible to tell how deeply he was frowning.

"Hi, Mr. ..." I should have asked Sarita for her last name.

"Patel," he said. "Greg Patel. I'm Sarita's father," he added, as if he had not been standing there yelling for Sarita for what seemed like hours. "What is she doing here? This is not Bible study."

"No, really, it is. I'm Dr. Jenkins. Mary. This is my home. My office is downstairs."

"What kind of doctor?"

"I'm a psychologist," I said primly. Hopefully he would not be tempted to test my skills.

"Which church are you from?"

What was the name of that church Evelyn and Yvette went to, where we had the benefit? I couldn't remember, but Greg wouldn't believe I went there anyway. Hardly any white people did. Of course I knew the name of Nell's church, but in the moment, it wouldn't surface.

"I don't belong to a church yet, I've only been in town a short while. I'm still shopping around. Perhaps you have one to recommend?"

His face lit up, thankfully. I sensed he was one of those guys who liked being asked his opinion on every subject.

"What denomination are you?" I didn't think "pagan" or "Jewish atheist" would satisfy.

"Back in Oakland, where I moved from, I attended The Church of Religious Science," I said. At least I'd set foot in there once. Greg's mustache-crowned lips turned down.

"I don't think we have one of those in Richmond." His voice was musical as well as intimidating.

"Probably not."

"You are not teaching my daughter about evolution," he said. There was no question mark at the end.

"As a matter of fact, I am not teaching at all. My young colleague, Josie, is."

"Josie Singh?" he leaned toward me eagerly. I hated to burst the momentary good vibe.

"No, Miyamoto," I said. I shouldn't have given her real name, but I was afraid to use a fake one in case he turned out to know her.

"I don't know her," he said, shaking his head slightly.

"Why don't you come in and meet everyone? We're about to have a snack."

His eyes softened at the mention of food. I opened the door very slowly, trying to think of something to do if I heard a gasp or a squealed "I'm not ready!" Before next time, we would have to come up with a safe word. Hearing nothing alarming, I led Mr. Patel into the apartment. It looked like a normal living room, no trace of perversion. *A New View of a Woman's Body* had been safely stashed somewhere. Someone had even taken down the poster of Emma Goldman saying, "If I can't dance, I don't want to be part of your revolution." Mr. Patel appeared satisfied that this was no den of iniquity.

"Everybody, this is Sarita's dad, Mr. Patel," I announced.

"Hey, Greg," India and Ming chorused. So he wasn't quite so much of an old fogey as I had thought.

"Girls," he replied.

"Greg's going to join us for supper." I kept my tone bright, as I imagined a Bible study leader would.

I hastily set out plates and silverware while everyone filed into the kitchen. I thought about offering Greg a beer, but he might be Baptist, so I decided against it. He ate two helpings of macaroni and a veritable mountain of potatoes. In between bites, he quizzed Josie about her religious beliefs. Josie, at least, had obviously been raised Christian, and was holding her own, but I was infinitely relieved when Evelyn showed up and interrupted the interrogation.

By nine thirty, everyone was putting on their coats and I was congratulating myself on averting disaster. Greg had been deep in conversation with Evelyn, and now he was handing her a business card. She reached for it but in one of those annoying moments of mixed signals, he let go just before she grasped it and it fell to the ground. He bent to retrieve it, and suddenly he was half-lying on his side, looking under the couch. Before I could get over there to ask if there was something he needed, he reached in with a long, narrow index finger and poked a small plastic item out into the room.

"What's this?" He held up the 50 millimeter syringe I had brought to show the girls what they would be using later on, to suck out their menstrual blood and anything else hanging out in their uterus. It must have rolled under the couch when the girls stretched out. Now Greg was holding it aloft like the Sacred Chalice and glaring at me accusingly.

"It's a turkey baster," I said, taking it firmly from his hand. "For basting turkeys," I added.

I marched into the kitchen and threw the syringe into the sink along with the congealing dishes.

CHAPTER TWELVE

Sonic Youth

"We need an ultrasound," I told Josie. We were sorting dilators and cannulas in the supply closet. It was appalling how many could end up in the wrong bins within a week. "That Caitlin disaster was the last straw."

We both laughed at the metaphor, given that we were surrounded by straws. Josie tossed a plastic-covered cannula at me. I glanced at it and threw it into the proper carton.

"I don't see how we can afford one," she said. "We're struggling as it is just to keep up with all the supplies we need. Another med abortion group got busted last week, and the other suppliers are a lot more expensive."

Under pressure from Republican governments, the FBI had stepped up its efforts to shut down the pipeline for abortion drugs. A few years ago, it had been easy to order them online and get them delivered through the mail. One by one, those outlets were being shut down. Last month, we had to pay someone to go to Mexico, where the ulcer treatments that were also abortifacients could be purchased over the counter. Smuggling controlled substances carried a much bigger risk, and meant a much higher price tag. Even medical devices like the ones we were now sorting had become harder to get. The Virginia health department had demanded to be informed of anyone ordering cannulas and dilators in bulk. We were now ordering them through the Maryland clinic that handled our waste, but that had a cost too.

"It's a safety issue," I insisted. "I'll see if some of my friends from home will kick in for it. But I don't want to wait very long."

"We can discuss it at the meeting tonight," Josie said. "But where would we keep it?"

That was indeed a problem. To be most useful, the sonogram should be at the safe house, so that volunteers could verify the age of the fetus and make sure clients were scheduled for the right kind of procedure. But we had agreed that all medical equipment would be kept at the clinic under lock and key, except when we were here. Of course, the presence of an ultrasound didn't actually prove anyone was practicing medicine.

"Crisis Pregnancy Centers have ultrasound equipment," I said.

"True," Josie replied. Crisis Pregnancy Centers were anti-abortion centers that pretended to offer comprehensive pregnancy care. Where abortion was legal, they set up near legitimate clinics, luring unsuspecting pregnant women with big signs advertising free pregnancy tests. Ultrasound was their secret weapon and they wielded it proudly. Once a young woman saw the fetal heartbeat, her resolve to end the pregnancy frequently evaporated. Now that abortion was illegal in Virginia, the CPCs would be moving on, seeing their fight as won. But right now there were still a few relics around, and the Options for Women's Life Situations Counseling Center could pass for one of them, if somehow the health department got wind of it and showed up to check it out.

"Sonography needs a private space," I thought out loud. "Plus it can be helpful during a D&E. It would be better to keep it here."

"But then every woman who comes for counseling needs to come here," Josie objected. "We'd need twice as many drivers. Right now we don't have any on counseling days."

"God, that's right," I said. "I don't know – everything's so complicated."

"Well, don't worry about that right now. We haven't even gotten the go-ahead to buy it yet. Let's just see how it goes at the meeting."

"Sounds good," I said. This was my light day – I did D&Es until noon, then inventory and catching up on notes. I didn't need a headache.

"So, how's the dissertation going?" I asked.

"It's okay." Did I imagine it, or did her voice lose a bit of verve? I looked over at her; she was busy scanning packets across her iPad, her eyes scrunched in concentration.

I waited until she swiped right, meaning the inventory was complete, before saying, "Is it really okay?"

Josie ran a hand over her head, pushing an invisible forelock behind her ear. She'd had a crew cut since I had known her, but I'd noted that gesture before, so she must have worn her hair longer until fairly recently.

"I sent three chapters to my advisor last week, and she said it's really good." She moved to where I stood, and I hovered in the doorway as she scanned the contents of the last box.

"Let's have some tea before I have to go face my charts," I offered. I led the way to the kitchen. "Tea" of course was a euphemism, at least for me. I put water on for her, and thought about what I wanted. It was late in the day for coffee and early for wine, which we didn't keep in the clinic anyway. I settled for a glass of filtered tap water and fished out a box of chocolate-covered shortbread. We kept a lot of food around, since clients couldn't eat prior to their procedures.

"You sound like there's a problem," I said, returning us to the conversation. I broke off pieces of a cookie to nibble one at a time, and shoved the plate in front of her. She picked one up, dunked it in her tea and then licked around the edge.

"I don't know – I'm just not that into it," she said after a few moments. She blew into the steaming surface of her cup, then put it down without drinking.

"She's just not that into you," I said to her iPad, a stand-in for the laptop I knew was stowed in the backpack in the other room. She didn't smile.

"I'm not making fun of it," I said. "Maybe you just need a break."

"That's what my advisor said."

"Great minds," I said.

She lifted the cup to her lips and apparently judged it safe to drink. "It seems too erudite," she said after a few sips. "I wish I had picked another topic, something that might be useful for our work. Maybe I should write about Atwood instead of Austen."

"Sticking with the As," I said, and was rewarded with a half-smile. "Look," I went on. "My father taught Classics, a field not known for its practical application, but every now and then he had a student who wanted to use Greek or Latin literature in the service of contemporary efforts to build social democracy. I heard him advise one of them, 'Write your dissertation about something you're not passionate about. If you set out to find answers to the questions you most want answers to, you'll be working on it for the next forty years.'"

"Hmmm," she said, propping an elbow on the table and resting her chin on one hand.

"You want my advice, stay the course. You might find out Austen has more relevance to underground abortion than you think."

She hadn't asked for my advice, and I had just told Yvette my father taught Forestry. In fifty years, you might think I would have gotten my stories straight.

CHAPTER THIRTEEN

HillaryCare

It was the Ides of June, more than halfway through my planned stay in Richmond. I was so busy, I rarely had time to miss home. Or perhaps more frightening, Richmond was starting to feel like home. I wondered what the OWLS would say if I announced I wasn't leaving after my six months were up. Would they kick me out of the apartment and not let me do abortions? They had a carefully laid plan. But lots of our plans had been modified by now.

Sundays were no longer as free as they had been when I first got here. The clinic was still closed, but there always seemed to be an emergency follow-up to see to or charts to finish or new medical volunteers to train. I wasn't officially on any of the committees, but I had gotten into the habit of dropping in on meetings, at first because I was bored or lonely, more recently because my friends would be there. Occasionally, they even requested my input.

The comfortable Sunday routine Toni and I had developed during the first couple months had been disrupted by the cursed softball. Now she set an alarm for nine so she could shower and drink coffee before practice. Today she popped out of bed even earlier, raring to go. The Lady Dianas were playing their first game of the season, against the southside-based Sapphic Storm. I'd agreed to come cheer the team on.

When Toni appeared in her beige uniform with Lady Diana emblazoned in royal purple on the front and a big number 10 on the back, I was still sitting on the edge of the bed, rubbing a callous on my foot.

"C'mon," she said. "Spit spot. I don't want to be late."

"Let me just make some coffee," I said. "I'll put it in a to-go cup."

"I'll make it while you shower." Toni was already moving toward the kitchen so I obediently hustled off to the bathroom. Half an hour later, I sat sipping my coffee on the bleachers of Thomas Jefferson High School, watching the Lady Dianas warm up. The school board was mired in endless debate over a suitable name to replace the slaveholder president. In the meantime, a black cloth had been taped over the offending name atop the scoreboard, so it read simply "High School."

Toni stood on the pitcher's mound, tossing balls back and forth to Nell, in the catcher's crouch behind home base. Even I, who found sports involving bats a consummate bore, could see that Toni had natural talent. As she pulled back for each throw, her torso pivoted on her right foot, balanced nearly on toe like a ballet dancer, while her left leg lifted in a side arabesque. She fired fast balls and sidewinders and loopers that carved an arc through the air, looking like they were going to be balls until just before they would dip into the strike zone. After fifteen minutes Nell called for a break, standing up slowly and massaging her thighs with her fingertips. I could only imagine the pain she was in. Her mind might still be thirty-five, but her body was the same age as mine.

A woman I didn't know, forty-ish with a thick chestnut ponytail, jogged up to the mound where Toni was doing exercises that involved bending at the waist and turning quickly from side to side. Ponytail was medium height and Toni had to stoop to hear her over all the other commotion around them. Toni turned that into an exercise too, lifting her left heel and using her left hand to press it to her butt. She placed her right hand on Ponytail's shoulder to steady herself. I felt a little lump in my throat.

"Mind if I sit here?" I peeled my eyes from Toni's little dance with Ponytail to look at Hillary, who had plopped down next to me without waiting for actual permission. She sat, her eyes glued to the woman one bleacher below us: Linda, Nell's new squeeze, spreading out an array of snacks and beverages. Linda was a light-skinned Melissa Harris-Perry type. She was a good twenty-five years younger than Nell, no surprise there. Nell had always liked them young and pretty. Nell trotted over from the field, grabbed a handful of apricots and took a swig of Gatorade. She kissed Linda on the lips before returning to the field. I should have brought snacks too, so Toni would come get them from me and give me kisses instead of playing babe at the barre with Ponytail. Plus I was hungry.

I turned back to Hillary, willing myself not to think about food or look at the pitcher's mound. She was staring at the back of Linda's head, her lips firmly pressed together.

"You don't play?" I asked. Seemed obvious, but I wasn't sure what else to say other than, "Why are you torturing yourself by coming here to watch Nell and Linda?"

"God no," she said. "I'm a disaster at anything that requires eye-hand coordination. Except tennis, sort of."

"Oh, you play tennis?" I said. "So do I."

I don't know why I said that. I hadn't hit a tennis ball in years, except occasionally for a few minutes against a wall.

"We should play sometime," Hillary said. At least her eyes were no longer fixed on Linda's curls.

"I'm really not good enough to play with anyone," I said. I heard the thwack of bat on ball. Practice had resumed. The batters lounged behind the plate, chitchatting as each woman took her turn. Nell signaled the pitches to Toni, like Kevin Costner in Bull Durham.

"I'm no good either," Hillary said. "I just like to hit stuff."

"That sounds like my speed," I said. I don't know why I was semi-agreeing to play a sport I didn't really play with someone I didn't particularly want to hang out with. But then I scolded myself. Hillary and

I had always gotten along fine, and she was hurting. It would be good for me to get some exercise, and I could use an activity that had nothing to do with the clinic.

"How about this afternoon?" I said. "Why don't you have lunch with Toni and me and then you and I can find somewhere to play. I bet she has a racquet I could borrow."

"I'm on my way to church," Hillary said. "I just stopped by to ..."

She didn't need to finish the sentence. We both looked at Nell, deftly catching strikes and balls.

"Which church?" I asked.

"Holy Redeemer."

That explained what she was doing here. Holy Redeemer was just two blocks away, on Monument Avenue. Probably Hillary couldn't resist walking by and seeing Nell, and when she saw Linda, she took refuge in me. Any port in a storm.

The other team had arrived, wearing bright orange shirts that made them look like a herd of pumpkins. They claimed the set of bleachers opposite where we sat. I flashed back to my high school days in Portland, when my biggest worry was whether Tommy, the quarterback of the Horace Mann Manatees, was going to try to cop a feel at the Dairy Queen post-game outing.

The pumpkins trotted onto the field, leaving a modest entourage to keep an eye on their gear.

"How about tomorrow night?" Hillary said. She stood, one sandaled foot perched on the row below us.

"For what?" I said. "Oh, you mean for tennis?"

"There are courts here – see them over there?" She pointed to a fenced area I could just make out, between the field and the school building.

"I don't get done at the ..." I'd almost said "clinic," stopped myself just in time. I wasn't sure what Hillary knew about OWLS' real purpose. She and Nell had broken up before the abortion ban passed.

"… at work until six thirty," I said. "By the time I change and get over here, it'll be getting dark."

"I'll pick you up at seven," Hillary said. "We'll have at least an hour of light, and anyway the courts are lit. I have an extra racquet."

"Okay, great," I said, wondering what I had gotten myself into. I gave her the address, being careful to specify the top floor. I didn't know whether she knew where the clinic was. But hey, I had the right to have friends over to my apartment, didn't I? I wasn't a nun.

Hillary arrived promptly at seven. I hadn't showered, as I usually did after closing up the clinic, but I'd changed into Spandex and a Free Them All t-shirt. Hillary was sporting an actual tennis dress, an ice blue crepe de chine with a swirling skirt and fitted top, and some kind of bloomers underneath so no one would see her underwear when she ran for the ball, or more likely bent over to pick up ones I'd hit into someone else's court.

Thankfully, there was no one else on the courts behind the high school when we arrived. Whenever I drove past the courts, they seemed to be full, but the enthusiasts must have gone home to dinner, leaving us to spray balls all over the four courts, which I certainly did. I managed to hit the occasional shot into Hillary's striking range, and a handful of times even caught one of hers on the first bounce.

"Wanna play a set?" she asked after we'd hit for about half an hour.

"Oh, no," I said. "I'd have to concede before the first point." I was already feeling the unaccustomed exercise in my aging thighs, and she was just getting warmed up. This was not going to work.

"Okay, how about a break?" She strolled over to the bench where we had lined up our water bottles and ball cans and her extra racquets.

"You're not bad," she said, sipping water from her glistening Kleen Kanteen. I swigged from a misshapen Evian bottle I'd discovered in a closet at the office. I would have to invest in a decent water bottle before our next foray.

"You're sweet," I said, laughing.

"No, really," she said. "I bet you used to be good."

"Well, I was on the tennis team in high school," I admitted. That was actually true. No reason to mention that our team never won a tournament. Maybe tennis was like driving, and you never forgot the mechanics, although I saw no evidence of that in my strokes.

"See?" she lifted her Kanteen in a salute. "I could tell. You'll be back in shape in no time."

"What about you?" I didn't want to dwell on my high school years. Even the mention had me feeling a little woozy. "Where'd you learn to play?"

"Oh, here and there," she said. She was not going to make things easy. "So, when you were in high school, did you travel all over the state for tournaments and stuff? You were in Oregon, right?"

Had I ever told Hillary I'd grown up in Oregon? I couldn't remember that it had ever come up, but Nell knew, of course. It wasn't a secret. Still, I wished she would drop it.

"Yeah, that's right. We mainly played other teams in our district. Only the good teams went to state competitions. That wasn't us. Are you a lifelong Richmonder?"

"Born and bred. Proud graduate of Douglas Freeman High, on the Southside."

"Who was Douglas Freeman?"

"Hell if I know. Some old racist, I suppose."

"Guess so." We were quiet for a few minutes, looking out at the lone individual running around the track just beyond the fence. "Did you grow up in Holy Redeemer?" I asked. I don't know why I chose that topic. It's not like I knew anything about Richmond churches. Talking about Oregon was always unsettling.

"No, I grew up Catholic. But after I came out, I couldn't deal with the pope's homophobia so I started trying the Protestant churches. That's how I met Nell. I checked out her church too."

"You didn't like it?" I didn't know that much about Nell's church, but I'd gone to a lesbian potluck there once since I'd been in town. It seemed quite homey.

"I loved it," Hillary answered.

"So why didn't you stay?"

"I figured she'd never have sex with a parishioner."

Smart woman. Nell definitely would not have done that.

"Ready for Round Two?" she asked. She was already hopping up and down, racquet in hand.

"Not sure I'll ever be ready," I said, but I picked up my racquet too. As the sun sank, it was cooling off slightly, and the sweat was cooling me off rather than making my shirt stick to my skin. In the next half hour, I actually hit one solid backhand down the line and two cross-court forehands that went somewhere near the spot I was aiming for. Not too shabby for an old broad, I supposed. We made a date to play again on Saturday afternoon.

CHAPTER FOURTEEN

Herbie Fully Loaded

The shiny, slightly used SonoSite sat proudly in the corner of the procedure room. When I'd pulled it out of its box, I'd felt a thrill akin to when I caught my first baby, decades ago. We still hadn't worked out the ultrasound's permanent housing arrangement, but for now, it lived here. It looked like a skinny robot, and I called it Herbie.

It wasn't even paid for. Toni had put the five grand on her credit card and would hopefully get it back after the fundraiser on Halloween. Given all the other bills we were behind on, the events team would need to kick their outreach into serious gear for this one. I, who didn't know anyone who wasn't already an OWL, couldn't do much besides cheer them on. And make the best use I could of Herbie.

Today was a perfect day to inaugurate him. Miranda, a nurse midwife from Birmingham, was bringing three women for D&Es. It was becoming harder and harder even to get abortion medications in Alabama and the surrounding states, and these women were too far along for that anyway. All four women were sharing the guest room in the basement of Nell's church, and she escorted them into the clinic promptly at ten.

In passable Spanish, Nell introduced me to Gabriela, Esperanza and Carmen. Gabriela was the youngest, I thought maybe not even out of high school. Carmen appeared to be in her late thirties, with pocked skin and misery-filled brown eyes. Her face and hands were puffy in a way that suggested her body wasn't handling fluids well. Esperanza had a long thick braid, and was talking excitedly on her phone in Spanish.

"Bienvenidas," I said, trying to sound cheerful. "Um, we can't allow anyone to have a cell phone here." Though my sojourn in Chiapas had been partly a language-learning expedition, I couldn't summon the words to outline our security protocol. Nell obliged, gathering up the phones with only a brief protest from Esperanza.

Miranda was small and chunky, with springy black curls and snapping black eyes. She wore what back in the day we called a muumuu, but I was pretty sure that was a politically incorrect term for a dress with bright flowers and no shape. She quickly established rapport with me, complimenting our setup and expressing suitable appreciation when I introduced her to Herbie.

"Our newest team member," I said with a flourish.

"Oh, que lindo," she said, laughing. The other women followed her glance but clearly didn't get the joke, even after she said something in Spanish. I decided that was our cue to get started.

"Would you like to go first?" I asked Gabriela. They would not have been able to eat this morning. Whoever went first got to break her fast the soonest.

"Sí," she said, after Miranda translated.

"Do you want to assist, or wait with the others?" I asked Miranda. "Nell is prepared to assist and translate, but we could switch it up if you want."

"No, it's better if I stay with Carmen and Espy," the midwife said. I thought that was the right call. She was probably breaking some laws by bringing the women across state lines for this purpose, but she didn't need to compound the risk. I ushered Gabriela into the PR while Nell got the others settled in the waiting room.

I managed to use my first-grade Spanish to tell Gabriela to knock on the door when she was ready. I demonstrated, just in case my words were all wrong, and she smiled to indicate she understood. By the time she knocked, Nell was with me and we entered together. Nell showed her how to position herself on the table, and I wheeled Herbie over.

"This'll be a little cold," I said, before smearing the jelly onto Gabriela's belly. The image came onto the screen, and Nell said something to Gabriela, I didn't hear what, just anything to get her to look in her direction, rather than at the tiny, perfectly formed fetus swimming in her uterus. I'd made sure to turn the sound down, so she wouldn't hear the heartbeat.

I didn't need it, but it still thrilled me to let the ultrasound guide me through the simple procedure. It was over almost before it started, and Gabriela walked out with Nell, chatting about soccer, which she was hoping to play professionally. At least, that's what I thought they were saying.

Nell set Gabriela up with juice and a snack in the recovery room, and Esperanza took her place on the table. I got the ultrasound going, and when Nell returned, we took care of Espy in a few minutes flat. No doubt Miranda would tell her colleagues what a smooth, professional operation our guerrilla clinic was running, and we would soon be inundated with women from the Deep South. OWLS might have to recruit more providers. Of course that wouldn't be my problem, I'd be safely back in California before long. That thought, which a few months ago would have lifted my spirits, had the opposite effect now. Oakland meant no home, no job, and the mess that was Sidney, Jenny and our deeply interwoven community of friends and comrades. Richmond was quiet and provincial, but it had Toni, whom I might be falling in love with, Nell, who was like a sister, Yvette and Josie, who were becoming friends, and Hillary, a slightly annoying tennis partner. And I had a purpose. I might fit like a slightly awkward Weejun, but at least I knew where I fit.

Nell showed Carmen in and we left the room so she could get changed. When we went back in, she was sitting on the edge of the operating table, dabbing at her eyes.

"Are you okay?" I asked. "¿Estás bien?" I looked at Nell to make sure my rudimentary question was understandable. She nodded imperceptibly, said something I didn't hear to Carmen.

"Estoy asustada," she said. I looked at Nell.

"She's scared," Nell said. She sat down next to Carmen, took Carmen's left hand in her right, stroked the other woman's knuckles with her thumb. I sat on the wheeled stool and scooted back to give them some space.

"Yo entiendo," I said, I understand. I could only imagine why she would be scared – far away from home, two homes, maybe, about to have people she never met before half an hour ago do something to her body she'd probably never have considered if her life were different. I wished there was anything I could say to make things better, but even if she'd spoken English, I wasn't sure I would have found suitable words.

"¿A qué le temes?" Nell asked. I knew "que" meant what, so I assumed she was asking what she was afraid of.

Carmen's answer was too low for me to hear, even from where I stood six feet away. I was about to suggest to Nell that I go get Miranda, when Nell looked up at me and said, "She's afraid of going to hell."

I nearly put my head in my hands, stopped with them halfway to my face. I looked at the clock. Ten fifty. We had allotted three hours for these procedures, which had seemed more than ample, leaving time for cleaning and lunch before local clients arrived in the afternoon. But I hadn't anticipated a religious crisis.

"You're the priest," I said. "I'll go update the others."

I wasn't sure what to tell Miranda, who was chatting with Esperanza and Gabriela while they munched on crackers and apple slices in the sun-drenched recovery room. In there, everything seemed so normal. The procedure room had only a small window and it was covered with a heavy curtain. That made sense from a security perspective, but I wondered for the first time if it contributed to an atmosphere of doom.

Miranda greeted me with a smile, which faded when she caught sight of my face.

"Everything okay?" she asked, setting down the cup of juice she'd been about to drink.

"Carmen has some questions," I said. "Nell's talking with her."

"Questions?" Miranda inclined her head and lifted her shoulder so they nearly met.

"About the procedure," I said, and she nodded. "It will be a little while longer. We have some videos." I pointed to a stack of random DVDs which had been donated by various OWLS. Miranda fingered through them, "Runaway Bride", "Rashomon" (must be Josie's), "Bridesmaids" (who thought weddings was a good theme for an abortion clinic?), "Parasite" (I expected a Korean thriller with English subtitles was exactly what Latin American immigrants who'd just had abortions wanted), "Get Out" and "Twelve Years a Slave" (if they watched either of those, they would probably go flying out of the building to escape the white devils within). I showed Miranda how to work the ancient television and left them to their own devices.

I sat in the office, unable to do any work or even compose an email to my sister. Nearly half an hour ticked by before Nell poked her head in.

"She's ready," she said. She looked exhausted. I never thought of pastoral counseling as physically taxing, but I'd need to think again.

"You sure?" I asked. I really didn't need the bad karma associated with taking someone's soul. She nodded. If she was confident, I guessed I should be too. But she had a relationship with God. I spoke religion about as well as I spoke Spanish.

Carmen did seem more relaxed when I re-entered the PR. She managed a weak smile as I wrapped the blood pressure cuff around her right arm. Nell stood at her left side, holding her hand once again.

Her blood pressure was on the edge of worrisome, 125 over 82. I decided that was acceptable, given her level of stress. Her other vitals were okay. I eased her back onto the table and wheeled Herbie into place, rubbed the gel onto her belly and picked up the wand. Nell spoke to Carmen quietly in Spanish, keeping her focus away from the screen as I scrutinized its images.

Which were not comforting.

The fetus appeared to be about twenty-two weeks' gestation, not the seventeen she had estimated. She was still inside the window for the procedures I could do, but the fetus was in a highly agitated state. That was no surprise given its mother's emotional condition, but it could cause a host of problems. And then there was the scarring, indicative of a prior Caesarian section with a classical incision. Classical incisions are rare in the U.S. but still practiced in many less developed countries. I wasn't sure where Carmen was from, but she'd likely had at least one baby there. To make matters worse, I detected some uterine fibroids, causing her uterine cavity to distend so it resembled a rare steak.

Essentially, Carmen's uterus was a ticking time bomb on my operating table.

"Can we talk outside?" I said to Nell. She said something to Carmen and followed me into the hall.

"I can't do it," I said, leaning against the wall. I was shivering, though it was a hundred degrees outside and we kept the air conditioning at a comfortable seventy. "The procedure she needs requires three or four days and a much better equipped facility."

Nell wrapped her arms around my shoulders, pulled me to her. I stiffened at first; this wasn't the time for comfort. But her touch was familiar and welcome and my body softened in spite of my stern mind. I inhaled and exhaled deeply, and it felt like the first breath I'd taken in an hour.

"Tell me what you would need to do," she said, when I had stopped quivering like a caged squirrel.

"Soften her cervix with misoprostol, wait two days, then give misoprostol and mifepristone to induce miscarriage. But it's only been successful up to twenty weeks and she's at least two weeks past that. So she would probably need an evacuation of the remaining pregnancy.

In a hospital, she could have an MRI-guided ultrasound to ablate the fibroids."

"I don't think a hospital is an option," Nell said. "So what's the best *you* can do for her?"

"I'm not sure. Maybe give the meds and wait. But the others would have to agree to stay several more days. And even then, what if she doesn't miscarry, or goes into crisis because of her blood pressure? We'd need a hospital. They'd be better off going to Maryland, to Brenner's clinic. But I don't know if he could even see her with no notice, and he doesn't normally go that late."

"And then there's her mental state," Nell said. "A long process of miscarriage could trigger her guilt feelings, which could impact her healing. Let's go talk to Miranda."

It was past noon when the four of them walked out the back door. Gabriela and Espy's high spirits were gone. Each had an arm draped around Carmen, who had opted to do nothing for now. We agreed to meet the next morning and discuss her options, and the others could get any follow-up care they needed. In the meantime, I would convene an OWLS URGCON, an urgent consultation committee, made up of whoever from the inner core was available that night. I retreated to my apartment for a coffee to wash away the bitter taste of being no help to someone with so much need.

Herbie's first day in the office had not gone according to plan.

CHAPTER FIFTEEN

Where in the World Is Carmen Miranda?

"Come quick. She's not breathing."

The woman on the phone was shouting. I squinted at the clock. I had jumped out of bed when the phone rang and stubbed my toe on the radiator. It was four fifteen in the morning. My head felt like a pincushion, an ocean rang in my ears. Outside it might be ninety degrees, but I had the air conditioning cranked up to a climate-destroying sixty-two. I sank onto the couch, cradling the phone between my ear and my neck, trying to wrap the blanket around my naked body. A combination of cold and fear had my teeth chattering so hard, I feared I would crack one.

"Who isn't breathing?" I interrupted Miranda, whose Alabama accent was so thick I could barely understand a word.

"Carmen," Miranda snapped, as if she didn't have two other women with her who had just had abortions. But what could be wrong with Carmen? Her hypertension acting up? I didn't want to waste time asking questions.

"Miranda, if Carmen isn't breathing, you need to call 9-1-1. By the time I get there, it will be too late." If she really wasn't breathing, it was probably too late already.

"We can't call 9-1-1. They will ask questions."

"They aren't allowed to ask about anyone's immigration status."

"They will ask why we are in Richmond."

"You say you're visiting friends. Anyway, they won't."

I could hear frantic chatter in the background. Hopefully someone was doing CPR.

"Miranda, where's Nell? Isn't she there?" Nell had promised to stay at the church while our guests were there. She had a fold-out couch in her office.

"She is upstairs. But you said to call you."

"That was for a complication from the procedures we did. We didn't do anything to Carmen, you know that. Look, I'm hanging up now. I'll call 9-1-1 and then I will come."

I made the 911 call, pulled on sweats and grabbed my car keys. While waiting for the windows to defrost just enough so I could see, I pounded out a text: "Get over to the church. Emergency." Hopefully Toni, Josie and Evelyn all slept with their phones. If the text didn't wake Nell, I'd bang on her door.

The traffic lights were flashing, as they did after midnight, and I didn't stop at any of them. I made it to the church in ten minutes. I'd heard my phone buzzing several times, so I figured at least a couple of the others were on their way. Maybe I should have insisted Nell sleep with the Alabamans in the church basement, or maybe I should have. But it seemed unnecessary. Nothing was going to go wrong, and Miranda was a nurse herself.

I tried to turn the car off without putting it into park, and just managed to pull the emergency brake before I rammed the car in front of me. The door of the church was open and Nell was standing in the doorway.

"Did the paramedics come? Where is she? Is she alive?"

I saw Toni's Mini Cooper zooming up the street.

"See for yourself," Nell said. If Nell was any calmer, she might not be breathing either, I thought. Why wasn't she downstairs, helping keep everyone else calm? I felt like shaking her.

I tromped down the stairs, Nell at my heels. I heard Toni set her car alarm. Even to save a life, she wouldn't risk someone breaking a window of her car.

The basement was empty except for the foam mats and blankets Josie had bought at Kmart. I spun around and glared at Nell, as if she had hidden four women in her pocket.

"Where are they?" I demanded.

Nell shrugged. "They split."

"What do you mean, split? How could they get out that fast?"

"I have no idea. I got out of bed the second I got your text. By the time I got down here, they were all gone. Without a trace, as they say on TV."

"Maybe they decided to take her to the hospital themselves. It's only four blocks away."

"How would they have known that?"

"I couldn't tell you. But I'm going to check."

I ran to the car, gesturing wildly for Toni to get in.

"This is stupid," she said. "You have no idea where they went. We should stay here and call."

"They won't tell us on the phone," I said. "Come on!" I sped off before Toni had even gotten her door shut. She fastened her seatbelt for the short trip. Not a bad idea, considering how I was driving.

I had never been to the Medical College of Virginia Hospital before. We had scoped out St. Mary's, which was closer to the clinic, in case we needed to drop someone off. MCV was much bigger. Signs on the street pointed to this building and that, radiation this way, main hospital that way. I followed the signs to Emergency and parked in the white zone, clearly marked "Drop Off Only."

"I'll stay with the car," Toni said as I took off at a run. I could have given Usain Bolt a run for his money as I tore through a maze of gurneys and waiting rooms and finally found a reception desk.

"Did a Carmen— did a Spanish-speaking woman from Alabama come in here?" I tried to sound intelligible. Now that I was standing still, the unaccustomed run was catching up to me. I couldn't catch my breath.

The startled receptionist shook her head.

"Well did – did you see a group of women – or anyone named Miranda?" By policy, I did not learn clients' last names. I had no idea if Carmen or Miranda were even their real names. In fact, now that I said them together, I suspected they were not.

The blonde-streaked woman shook her head again, making her fashionista glasses bob.

"What would they have been here for?" she asked.

I wondered how to answer. "Cardiac arrest," I said. "Or an overdose."

"Well, in that case, they might not have come here. They might have gone straight to the ER through the ambulance bay."

I started to ask the young woman to check, but I didn't want to wait, and wouldn't trust the answer anyway unless it was the one I wanted. I tore out of the waiting room, and ran out of the hospital and around the back to where the ambulances pulled in. I got nothing for my trouble but a set of angry utterances from stressed out orderlies. I thought for a few seconds back to the hospitals where I'd worked when I was a new nursing graduate. I marched toward the elevator marked "Staff Only," and sure enough, in the alcove next to it, stood a hamper full of laundry. I located a white coat that fit and didn't have obvious blood or urine stains. Forty-five minutes later, having combed through every floor of the hospital, I was forced to conclude that the women were not there. Could they have gone to another hospital? More likely, they were driving around hunting for one. People could be so stupid. If they had only waited for the ambulance, Carmen would probably be fine.

"You don't know that," Toni said, as I huddled in the deep armchair in Nell's office.

"Of course I don't. I don't know shit. Except that I could have helped her and I didn't."

Evelyn was on the office phone with the Yellow Pages open to "Hospitals." I could hear her saying over and over, "Thank you for your time." In the opposite corner, Rabbit was also on the phone, trying to reach Rita from the Birmingham Planned Parenthood for the thirteenth time. Josie was still en route to Maryland with this week's medical waste. For once, I envied her.

Nell crossed the room and stood over me, grasping my arms tightly with her sturdy mother's hands.

"Mollie, you couldn't have done anything for her. Even a legal clinic, with all the best facilities, would not have given that woman an abortion."

"Tiller would have done it," I objected.

Nell reached for my chin, tilted it up so she could look directly into my eyes. When I tried to look away, she tightened her grip until I winced.

"Tiller," Nell said, measuring every word, "is dead."

That stopped the conversation for a few minutes. George Tiller had been a legend. When he was shot during a church service in 2009, it put the fear of God into providers across the country. The doctor who had taken over his practice had started the Maryland clinic where we took our waste for disposal. He'd originally been in Nebraska, but after a while no one would rent him a space. Now, even he didn't do abortions after twenty-two weeks of pregnancy. The new laws in Maryland made it illegal and he didn't think it was worth relocating, since every other state was likely to follow suit.

"We could have sent her with Josie," I said. "If Brenner had seen her, he might have done something."

"Probably not," Nell said. "She wasn't just late, she had had a prior Caesarian with a classical incision. She had high blood pressure and fibroids. You called her a time bomb yourself. Anyway, how would we have gotten her back to Alabama after Brenner turned her away? You're being ridiculous."

"Don't tell me that!" I jumped out of the chair, shaking my fist. Nell took a step back. Rabbit looked over at us and held a finger to their lips. I lowered my voice to an angry whisper.

"There were lots of things I could have done. I could have offered to call Brenner and beg him to see her. I could have broken her water and dropped her at the hospital. I could have done the fucking abortion. Even if I botched it, at least I would have known it, and we could have gotten her to the hospital. She wouldn't be dying somewhere on Highway 95."

"Oh, so now you know where she is?" It was Evelyn, who was done with her calls.

"Well I know she isn't here, don't I? I should get on the road, go after them."

"And do what? If you found them – which you wouldn't, what could you do?" Evelyn challenged.

Our voices were rising again. Rabbit glowered at us and walked out of the room into the adjoining kitchen, still holding the phone to their ear. I couldn't understand what they could still be talking about. How long did it take to get a yes or a no?

"More than I'm doing now." I didn't want to talk any more. My stomach felt like it held a cannonball inside. My breath tasted like vomit.

Evelyn picked up a squat, cushioned armchair and brought it over to sit by me. She put one hand on the arm of my chair, reaching out without invading space.

"Mollie, tell me something," Evelyn said. Her voice was vanilla ice cream and strawberry shortcake. I turned toward it like a sunflower to the sun. "If you thought you could help Carmen, why didn't you?"

I dismissed the angry retort that came into my mind – *because you wouldn't let me*. That might be what I would tell myself if Carmen was really dead, but it wasn't the real reason.

"Because the group decided," I said. "We're a collective."

"And why is that important?" Evelyn asked. Evelyn did executive coaching for nonprofits. I could tell she was good at it.

"No woman is an island," I said, smiling for the first time since I'd answered Miranda's call.

"That's right. You're not an island. I'm not an island. Carmen isn't an island. Everything we do affects each other. Carmen isn't an innocent victim here. She had a choice. She could have started this process six weeks ago, instead of two. Or she could have remembered to take her damn pills."

I laughed, an unfunny sound. I'd never heard Evelyn curse before, not even a benign curse like "damn."

"I just felt... I had the notion that she would do something to hurt herself. I could have argued harder with all of you."

"You could have argued 'til you were blue in the face," Nell said, "and we would not have agreed. Because there was nothing you could do safely, and we're not the Weather Underground."

"Don't start in on Weather again," I said.

Nell's older sister had gone underground with the radical group Weathermen in the late sixties. They'd thought they were going to spark a socialist revolution. Nell always used Weather to stand for people making rash and dangerous decisions. As much as I believed in nonviolence, I had a soft spot for Weather. Some of its members had done me a big favor once. I thought Nell hated them mainly because they'd taken her sister away at a time when she needed an ally in her family.

Linda entered with five mugs and a honey bear on a silver tray. I accepted a cup of the ginger tea and added a generous drizzle of honey. I held it under my nose and breathed in the pungent sweetness. It was still too hot to drink, but the steam felt great on my face and hands. I no longer felt so frantic. Rabbit came back in, the phone a bulge in their pocket now, a grim look on their gentle face. My pulse began to race again. I took a gulp of the tea, even though it was still scalding. I burned my tongue, jerked the cup away from my lips and spilled it on the leg of my jeans. I decided to ignore that for now.

"They're headed south," Rabbit said. "Rita hadn't heard from them, but someone else from the clinic had. Carmen's alive," looking at me, "but she's not conscious. They think she took pills from one of the other women's purse."

"Pills we gave them?" I had finally started to believe whatever happened to Carmen was not my fault. Was that all about to come crashing down?

"Thankfully, no. OxyContin she brought with her. She didn't have a prescription for it."

That explained the flight. At least some of the women were almost certainly undocumented, and now they had an overdose on illegal drugs. They were probably smart not to go to a hospital. Except that Carmen might never wake up, and if she'd had her stomach pumped, she would have had a good shot.

A good shot at what? I wondered. A prison term and deportation with a baby she didn't want, or couldn't care for?

"Shit, why did I tell her I was calling 9-1-1? I'm such an asshole," I said.

"Don't even start," Evelyn rolled her eyes.

"What are we going to do?" I asked.

"What can we do?" Toni said. She had been so quiet, I had almost forgotten she was there. "They'll be in Alabama and we'll be here."

"Well, they're going to have to tell Carmen's family something, aren't they? And if she lives, she'll eventually get to a doctor. How do we know they won't tell someone about us?"

"They broke the law too, coming here. In Alabama, it's a crime to go out of state for an abortion. That's our insurance," said Nell.

I hoped so. I sipped my tea and blotted at my jeans with a paper towel. The others were chatting quietly among themselves now. I had no interest in joining in. The stress of the day had worn me out. My eyes started to droop, and for a second I closed them, just cherishing what felt like my first quiet moment in months.

"I think we should start a clinic in the Deep South," I said when I opened my eyes.

Five pairs of eyes gaped at me. I would have gaped at myself if I could. What the hell was I saying? My self-imposed exile in Richmond was nearly over. Now I was proposing another whole project. Of course, you don't have to do it yourself, I thought.

No, I didn't. But somehow, I knew I would.

CHAPTER SIXTEEN

Balls in Her Court

Hillary and I had been playing tennis regularly on Tuesday evenings and Saturday afternoons. I looked forward to it more as my backhand got surer and I no longer huffed and puffed with every jog. Now I could occasionally hit a winner that wasn't an accident.

Hillary wasn't quite as much of a lightweight as I'd thought. She wasn't very political, but she had a wicked sense of humor. She called Nell "Schweitzer with a Schnoz," which made me laugh guiltily. Nell was Swedish on one side, Polish on the other, but her nose definitely came from the Polish side.

I was wheeling Herbie into the supply closet when I heard a horn toot lightly in the parking lot. I looked at my watch. It was nearly seven. I had expected to be upstairs already, changing into tennis gear, but the day's appointments had gone a little long. Yvette was changing out the sheets in the Procedure Room. Before I could say anything, she had opened the back door. I heard murmuring, and then Hillary was standing in the clinic hall.

"See you on Friday," Yvette called to me.

"See you." She hopped on her motorcycle and sped off in a roar of engine.

"Why don't you wait upstairs?" I said to Hillary. "I just have a couple other things I need to do here, and then I'll be up to change." I started toward the door, fishing in my pocket for the apartment key. No one who wasn't an OWL was supposed to be in the clinic. Hillary had been hanging around so much, Yvette must have forgotten she wasn't part of the group.

"That's okay, I can wait in the car," Hillary said. She started out into the lot. I could not let her sit in the hot car in mid-August heat. Even having the door open for a minute was letting in blasts of heavy sauna-like air.

"No, no, it's okay. You can sit in here." I showed her into the reception room. She flopped into an arm chair and picked up an ancient copy of *Teen Vogue* with the cast of *Pose* on the cover.

"Can I get you some water or something?" I asked.

"Yes, thanks."

I went back into the kitchen and returned with a tall glass of water and some cheese crackers. I really wished she would go upstairs, where she could serve herself, but it was too late to make a fuss over it. I went back to the PR, gathered up the remaining instruments and placed them in the cleaning solution. After tennis, I would run them through the autoclave. I took everything that was still in sterile packaging back into the supply room. I was just setting the alarm on the keypad when I heard footsteps behind me. I wheeled around, to see Hillary only inches behind my left shoulder.

"What are you doing in here?" I snapped.

"I need to pee."

That was fair. I'd given her water, after all. I showed her where the bathroom was, and rested against the wall while waiting for the toilet to flush. How long had she been behind me? Had she seen me enter the alarm code?

When she came out of the bathroom, we went upstairs and she played with Bunny while I changed into tennis clothes. As she drove to Jefferson High School, I told myself to settle down. I'd known Hillary for years, not well, maybe, but Nell had good taste in women. And she was a school teacher. They did background checks, right? Hillary must be a reliable sort.

I won the first set six games to four, then ran out of steam and lost the next six-two.

"I need a break before the third," I said. We sat knee to knee on the frayed wooden bench at the side of the court, sipping from our water bottles and fanning ourselves. There was a scant breeze as dusk settled in. The court lights hadn't come on yet, and everything was washed with a gray haze.

"I wanted to talk to you about something," Hillary said.

"What's that?" I asked, my throat tightening. What had she seen in the clinic that freaked her out?

"It's about Nell," she said. The breath I didn't know I'd been holding coursed through my chest. "I can't stand not being with her. Do you think she's really serious about Linda?"

I rested against the back of the bench, thought before answering.

"They haven't been together that long, but in my experience, Nell moves on pretty quick."

A month after Nell had moved out of our apartment, she'd arrived at my birthday party with someone else on her arm. I'd been cherishing the notion that we were just taking a break, but she had already tossed me into the friendly-ex container.

"Do you think... Could you talk to her? Tell her I still love her?"

"Oh, Hillary, I don't know. Nell's never listened to me about romance. Why don't you tell her yourself?"

"I've tried. She just laughs. We were together for five years. She can't have stopped caring for me all of a sudden."

It was true, that was a long relationship for Nell. But she seemed pretty solid with Linda now.

"She has so much respect for you," Hillary said, and I felt myself weakening. Flattery gets me every time.

"I can't promise anything," I said. "But if I get a chance, I'll feel her out."

Hillary won the last set. The sky was a deep violet by the time we got back to her car, a few stars already twinkling. I was opening the passenger's door when two men passed by, clicking their car alarm.

"Hillary!" one of them said in surprise. I looked at him, then looked quickly away.

"Greg," she said. "This is my friend, Mollie."

"Mollie?" Greg Patel flung a racquet bag into the trunk of a late-model Hyundai. Shit, he not only recognized me, he remembered I'd told him my name was Mary.

"Pleased to meet you," I said, hoping I sounded unbothered.

"You too," he said. We climbed into our respective cars and took off. I hadn't noticed anyone playing on the other courts, but I hadn't been paying attention. I recalled hearing a few grunts.

"Who is he?" I asked.

"Just some guy from my church," Hillary answered.

"How well do you know him?" I asked.

"Not well. I've met him a few times."

When she dropped me at my building, I went straight into the clinic. I finished my charts while the autoclave ran, then packed all the instruments into their proper cases in the supply room. After resetting the alarm, I twined a strand of hair around my middle finger and nicked it out of my head with a flick of my thumb. I threaded it through the second row of keys on the key pad. From a distance you couldn't see it, but when I got in the next morning, it was comforting to find it still there, undisturbed. I made a point to replace it every night when I left.

CHAPTER SEVENTEEN

The New Midwife's in Town

"Here it is," I announced, sounding like an over-eager realtor. "Your home away from home."

"*Your* home away from home," Kimberly said drily, "except it seems to be your new home *at* home."

"Don't knock it 'til you've tried it." She was right, Richmond had grown on me, day by day. It wasn't just Toni's sexual energy or even the fact that we had upped our romantic encounters to twice a week. I sometimes missed being in the lesbian feminist hub that was the Bay Area, but I didn't miss all the drama. Richmond, with its small, tightly knit women's community, had a more forgiving culture. Though maybe it was just because I was still the new kid that people were more tolerant of me.

The lilacs down the street were in full bloom, their powerful perfume wafting like a curtain on the summer air. I breathed in deeply before ushering Kimberly around the apartment as if it was some great mansion. I pointed out the trash compactor and started to explain the intricacies of the washer/dryer, how if you ran both at the same time, the dryer wouldn't get hot. I showed off the air conditioning, which was cranked to a modest 70. I was nervous, I realized. I wanted my friend to be impressed with what I'd done here.

Kimberly did her best to look interested and not in need of a nap. She had just arrived after a seventeen-hour trip from Crescent City.

"Are you hungry?" I asked finally.

"Well, yeah. They don't feed you on planes anymore, you know. I ate breakfast in Portland but I thought I'd have time to pick up something in Chicago and I didn't. I barely made the connection."

The mention of Portland made my throat constrict. I had a momentary image of a favorite café, probably long converted into a spa or something. In my fifty years in California, I had not allowed myself to go north of Eureka.

"I'm afraid I don't have that much at the moment," I said. "Grilled cheese or peanut butter?"

Kimberly wrinkled her nose and went for the grilled cheese. She was unfamiliar with the joys of Richmond grocery stores, at least the ones convenient to the clinic. Ellwood Thompson's had good fresh produce, but I didn't usually have time to get there on clinic days.

I slathered two pieces of whole wheat bread with butter, and cut thin slices of cheddar and pepper jack with one of those old-fashioned wood-handled cheese slicers.

"I might have a tomato if that'll make you feel better," I said.

"Please." Kimberly was a typical California healthy eater. My only food rule was to try to eat fruit or vegetables every day, but I didn't specify how much, and some of what I allowed to qualify would have made Ronald "Ketchup-Is-a-Vegetable" Reagan happy.

Kimberly and I had worked together at Alameda County Medical Center, but when she retired, she and her girlfriend moved up to Crescent City, near the Oregon border. I thought a sleepy southern town would suit her well. I had recruited her to replace me in Richmond, but now that plan had been modified. She would shadow me on Monday, then take over doing procedures on Tuesday. Yvette and Josie would alternate running the clinic for the three weeks that Toni and I would be on our tour of Alabama, Georgia and Mississippi. When I got back, we would decide which of us would stay in Richmond, and which would go start the new clinic, wherever it was going to be.

The OWLS had not yet discussed whether I could stay at the clinic indefinitely. I hadn't even told anyone I wanted to. I didn't see why it would make a difference. It was true that every time I went to the grocery store, I worried that I would be recognized by a client, but the clinic volunteers were just as much at risk.

I put the tomato and cheese sandwich in the frying pan with a quarter inch of butter, and flattened it with the spatula the way my mom used to. Kimberly took a stool at the counter, facing my back as I stood at the stove.

"Have you seen Sidney or Jennifer lately?" I asked, trying to keep my tone light. It seemed safest to ask when Kimberly couldn't see my face. Though Crescent City was an eight hour drive from the Bay, Kimberly got back there a few times a year.

"I saw Sidney at a butch gathering," Kimberly said. She didn't seem eager to supply any more information.

I turned the sandwich, observing the perfect golden filigree on the upside with unabashed satisfaction. I might be terrible at love and a poor shopper, but you couldn't say I didn't know how to cook.

"How did she seem?"

"She seemed – great."

What did I expect her to say – she seemed malnourished and lovelorn? I'd given Sidney and Jen my blessing – what else was I to do when two people I loved, loved each other? That didn't mean I wanted to hear that all was perfect in Whoville.

I lifted the sandwich on the flat of the spatula and inspected the underside to make sure it perfectly matched the top. I put it on a flowered plate and sliced my last apple to make a garnish, then placed it in front of Kimberly with a flourish. She immediately began devouring it in large bites. Maybe I should have made two. I scoured my pantry for some chips or something. Finding none, I broke out a package of Oreos, making two concentric wheels on a glass plate.

"Want tea?"

Kimberly nodded assent, the remaining quarter of the sandwich half-way into her mouth. I went to the sink to fill the kettle. While it filled, I glanced out the window, which faced the sidewalk in front of the clinic. A man stood outside, looking up. He was short and dark-skinned, about Greg Patel's size, but wearing jeans and a hoodie, not an Italian waiter's uniform. He had a phone in his hand, and I was pretty sure he was taking a picture. From the angle of his hand, it could only be a picture of me. Should I turn away, stare him down, or run downstairs and confront him?

I put the kettle on.

"I think I heard the clinic phone ring," I told Kimberly. "I'd better go down and check."

"I didn't hear anything," Kimberly said.

"Well, it's not that loud but you know, you get attuned – I just need to listen to the messages. I'll be right back."

"I'll come with you. I'd like to see the clinic."

"No, no, stay and relax. You can see everything after you've had a nap. When the water boils, make your tea." From the shelf next to the stove, I grabbed two boxes of herbal tea in each hand and dropped them on the counter where Kimberly sat. One bounced off and landed on the floor. I left it there. I snatched the clinic keys from the hook by the door and bolted down the stairs.

I was almost sure the guy would be gone by the time I got around the building, but he was still there. Greg Patel wasn't trying to be in-conspicuous at all, just standing in the middle of the sidewalk, filming my apartment. He didn't even lower the phone when he saw me coming toward him. He put his hand over the screen so I couldn't see what he was shooting, but I didn't need to see it.

"Hi, Greg," I said. "What are you doing?"

"Taking pictures of you," he said.

"Pictures or video?"

"A bit of both." He sounded like there was nothing weird about standing outside someone's house filming them.

"If you don't mind my asking, why?"

He didn't say anything for a few seconds, which was why I expected a more circuitous answer when he opened his mouth.

"Let's just say I don't believe you teach Bible study," he said in his musical, almost friendly voice.

I stood facing him, hands on hips. The late afternoon sun gave Greg a golden aura. I supposed it must be giving me one too.

"You don't have to shoot through my kitchen window. Let me pose for you," I said. I lowered my arms and squared my shoulders, lifted my chin and smiled, peeling back my lips and exposing my teeth as if I'd just won an award.

He snapped one photo and put his phone in his pocket. I supposed my bravado might have worked. Except there was one problem.

"Mr. Patel, Greg, what are you going to do with the pictures?" He had turned toward the Hyundai parked at the curb.

He didn't answer. He unlocked the car and got behind the wheel. The night he crashed the menstrual extraction class, Greg had given Evelyn his card. I made a mental note to ask her what it said he did for a living. Though if he was some kind of undercover cop, it was unlikely to say that.

After seeing him turn the corner, I went back upstairs. Kimberly had abandoned her tea and was crashed out on the couch. I envied her. I sat at the counter and drank the now-cool white pomegranate tea and comforted myself with the knowledge that I would be out of state for a while.

CHAPTER EIGHTEEN

The Ex Factor

Even though I would only be gone a few weeks, I wanted to leave Richmond with all my ducks in a row. So I invited Nell to have dinner with me and Hillary at The Magic Mushroom in Carytown. Nell had wanted to bring Linda, but I insisted on a three-way.

"It's a conspiracy of your exes," I said. "You wouldn't want to scare her."

"Good point," Nell said with her gravelly chuckle.

Hillary and I wedged ourselves into one side of the wooden booth, leaving Nell to sprawl out across from us. Between us, the pizza oozed garlicky red sauce and browned mozzarella cheese, glistening with less-than-virgin olive oil, sending up a faintly noxious eau d'anchovy on a cloud of steam. A perfect triangle with a gooey, messy circle in the center.

"How are things at the church?" I asked Nell, who held a folded triangle of pizza before her eyes then aimed it like a dart into her open mouth. She bit off half the slice, held the other level with her nose.

"Good," she said. I swiveled the metal plate so I could take from the pizza's non-anchovied side. The thought of teeny-tiny fish bones sliding into my gullet gave me the creeps. "We hired a new youth minister, and she's trying to make contact with the BLM activists at the high schools. We're also holding a series of discussion on reparations. Some of the older folks are concerned, but I'm working on them."

"Older white people?" I asked.

"Actually, it's the Black people who have the most problem with it," she said. "We're a pretty liberal church – obviously." She pointed to her chest. "For the white members, it's a chance to feel like they're helping without actually doing much. The Black members are afraid of becoming a target, setting things in motion that could spin out of control. No one wants to be the next Mother Emanuel."

I nodded. The mention of the Charleston massacre brought conversation to a momentary halt, as it nearly always did.

"What about that?" I asked after an appropriate interlude. "You're a mixed church, you can't guarantee that no undercover Nazi walks in."

"We're small, everyone knows everyone," Nell said with a shrug. She took a swig of amber ale, so I figured I could sip from my wine glass without conveying disrespect for the dead. "Anybody new comes in, someone's on him like ants to sugar."

"I hope you're right," I said. I flashed on Greg Patel, who seemed to have a nose for people who did and didn't belong in church. I wondered how he'd fit in at Nell's liberal church.

"What about your church," I said, angling my head toward Hillary. "Think they'd get behind reparations?"

Hillary jerked, as if I'd poked her with my fork.

"Nah," she said. She gulped water from the heavy mason jar-type glass. "We try to stay away from politics. We want everyone to feel comfortable."

"That's a cop-out," Nell said. She sounded cheery, as always. Verbal combat was her favorite form of entertainment. "Every church is political. Being nonpolitical is a political act."

"What does that mean?" Hillary demanded.

"Saying you're not political is just another word for maintaining the status quo," Nell said.

"Well, it's actually several words," I said, hoping to head off a collision. Hillary didn't seem like she was in the mood for jousting. I'd started us off on this line of conversation; if it went haywire, Hillary would no doubt hold me responsible.

"Just because we aren't calling for radical change doesn't mean we endorse the status quo," Hillary said. "You always have to make a dramatic gesture."

"It's not a gesture," Nell said, swinging her long arms in a dramatic gesture. She nearly knocked the cap off the head of a VCU sweatshirt-clad man in the booth behind her. He glanced around, lips parted to exclaim, but chose not to make an issue. I guess he figured the old woman might be having a stroke, and he didn't want to have to call an ambulance.

"It's changing consciousness," Nell continued.

"That's what education is too, right?" I said, angling my head in Hillary's direction. "Do your students talk about reparations?"

Hillary shook her head vigorously, her upper lip curled slightly upward. "They're ten," she said. "They talk about farting."

We all laughed, grateful for a tension break. But then Nell leaned forward, a cheese-dripping slice between the fingers of her right hand.

"Ten year olds are the perfect age to discuss new ideas," she said. "They're old enough to understand the problems they see and young enough to be open. You should do a unit on reparations. Linda's working on a school curriculum. She'd love to try it out on your kids."

"I don't need LINDA to come talk to my class," Hillary said loudly. "If I want to do a unit on reparations, I'm quite capable of planning it myself. And my class isn't a petri dish for your girlfriend's embryonic educational theories."

The VCU students in the next booth turned to see what the commotion was all about, and the birthday party in the middle of the room simmered down to catch whatever soap opera was playing out. Unfortunately, Nell loved an audience.

"It was just a suggestion," she said, forcing a chuckle. "You don't have to get your panties in a twist."

"Don't talk about my panties!" Hillary shrieked.

"Oh, please," Nell said. She pressed her palms to the sides of her head, as if her brains threatened to leap out.

"It's just an expression," I said. "Do you want another glass of wine?" I waved frantically to the waitperson, who was about to light up a pizza in front of the birthday celebrant.

"God, no," Hillary said. "I just want to get out of here. Why'd you set this up anyway, just to thoroughly humiliate me?"

"Hillary, wait," I called but she was already racing for the door. I got up to follow. She was younger and faster than me, and by the time I got to the sidewalk, her car was pulling into the street. I stared after it for a few seconds, then retreated to the restaurant.

"Don't worry about it," Nell said, when I got back to our table. She had already put a credit card on top of the bill and waved away my offer to contribute. "She'll be okay."

"She's still into you," I said; just as she muttered, "I can't figure out what I ever saw in that woman."

On the way to my car, I wondered if Hillary's use of the term "embryonic" held any significance.

CHAPTER NINETEEN

On the Road

The plan had been for Josie and me to travel south, talking to women's organizations and health care advocacy groups, until we found a suitable place for the OWLS' next clinic. At first, we'd thought it would be pretty easy. There were already a number of projects, mostly created by Black women, offering options counseling, helping women get drugs from Mexico or arrange travel to states where abortion was legal. But when we'd reached out to them, none had even wanted to talk to us. They were already under scrutiny, some had been harassed or shut down by local law enforcement. We figured we'd have better luck in person. We calculated it could take several weeks to find a group ready to take on the risk of an underground clinic.

The problem was that Josie was scheduled to make a presentation to her thesis committee before the fall term began. Her advisor warned her that if she delayed the presentation, her teaching assignment could be jeopardized. If she couldn't teach, she couldn't afford to stay in school. Josie reluctantly backed out of the trip, and Toni volunteered to go in her place. Toni wasn't as well versed in the national reproductive justice community as Josie, but she'd met some of the major players at National Women's Studies Association conferences. Though I had looked forward to spending time with Josie, I wasn't disappointed. Toni was supposed to be preparing for her fall classes, but she assured me she could fit it in between meetings and driving. I looked forward to distracting her from her course prep in pleasant motel rooms with jacuzzis and no clinic upstairs.

I insisted Alabama and Mississippi were a waste of time. I was sure Atlanta or Athens was the southern hub we were looking for. They had large progressive and lesbian communities, well organized self-help circles of all types, and money. Athens had a medical school where they could surreptitiously ferret out people who might help them, either as practitioners themselves, or at least medical backup if they needed it.

Toni said Georgia was too class-conscious and liberal. Atlanta had what she called a "femocracy," big well-funded feminist nonprofits that wouldn't want anything to do with a little underground project. The communities in Mobile, Birmingham and Biloxi were used to being under attack and banding together. They were resourceful, like the Richmond women. She thought Mississippi's proximity to Mexico might come in handy. I pointed out that Mexico had no land border with Mississippi. The technical proximity would be useless unless the new collective had a good boat.

We argued and argued for our respective positions, as Richmond faded in our wake. Finally we agreed that whoever was right would pick the restaurant where we'd eat the last day on the road, and the loser would pay.

"This weird thing happened yesterday," I said, as we sped down an empty stretch of highway between Petersburg and Durham. We were in Toni's Mini Cooper, but I had volunteered to drive the first shift. Greg Patel's visit had made me jumpy. I paid close attention to any vehicle that stayed near us for more than a few minutes, speeding up or slowing down to make sure they weren't following.

I could tell Toni about Greg because it didn't have anything to do with Renata Kellam or any of my errors in judgment. If he was building a case against us, it was because of the work we had all signed on for.

"You know how I told you this girl's father showed up in the middle of the ME class?"

"Uh huh. Indian guy, you said."

"Yeah, him. He came by the apartment yesterday."

"He did? What did he want?."

"He didn't exactly want anything. He was standing outside taking pictures of me. I saw him and went out. I asked him what he was doing, and he said he didn't believe I teach Bible study. Can't imagine why not."

"He doesn't know anything. You didn't do anything illegal. Doesn't matter what pictures he took."

"I hope not," I responded. I wondered. Probably, if Greg got Sarita to admit to what we had done, he could find some way to criminalize it. Adult women watching teenagers get naked? Didn't seem like a big stretch. I moved into the left lane to get around an eighteen-wheeler with a bumper sticker asking "How's My Driving?" The truck sped up too. I drove alongside it for ten minutes, slowing down, speeding up, which I could do because there was not a single other car in view. I could not shake the truck.

I wanted to say something to Toni, but I felt silly even bringing up my concern. It was improbable that anyone would be watching us this far out of Richmond, and even less likely that they'd use an enormous truck to do it. I tried to catch any markings saying what kind of truck it was, or get a read on the license plate. Not that I had any idea what I could do with the plates. Was I imagining it, or was the driver slowing down every time I got close to being behind it and speeding up before I could get in front?

We were approaching a curve, not a really sharp one, but it would be a lot harder for the big vehicle to make the turn than the Mini Cooper. As I reached the sharpest point of the curve, I jammed on the accelerator. For a blissful few seconds, I didn't see the truck. I pushed the speedometer higher than I was comfortable – 80, 85, 90. I couldn't make myself go faster than that, and I heard the engine groaning. I sensed Toni was about to complain about putting so much stress on her car.

Then the truck came back into view, gaining on us once again. I was being stupid. Maybe I should suggest we stop for lunch, but it wasn't even eleven. We'd agreed to eat in Charlotte and then switch drivers. Should I say I was tired, wanted to switch early, or needed to use the bathroom? But if I got off the highway, and the other driver did too, then I would know we were being followed and what would I do then? I'd almost rather not know. I switched to the right lane, directly in front of the truck, which was closing. If he would get in the left lane and pull alongside us, I could exit at the last second and leave him on the road. Problem was, I had no idea how far the next exit was. I tried to maintain my speed. Toni clutched the hand rest on her door as the car hit a pothole and jolted briefly into the air. I could see the truck driver in my rear view mirror, laughing at my attempt to pass for a race car driver. I slowed down precipitously, hoping to force him to change lanes, but when he didn't, I had to speed up again to avoid being hit.

I heard the siren before I saw the flashing lights. Shit. I couldn't slow down to speed limit without getting rammed by the truck. The highway patrol was in the other lane, and I didn't think I had enough time to swerve in front of them without crashing, or at least coming close. I didn't need to add reckless endangerment to the speeding ticket I was sure to get. The truck slowed down, enabling the patrol car to move behind me. Why were they stopping me and not the damn trucker? I didn't have too much time to wonder. The voice on the bullhorn ordered me to pull over and put my hands on the steering wheel. I pulled over. The trucker zoomed past us, holding up his middle finger and laughing hysterically. In my side view mirror, I saw the two troopers get out of the car, leaving their doors open, and head toward us. I rolled down the window.

"Didn't we tell you to put your hands on the steering wheel?" The cop chiding me was grizzled, probably in his late fifties and not well kept. He had a paunch and a raspy smoker's voice. His partner appeared twenty years younger, half a foot taller and lean. The older guy had his hands in his jacket pockets, but the younger guy's hand was on his holster.

I placed my hands so tightly on the wheel, my wrists started to cramp.

"I asked you a question," Grizzly Bear said.

"I'm sorry," I said. "I just figured I was going to need to talk to you."

"You sure were right about that. You always drive that fast?"

"No, actually, I never drive fast at all," I answered. "I just …" Just what? Thought someone was following me? They would ask why I would think that, and Toni would hear. Better to just shut up and let him give me the ticket.

"We're in a hurry," I said. "We are trying to make it to Georgia, and I don't like driving at night."

"Well, you don't have to worry about that now," he said. "You're going to be spending the night here."

"What do you mean? I have my license and registration."

"Well, see, it don't work that way here. We do stuff differently than – where you from?"

God, I didn't want to say California. He was obviously reading my accent, and not liking it.

"Richmond," I said.

"Let me see your license."

"Okay, but I'll have to get my purse out of the trunk."

The younger cop opened the door, and stayed close as I moved around to the back. He skulked as I found my purse and fumbled for my ID. My hands shook. I tried to force them to stop, but that only made me tremble harder.

I handed the ID to the younger guy, since he was closer, hoping that would make him leave me alone for a second. It didn't. He held it out to Mr. Grizzly, who walked over and plucked it from his hand. The younger guy put a hand on the door of the trunk as I tried to close it. He pawed around, moving luggage aside. I wanted to tell him to stop, but I was in trouble already, and there was nothing incriminating in the trunk, so I said nothing. He picked up the only questionable item, a copy of *Curve* magazine. I didn't even know why Toni had that rag. Probably got it at a Pride parade or something. The young cop flipped through it, chuckled at something and handed it to Grizzly. The older guy's eyebrows did a little dance.

"Mollie O'Shay? That's you?" asked Grizzly.

I nodded. No harm in that; it was obviously my ID.

"This here says you're from Oakland, California. You told me you were from Richmond."

"I am from Richmond, but I only moved there recently. I haven't had a chance to change my license."

"How recently?" He ran his hand up and down the night stick hanging from his belt.

"Three months ago." I figured that wasn't as egregious as six. If I'd said three weeks, or however long the law said you had to apply for a Virginia license, it would seem too much like I was visiting Richmond, not "from" there.

"Well, see, that's an even bigger problem," Mr. Grizzly said. "Because by Virginia law, you only have two weeks to change your license."

"Well, I guess it's a good thing I'm not in Virginia now."

Wrong. Why, why, why was I such a dumbass? He pulled the night stick out of its strap, held it under my chin, pointing up.

"Guess that's where you're wrong." I would have nodded, but I couldn't without impaling myself on the stick.

"You want to turn and face the car for me? Put your hands on top of the car and spread your legs."

I obeyed. He holstered his stick and began the pat down. He felt my breasts the way doctors checked for lumps, and cradled each buttock in both hands. I closed my eyes and ordered myself to stand still and not cringe. Toni jumped out of the passenger's side door. The younger cop dashed around to stop her.

"Get back in the car."

"Isn't he supposed to get a woman to search her?" Toni's voice was low and even.

"Get in the car."

Toni hesitated. I thought about the carry permit I'd seen in her bedroom. Did she have a gun in her glove compartment? What would happen if the cops found it? I wondered if that's what Toni was thinking about too. I tried to make eye contact, but she was looking down.

"You're not in trouble yet," the younger cop said to her, "but you sure could be."

Toni sucked in her cheeks and climbed into the passenger's seat.

Grizzly rammed his hand into my crotch, thumb up. I jumped uncontrollably. He flattened out his hand and placed it between my legs, moving his fingers back and forth, like something crawling inside me.

"Drop your pants," he said in my ear.

"What?" I must have imagined it. I'd heard about sadistic highway cops, but I'd never heard of this.

"You heard me. Pull your pants down. I felt something between your legs. It could be a weapon."

"I am not going to do that."

Seconds later I felt the night stick against the back of my neck, smashing my face into the scalding hood of the car. I heard a car whizzing by. I supposed it was too much to hope for that there was a Cop Watch type or a human rights lawyer on this deserted North Carolina road.

"You better think about that again," said Grizzly. His voice had gotten increasingly low and his drawl more pronounced. At this point, I would have sworn he was from Mississippi. For all I knew, he was.

"I can think about it all you want, but I'm not doing it."

Next thing I knew, I was on the ground, my face pressed into gravel and dirt. He was kneeling on the small of my back so that I gasped for breath, while clamping metal handcuffs on my wrists. At least they weren't too tight, I thought – and then, as if reading my mind, he squeezed the rings until they bit into my skin like an asp.

I almost protested, but then figured he would make them even tighter.

"I was gonna let you go with a warning," he whispered in my ear, as he led me to the patrol car. "But now you're in a world of trouble."

I hoped Toni would be able to keep up with the cops' car.

CHAPTER TWENTY

The Prisoner's Bible

It wasn't my first time in handcuffs, but that didn't make it any more pleasant. I sat silently in the back seat of the patrol car, leaning my right shoulder against the door to take some of the strain off of my hands. The cuffs pinched whenever I moved the slightest bit. I could feel my wrists swelling under the metal. It was about 90 degrees in the car and they didn't turn on the air conditioning. I wondered if they did that just to plague me. They must be hot too, under all those clothes. The younger guy drove, and Grizzly chewed tobacco – really! chewed tobacco! – and made sick jokes about prison rape.

They drove for a long time. I saw signs letting me know I was in Winston Salem before they finally pulled into a huge parking lot behind a classic white stone institutional building. They left me in the back of the car with the doors shut and all the windows rolled up – at least while they were driving, they had kept theirs down and I got a tiny bit of breeze from it. With the heat and my hands losing circulation, I thought I might pass out.

Finally, they led me out of the car and into a dark hallway of white cinderblock walls. I heard strange wailing sounds from beyond the walls. Probably just someone having a psychotic episode or going through withdrawal, but I had flashbacks of old newscasts, the Wilmington Ten, Bayard Rustin's "Twenty-Two Days on a Chain Gang."

I was pretty sure North Carolina no longer had chain gangs, but I better not be here twenty-two days.

I stood around for ten more minutes, hands still cuffed behind my back, until finally the young highway patrol guy showed up with the key. He twisted my hands painfully as he took the cuffs off, but then I was able to rub the deep red ridges in my wrists, which helped a little.

"Better put her in solitary," Grizzly Cop said as a brunette woman in starched khakis escorted me through a clanging barred door with peeling mustard yellow paint. "She's violent and she's a dyke."

"One out of two ain't bad," I said to the woman cop, trying to smile. The other woman looked at me with crossed and somber eyes that seemed to say "No jokes allowed." Later, I wondered if she really wasn't sure which one I meant Grizzly had gotten right. In a small room with nothing in it but a bench, I took off my clothes, lifted up my breasts, opened my mouth, showed the bottom of my feet, squatted and coughed, bent over and spread my cheeks. Years ago, I would have refused on principle to be humiliated, even though it would mean punishment. Now I just wanted to get it over with, be able to sit or lie down and think about how to get myself out of this mess. I put on my underwear and the orange jumpsuit they gave me, and watched my clothes disappear into a plastic bag, along with my ID, earrings and the twenty-eight dollars in my pocket.

"Commissary's not 'til Thursday," the woman told me, misreading my forlorn look after my clothes. "If you're still here by then, your friends can put money in your account."

At least the woman thought maybe I *wouldn't* still be here Thursday. That was the most cheerful thought I had had in hours.

They did put me in solitary, formally called "administrative segregation." I only knew that because the woman who searched me told the man who booked me that I was going to ad-seg. Solitary in this jail actually meant sharing an eight by ten cell with a white woman with stringy dull brown hair who hugged her knees and rocked back and forth all day. The only sounds out of my cellie's mouth were moans. I introduced myself anyway, but got no response.

The cell was more cinderblock and peeling yellow paint. It had an open metal toilet – I didn't see any toilet paper. I supposed you had to buy it from the commissary. I doubted I was going to be able to beg any from my cellie, given that we didn't seem to speak the same language, and I couldn't imagine the guards giving me any. I knew in many parts of the world, people managed with their hands, and at least I was lucky to have a sink with running water.

Though my cellie was doing her rocking on the floor, the sheets were crumpled on the bottom bunk, so I carefully climbed up to the top one. The top step doubled as the edge of the bedframe, so I had to hurl myself over. Only after I'd landed on the flimsy mattress did I realize that it was going to be hard to make the bed from up here. I should have done it from the ground before I climbed up. Well, I wasn't climbing down again. I thought about just sitting there for a while and worrying about it later, but then decided it wasn't going to get any easier. I had had an exhausting morning and the appeal of sleep was overpowering. I had no idea what time it was but reasoned it was probably after two. I hadn't eaten much breakfast and it was long past time for lunch. My stomach rumbled. I thought longingly of the grocery bag containing three kinds of chips and two boxes of Oreos in the trunk of Toni's car. Where was Toni now? Was she treating herself to a Howard Johnson's meal or calling around trying to get help for me? I wouldn't mind if it was the former. I liked to think *someone* was getting fed.

I'd been worried about getting arrested for the last six months, but I'd never imagined it being like this. How random – or was it? I had decided that the guy in the white truck had just been being an asshole, amusing himself by toying with me and not wanting to be outrun by a woman. But I couldn't be sure. Could he really have been following me? Or could someone have called the highway patrol and warned them to be on the lookout for two women in a Mini Cooper? But if that were the case, Toni would have been arrested too, right? Unless this could possibly have something to do with Renata, that strange phone call, or even Greg Patel.

I supposed eventually I would get to make a phone call. Unfortunately, I didn't know anyone's number by heart. I had gotten so used to relying on my phone. There was only one person's phone number I wouldn't have trouble remembering. I would call Sidney if I had to, but I wasn't looking forward to that conversation.

My general policy when in jail was not to ask the guards for anything. It let them know what your weaknesses were, and gave them an opportunity to fuck with you. I'd occasionally been arrested at protests, and jail guards generally saw protesters as softies who thought they were better than everybody else and needed to be taught a lesson. To the folks in charge here, I was just some stupid old lady who'd… well, I didn't even know what the patrolmen had said I'd done. I hadn't been there when they'd told the jail people what my charges were, and all that was written on the booking card were penal code numbers. I'd tried asking the guy taking my fingerprints what they meant, but he'd said it wasn't his job to tell me that.

"Ask your lawyer," was all he would say. As if I had a lawyer in this state. I knew not one soul in North Carolina. I hoped Toni might know someone, but I had no reason to think so. There were plenty of women's organizations and civil rights groups that would probably be glad to help us out if they knew what we were really doing, but Toni couldn't tell them that. As far as anyone knew, I had just been unlucky and run into a cop who didn't like Yankees or dykes.

I decided I had nothing too much to lose, or maybe I just needed to hear another voice speaking words. I walked to the door of the cell and banged lightly on the flat metal plate on the outside of the bars, where the lock was. I waited a minute, then banged a little louder, then a little louder.

"Shut the fuck up!" wafted from the cell across the hall. Even the angry utterance cheered me. At least I wasn't completely alone with my catatonic roommate.

"Sorry," I called back. "I was just hoping I could get a book and some toilet paper."

"You don't got toilet paper? When'd you get here?" A woman appeared at the bars of the cell. She was Black, maybe twenty-five or so, with neat cornrows framing her long, thin face.

"'Bout an hour ago."

"Yeah? What'd you do?" The young woman smiled, and two gold teeth glinted. Though the cells were dimly lit, the hall was bathed in garish yellow light. From experience, I knew it'd be on all night.

"Well, I really didn't do anything."

The other woman laughed.

"Course you didn't. None of us did."

"I guess I was speeding but other than that, I didn't do anything. This cop just didn't like me."

"Well, baby, you don't want cops liking you. You do something to piss him off?"

"He was pissed off as soon as he heard my voice, but I guess I was a little bit of a smart mouth. Then he told me to take my pants off and I wouldn't."

"That man told you to take off your pants by the side of the road?" The girl's eyes were wide and sparkling. I had impressed her without even meaning to. Maybe I'd get my toilet paper out of it.

"Yeah, can you believe it? Well, really, he didn't say to take them off, he said to drop 'em."

The young woman laughed again. "That's cold. I'm Greta, by the by."

"Nice to meet you, Greta. I'm Mollie."

"Hey, there, Mollie. So okay, here's the thing. When you go to dinner, there's two stalls in the cafeteria. If you get into 'em early, you can grab some toilet paper and stuff it in your pants. But then you might miss gettin' dessert. They never make enough."

Between dessert and toilet paper, there was no contest, even with my sweet tooth.

"Thanks, Greta, you're the best. How long have you been here?"

"Four months," Greta said. Her eyes lost their sparkle.

"Um, do you know how long you'll be in?" Stupid question, I thought. She couldn't know. This section would be for women awaiting trial.

"I don't think I'll be getting out," Greta said.

"You mean … ever?" I couldn't even imagine that. Greta had barely lived.

"Yeah. I did something real bad. And it's not my first time inside, ya know?"

"Got it." I wasn't going to ask what Greta might have done that was so bad. Even if she wanted to tell me, I didn't really want to know. I couldn't picture this sweet young person hurting anyone.

"Greta, you wouldn't happen to have a book in there, would you? I never go out without one."

"I got a Bible," Greta said. I smiled. That would be ironic – me, the unBible study teacher, reading the Bible for fun.

"I can't take your Bible from you," I said. I could tell Greta was relieved.

Greta's toilet paper tip worked like a charm. I stuffed so much in my underwear, I must have looked like I was wearing a diaper. When I came out of the bathroom, Greta was holding a seat for me at one of the long metal tables, covered with the trademark peeling yellow paint. After I got my tray, I slipped into the empty spot, and Greta proudly produced something wrapped in a napkin. I could see I was meant to unwrap it, so I did, revealing a piece of yellowish cake that was a bit hard to the touch.

"It's jello cake," Greta said with a flash of gold teeth.

"Jello cake?" I tried not to let disappointment seep into my voice.

"Yeah. It's got jello mix in it. Usually lemon or lime." That didn't sound quite as awful as strawberry or something. It was sure to be sweet, anyway.

"It was really nice of you to get it for me," I said. Greta nodded some combination of acknowledgment and agreement. "How'd you do it?"

"Told the line girls the truth. It was for the new girl, who was gettin' herself fixed up with TP."

I tried to think how long it had been since I'd been called a girl. I ate a few bites of mashed potatoes. I hadn't been able to stop the woman on the line from covering them with gravy, but I was too hungry for principles. The gravy didn't taste like it had much meat in it anyway. There were six other women at our table, and none of them were saying a word. I turned to the woman next to me, also young and Black. Her hair was done exactly the same way as Greta's, though it was shorter.

"Is it against the rules to talk?" I asked in a hushed tone. Two guards stood at the far end of the room, but they were talking and even laughing. They didn't seem to be paying any attention to what the prisoners were doing. If they glanced at anyone, it was the servers, probably making sure no one tried to eat when it wasn't their turn, or maybe secrete an extra piece of broccoli.

"Naw," the other woman said. She didn't look at me, but kept shoveling in bites of what was said to be roast beef. I decided not to push it, though I would have liked to use this little bit of time to get to know my fellow sufferers. I soon found out the reason for the silence. The guards stopped chatting and one blew a whistle.

"Now, ladies," the one without the whistle yelled, though everyone except me was already standing up and gathering up their mostly empty trays. I hadn't eaten half my meal, and I also hadn't gotten to peruse the bookshelf I had spied near the door. I rewrapped the jello cake and started to put it in my pocket. Greta shook her head furiously. I sat down quickly and shoved the cake in with the toilet paper, hoping the paper would keep it from getting too nasty to eat. This place was definitely going to change my ideas about hygiene.

We lined up by the door and I found myself conveniently by the bookshelf.

"Are we allowed to take books?" I asked Greta. I figured I could speak now since no one was trying to win a speed-eating contest, but Greta held a finger to her lips and shook her head for emphasis. At the same time, one of the guards yelled, "NO TALKING!" She scanned the line for the culprit, but thankfully, no one saw fit to point me out and the woman decided to let it go. I had assumed Greta's head shake meant ixnay on the books, but Greta barely moved her hand toward the shelf and gave a tiny nod. I scanned the shelf quickly, easier since we were facing the wall while the guards walked slowly down the line in opposite directions, counting. I saw a Sara Paretsky mystery I hadn't read, a big thick one called *Blacklist*, and Piper Kerman's *Orange Is the New Black*. The latter was very well worn. I could imagine it would be popular here, and appreciated the humor of whoever donated it. I grabbed both of those. Michelle Alexander's *The New Jim Crow* was there too. It didn't look very well read. I'd read it before and didn't think I'd be able to concentrate on it in present circumstances.

I stood in line with the books in my hand. Something had gone wrong with the count because the guards were doing it again. Or maybe they always did it twice. I made a note to ask Greta later. It might not be important, but it seemed good to have as much information as possible. This time apparently they got the same number because one of the guards yelled, "LET'S GO LADIES. ON THE DOUBLE."

I didn't know why they had to yell when everyone except me seemed to know the drill and be perfectly compliant. Everyone started moving toward the door, not really that "on the double" but steadily. In the hall, we lined up against the wall again, this time facing forward, backs pressed against the wall. We stood there for a long time, though no one seemed to be counting or doing anything else. As yet another woman with a whistle in her mouth came along and walked up and down the line, writing on a clipboard, a line of orange jumpsuits marched past us into the dining hall. A young brown-skinned woman with a fat pigtail sped up as she got even with Greta. Her round face lit up and so did Greta's. Quickly, she darted in between the two lines and caught Greta tightly in her arms. They did some heavy duty smooching until I, who had appointed myself lookout, coughed violently a few times. Greta and her girlfriend separated just in time for the Latina – at least, that was my take – to jump into the end of the line just before the cops had a clear view. Greta gave me a little smile, and I felt I'd earned my cake, which I could kind of feel crumbling in my panties.

I found out why Greta had said no to the pockets. Outside my cell, I had to turn my pockets inside out, run my hands through my hair and jump up and down. Obviously there would not be a strip search, or Greta wouldn't have told me to pack my pants. A few crumbs dropped to the floor, but the guard didn't notice or didn't care. She unlocked the door and locked it behind me.

"A reader, huh?" she said.

"Yes."

"Let me see."

I handed her the books through the bars, offering up a solemn prayer that I would get them back. The woman flipped through them, turned them upside down and handed them back.

"Don't get too many readers in here," she said. I read her voice as admiring, though that might have been wishful thinking. I didn't much care. With books and toilet paper, I could conquer the world. I climbed up to my bunk. My roommate was still on the floor, still rocking. An untouched tray sat in front of her, laden with the same fare everyone else had eaten, including a piece of jello cake. That reminded me to unload my treasure. I wriggled my hand inside my jumpsuit and extracted the cake, miraculously still more or less wrapped in the napkin. Much of it was crumbs, but lots of them were big enough to eat. Unwinding the spool of toilet paper from around my hips without taking off my clothes was more complicated, but piece by piece, I got it all out. I settled back against my pillow with a contented sigh, and opened up *Blacklist*.

The last time I'd been arrested was in 2003, just after George W. Bush sent troops into Iraq. I had been swept up with a few thousand other demonstrators, basically for standing on a sidewalk with a sign. It had been no big deal, but because there were so many of us, it took most of a day for us all to get booked and cited out. I'd been worried about getting out in time to get back to work, whether I'd get a sentence that couldn't be done on weekends or holidays, or be charged with something that would cost me my county job or my nursing license. This time around, I had nothing to fear. I had no job to lose. If I couldn't go back to the clinic, it would be their loss, not mine. I'd be warm and fed and my Social Security and pension checks would be waiting for me whenever I got out.

I hadn't had a real day off since I'd moved to Richmond. Days when the clinic was technically closed were nearly always occupied by meetings or emergencies, catching up on charting or inventory, shopping, laundry and cleaning. I loved spending time with Toni, but new relationships are not relaxing. Tennis dates with Hillary meant listening to her pining after Nell, trying to work out how to be a good friend to both of them.

Now here I was with absolutely nothing to do except read and think. I was almost disappointed when I heard the huge keys clang in the lock on my cell and a guard said, "O'Shay, get down here. You got a visitor."

I glimpsed Toni through a glass door when I passed, but I had to be strip searched again before I was allowed to go see her. This time the guard even shone a flashlight in my ass and my ears, as if she was a doctor looking for lice. A couple more times and I'd be used to it. I figured one of those times was coming after the visit.

They let me into the visiting room, locked the door and left me alone with Toni. I assumed someone was watching us through the glass; I wondered if they could hear too. I would operate on the premise that they could. At least I didn't have to talk to Toni on one of those phones through glass, the way I had had to do with my friend Clarence when he was in San Francisco County Jail on trumped up charges related to a thirty-year-old murder.

Toni and I hugged, then sat across from one another at the only furniture in the room, a metal table connected to metal benches and bolted into the floor. It was the first room I'd been in that wasn't white. The walls were a faded mint green, with graffiti scratched into nearly every square inch, people proclaiming their identities or their love or hate for one another or their hopes for when they got free. Or a bail bondsperson's phone number. That one might come in handy.

"Sorry it took me so long to get in," Toni said. "I couldn't find you at first. I tried to follow the cop car, but I don't drive as fast as you."

She smiled, and after a second, I did too.

"I don't usually," I said. "I thought that guy in the truck might be following us."

"Us? Why on earth would he?"

"I don't know – well, I told you about Greg Patel."

"Mollie, you can't believe this has anything to do with that." I was a little lost in all the *thises* and *thats*, but I shook my head.

"I don't, not exactly. But there are some things I haven't told you."

"Like?"

"Like I got a threatening letter, months ago."

"And you just decided to mention it now?" That was not the response I was expecting. She was supposed to be my girlfriend, but she was acting like a cop. But maybe I was being oversensitive. I knew I should have told someone about the letter.

"What did it say?" she asked. I told her, mentioning the part about the ransom note appearance.

"That's it? 'Dykes go home'? Not very specific."

"I know, that's why I didn't tell anyone. I figured it was just kids." I had figured no such thing, but it made a reasonable story.

"Doesn't sound like kids. When was this exactly?"

"About three weeks in, the first day you came to work in the clinic."

Toni leaned forward on her elbows, her head resting between her palms. She chewed her lower lip. I resisted the urge to tell her she wasn't going to have any skin left on her lips if she kept it up.

"It's not great, but it wouldn't be a reason for someone to follow us out of state."

"That's true," I said. I had mentioned the incident that would force me to reveal the least, but it only made me seem nuts. "I'm just tired. I haven't been sleeping well. Greg coming to take pictures of me in my home freaked me out." I squeezed my eyes shut, doing what I hoped was an effective impression of Woman On The Edge of Tears.

"I get that. I do," Toni stopped biting her lip and reached a hand across the table. She had changed from the tank top she'd worn in the morning to a white short-sleeved men's shirt. She looked crisp and wholesome, a stark contrast to the impression I must make in my rumpled, too-big orange jumpsuit. I swiped at my hair. I couldn't remember when I'd last combed it. Must have been this morning, but that felt like a week ago.

"Where are you staying?" I asked.

"There's a Motel 8 a mile away. The prison people told me about it," Toni said. She grinned. "They actually have a discount for inmates' families."

"Hopefully they didn't ask what kind of relative you are. I'll pay you back when I get out."

"Don't worry about it," she said. She leaned across the table, running her eyes across my face. "Doesn't look like they beat you."

"Sorry to disappoint," I snapped. I felt guilty when Toni recoiled.

"I didn't mean it that way," she protested.

"I know," I mumbled.

"I just thought they might have, because they're charging you with assault."

"They are? Felony or misdemeanor?"

"Felony. And reckless endangerment and a bunch of traffic stuff. Your bail's a hundred thousand dollars."

"You're kidding."

"I wish I were."

"Well at least if it comes to that, you can testify that I didn't assault them." I caught a flicker of uncertainty in Toni's eyes.

"Sure," she said, a beat too late.

"Toni? Is that a problem for you?"

Her head swung back and forth slowly. She bit her lip some more. I could see a raw spot.

"When they made me get back in the car, I couldn't really see you."

Could I have had it wrong all along? Could Toni somehow have set me up? But that made no sense. If she wanted to fuck with me, she'd had ample opportunities in Richmond. Imagining that she had been working a scheme to lure me to a jail in Winston Salem was even more nuts than thinking that Greg Patel could be some kind of government agent.

"Does it matter whether you saw me? You fucking know me."

I jumped up, almost ready to go pound on the window so the guards would come and take me back to my nice quiet cell, with my quiet rocking roommate, where I could read my novels and forget that I might be in this disgusting place forever.

Toni got up too, rounded the table and grabbed my arm.

"Mollie. Calm down."

"Don't tell me to calm down." All the fury I *hadn't* unleashed that day – at the highway patrolmen and the guards, the fingerprint guy who wouldn't tell me anything and the roommate who wouldn't talk, the strip searches and rushed meal and jangling keys and lack of toilet paper – came flooding through my body, and I couldn't stand being here one more second.

"Get out! Just get the fuck out! Leave me here to rot, why don't you? You have no idea what I've been going through. I've worked myself to the bone in that damn clinic, all 'cause you all were too lazy to keep your damn legislature from outlawing abortion. I've been threatened and rammed by an SUV and I don't know who I can trust and you don't even believe I didn't fucking assault two cops?"

"Mollie. Mollie," Toni was trying to pen me in, but I broke out of her attempted embrace. I was just getting started. I knew my face was red and I imagined my eyes were wild. Through the window I saw the guards getting up, pulling out their night sticks and a small can of something that was probably pepper spray.

Toni put her hands on my shoulders and pushed me down onto a stool, just in time. The guards came running into the room, but stopped short when they saw us sitting close together, me sobbing convulsively, Toni patting my shoulder ineffectually. Seeing them, I took a few gulps of air and managed to stop crying.

"Sorry," I said, wiping my eyes on my arm. I'd been going for my sleeve, but it was too short, stopping barely halfway down my upper arm.

"It's okay," Toni said. At least the presence of the guards kept her from asking what I meant about getting rammed by an SUV. I didn't suppose she was likely to forget. I wondered how much the guards had heard of my rant, and what they would have made of it. They were now prodding me to get up, it was time to go back to my cell. My outburst had probably cut the visit short, but I didn't really mind. I badly needed some quiet time.

CHAPTER TWENTY-ONE

Sisterhood Is Powerful

A lawyer named Beatrice Ross showed up the next afternoon. She was a short, skinny dark brown woman in a tailored gray suit with three strands of heavy gold around her neck. Her hair was salt and pepper, and I quickly learned that she had been a few years behind Evelyn at Spelman. Sorority sisters, she said. She'd do anything for Evelyn, she averred. That was no hyperbole, I concluded, since she'd driven an hour and a half from Charlotte to help someone she probably saw no reason she should care about.

"Tell me what happened." Beatrice pulled a yellow legal pad and a pen out of her shiny brown leather briefcase and wrote <u>Mollie O'Shay</u> at the top. Then she poised the pen over the paper, ready, waiting for something worth writing down.

"I thought a truck might be following me," I started. I kept my voice low. The guards on the other side of the glass were attentive, no doubt having heard about my outburst last night. I wasn't going to give them any excuse to end this visit early; it was the only thing that might shorten my time in this lovely facility.

"I am pretty sure it wasn't, but I sped up to see what the guy would do. Then the cops pulled me over, and they were pretty pissed off. They asked where I was from and I said Richmond, which is true, but my license says California and that pissed them off even more. Then they found a lesbian magazine in the trunk."

I hoped that wasn't a mistake. Evelyn and I had never discussed sexuality at all. I still had no idea if she and Yvette were a couple or just buddies. But half the OWLS were dykes, so I didn't think there was any homophobia lurking behind her impenetrable façade. Beatrice didn't react, just kept writing, her pen careening over the page, filling one with large, loopy cursive and turning to the next.

"Then what?" Beatrice asked.

I told her about the pat down and the order to strip. I felt ashamed telling the story, and then felt ashamed of my shame. How many survivors of sexual assault had I counseled? All those times I had said, "It's not your fault, you didn't do anything wrong," I hadn't really had a clue what I was saying.

Beatrice opened her briefcase again and took out a thick sheaf of papers, stapled together. She ruffled through them. I could read my own name typed on the top line of each page. Beatrice put on glasses and peered over the top of them at the report.

"One of the patrolmen, Officer Stanley, says he had to restrain you when you lunged at his partner," she said.

"That's garbage."

"He also says that you kneed him in the groin when he was trying to cuff you."

"I wish I had," I said, then regretted it. "Anyway, it would have been impossible. I was on the ground."

"How did you get on the ground?"

"Honestly, I have no idea. I assume they pushed me or threw me. I was face down on the ground, eating dirt. Here, I think there's a cut on my face from the gravel." I turned my right cheek toward Beatrice, lightly touching the spot where I had seen a scrape yesterday. My cell had no mirror, and we didn't get to go to the dining hall for breakfast and lunch. We only got out of the cells at dinnertime, and twice a week for showers, Greta had told me during a brief, shouted conversation.

"Your arraignment will be tomorrow," Beatrice said. "I'll be there. We'll try to get your bail reduced, but I have to tell you, I don't think we'll be able to get it down below seventy-five thousand, unless the judge dismisses the felonies, and that's also unlikely. The judges in this county never do that. I think you're going to be here a while."

"Don't they have something like own recognizance release here?" I asked. "In California, you can almost always get out if you have community ties."

"That's the problem," Beatrice said. She put the cap back on her ballpoint pen and tucked it into a little pouch in the briefcase. She put the legal pad in the case and locked it with a tiny key from her purse. "You don't have any ties in this community."

Shit, that was right. I was in frigging North Carolina. I had never seriously considered that I wouldn't be able to get out within a week. It didn't compute. I'd have to think of something, though right at this moment I didn't feel full of ideas.

Beatrice's prediction was spot on. The judge denied OR and declined to reduce the felonies to misdemeanors. She grudgingly agreed to lower the bail to seventy-five thousand, for all the good that would do. In the little holding cell off the court, where Beatrice and Toni – her "legal assistant" – were allowed to talk with me for five minutes before I was whisked back to jail, Toni asked if she should try to raise the bond. I rejected it out of hand.

"We'll lose ten percent unless we can put up the whole amount, and for that, I'd have to mortgage my house. I'd rather let it cost the state to keep me in jail."

Beatrice gently mentioned that the state of North Carolina would attach my assets to pay for my room and board, but I waved that away.

"I'd like to see them try," I said, with a bravado I didn't feel.

Back in my cell, claustrophobia started to set in. I was grateful for Greta's booming, disembodied, "How'd it go?"

I walked to the door to answer, but still didn't see Greta.

"Like I expected," I said. "Nada. Big waste of time."

"Yeah, I hear you." Greta appeared at her door with a pair of dripping wet underpants in her hand. When she saw me noticing, she put the panties over her face. When she removed them, she laughed, moisture glistening on her cheeks. Not a bad idea, I reflected. It was sweltering in these cells.

"So, that girl in line last night," I yelled.

"Angelina?" I watched carefully for any sign that I was crossing a line, but Greta's eyes sparkled as she said her girlfriend's name.

"That's her name? Pretty. Did you know her outside?"

"Nah," Greta disappeared again, I assumed to wring out her underwear. "We met here. Love at first sight."

"In the dining hall?" I thought I fell in love quickly, but two minutes a day with no talking allowed must be a world's record.

"Over on the other side." The other side must refer to a cellblock where women actually got to spend more than ten minutes in one another's company. I had just taken for granted that Greta had been in ad-seg all along, like me. After all, Greta said whatever she'd done was "real bad," and I wouldn't characterize my own offense that way. Then again, I wasn't a North Carolina cop.

I heard water running, and then Greta was back, this time with a pair of soaked white socks.

"That's why I'm over here now," Greta said.

"Because you're a ... in a relationship with a woman?" I knew North Carolina had reinstated its ban on gay marriage after *Obergefell* went the way of *Roe*, but putting someone in solitary for lesbian contact was awfully nineteen-eighties. I started making a list of LGBT legal services that might be interested in that.

"Excessive contact," Greta said.

"So how come you're over here and she's not?"

Greta whirled the socks around like pompoms, sending sprays of water flying. I even felt a sprinkle. "I got in a fight with her ex."

I dropped my plans to make Greta a cause célèbre.

"So you might get to go back over to the other side soon?" I asked.

Greta shrugged. "Doubt it. Her ex's a big snitch."

"You think Angelina'll be in the same place as you when you get sentenced?"

"Don't know. Hope so."

Greta walked away again, probably to hang her socks. I climbed up to my bunk and opened *Blacklist*. After a few pages, I put it down again.

The solitude and slow pace of life here were losing their charm fast. As much as I enjoyed reading, I would have liked to mix it with some trash TV time or go out to a movie. I couldn't let myself get this stir-crazy after only two days. I'd read a couple books by people who had spent years in solitary, and they all said you needed to set goals and make a schedule for yourself. Exercise featured prominently in preserving their sanity. I climbed down from the bunk and lay down on the cold stone floor. My roommate looked up from her rocking and growled. Greta had told me her name was Melody. I couldn't think of a less fitting one, unless it was Joy. I guess Melody felt the floor was her turf. I climbed back onto my bunk.

I lay on my back and lifted my left leg to a 90 degree angle, grasped it with both hands and pulled it toward my head as far as it would go, appreciating the tug in my hamstring. I held it there for ten seconds, put it down and did the right, then the left and the right again. I did as many situps as I could manage, using the cot springs for bounce. It turned out I could only manage twenty-two situps. I'd try for twenty-five tomorrow, or maybe even later tonight.

That whole regimen had eaten up maybe twelve minutes. I lay back down and opened my book again. I'd only gotten through a couple more pages when a guard appeared at my cell door.

"O'Shay, come with me."

"What now?" I hadn't meant it to come out quite so sharply, but it bugged me that they never told you what they wanted you for.

"Time for your medical intake."

"I'd really rather not. I don't have any medical problems you need to worry about."

"State law says you have to see the nurse."

I supposed that wasn't such a bad thing. I'd actually been part of a health workers' group fighting for better health care in California jails and prisons in the early oughts. Lots of incarcerated women died of medical neglect all over the country, told they were just trying to get over when they complained of unbearable pain or fevers or coughs. I followed the guard to the infirmary.

The nurse turned out to be a male physician's assistant according to his name tag, which said Alvarez. He wasn't old, but looked world-weary. He turned his back while I changed into the paper gown. I tried to bond with him by telling him I was a nurse practitioner, but he didn't say anything. He examined every inch of my body with his hands, but asked no questions. He did a reflex test, tapping my knees with a little metal drum and looked in my ears and throat.

I was starting to think maybe he couldn't talk, when he said, "Get on the table and put your feet in the stirrups."

"Look, I really don't think that's necessary," I said. "I'm seventy years old. I don't have sex with men. I've never had an STD. I'm a nurse. I get regular medical care. I can tell you, you're not going to find anything and I probably won't even be here long enough to get the results of a pap smear." I sincerely prayed that last part was true.

"It's part of the process," he said. "Please do what I say. Otherwise, I'll have to call a deputy to make you comply."

I considered his words. I knew exactly what would happen if I refused. I couldn't imagine having someone put a speculum inside my vagina while two guards held me down. I'd heard about pregnant women giving birth while handcuffed and shackled. I knew I stood no chance of avoiding this procedure. This young man – he was a young man to me – was just doing his job, and he wasn't going to risk it for some old white woman he'd never seen before. I took off my underwear and put it on the chair where the rest of my clothes were folded, then climbed onto the table. I tried to follow my own prescriptions and breathe deeply and relax my muscles as the PA slid the speculum into my vagina. I could tell he was trying to be gentle. I only felt a slight pinch. He took swabs and put them in a plastic bag, affixed the labels that had already been printed out.

When the exam was done, I dressed quickly and was sent into the hall to wait for the guard to escort me back to the cellblock. But when she showed up, she turned instead toward the sign that said "Outprocessing." We walked through two sets of metal doors that automatically opened and clanged behind us, and then we were in a small room that looked just like the one where I'd been granted this lovely orange jumpsuit. I saw the bag containing my clothes on a chair in the corner. After one more strip search – my protests that I'd just been examined inside and out by a trained professional went unheeded – I got to change into my own jeans and beloved Social Change Not Climate Change t-shirt. I tucked my twenty-eight dollars into a jeans pocket, put the amethyst earrings Sidney had given me through the holes in my ears, and was ushered through yet another set of clanging metal doors into a garishly lit lobby smelling of Pine Sol and the bodies of too many anxious people waiting too long to find out what had happened to their loved ones. Beatrice and Toni jumped up from a wooden bench and ran to embrace me. I languished a long time in the arms of Beatrice, whom I'd known exactly one day, and Toni, whom I had been so ready to cast off yesterday.

"How'd you do it?" I asked Beatrice.

"Seems they lost some of your paperwork," Beatrice said, sucking her cheeks.

We walked briskly out into the still September heat. Like most jails, this one wasn't in the nicest part of town. The block facing us contained four bail bonds storefronts with neon signs, flanked by a bar on each corner. My favorite was Hoods From The Hood Bail Bonds – No Crime Too Big Or Small! The air smelled of hamburgers and exhaust, but right now, those were the smells of Paradise to me.

"What do you mean, lost it?" I asked. "They lost it between this morning and now?" We arrived at Beatrice's silver convertible. I could see Toni's car just up ahead. Beatrice leaned against the shiny passenger's side door.

"Well, you know, I asked for the photos they took at the scene, and lo and behold, they were nowhere to be found." I opened my mouth to say something, then snapped it shut. I distinctly remembered seeing the photos clipped to the report Beatrice had shown me yesterday.

"That's crazy," I said.

"Crazier things have happened," Beatrice said. "It seems you weren't the first woman to be treated to Officer Stanley's unorthodox stop and frisk methods. That drop your pants routine is a bit of a signature of his."

"That isn't surprising," I said. "But why is he still on the force?"

"This is North Carolina." Beatrice opened her car door and threw her briefcase and purse onto the passenger's seat.

"I can't thank you enough," I said. Beatrice made an "all in a day's work" motion with her hand. "At least let me buy you lunch. I could really go for some Thai food."

"I hear they got good Thai restaurants in South Carolina," Beatrice said. Toni and I laughed.

"Oh, by the way, Mollie?"

"Yes?"

"Do you know someone named Renata Kellam?"

I froze. The way Beatrice had said it, "do you *know* someone," made it easy to just say no, so I did.

"No, who's that?" I asked.

"Just a name I saw in your file. When you come back, do me a favor and go through Kentucky."

"Count on it," said Toni.

CHAPTER TWENTY-TWO

A Long Walk on a Short Pier

Toni won the bet.

Athens was a waste of time, I realized, almost as soon as we crossed the county line. The students, even the very lovely interns at the women's health center, were too transient and everyone else too afraid to compromise their careers. I knew I shouldn't be as judgmental of that as I was. I had chosen to wait until my pension was set to go into crime.

The Atlanta women were hospitable and correct. Most of them were Evelyn's friends – some had never even left Spelman, morphing painlessly from students into teachers – but they didn't have her grit. There were plenty of collard greens with ham hocks I wished I could try, and cornbread laced with real corn kernels, which was delicious and doubtless contained lard, but I didn't ask. The comfy beds came with more feather pillows than I would have had if I stacked up every pillow I'd ever owned. The vice president of NOW brought a killer peach cobbler made with ripe peaches from her own front yard. They all pledged to hold fundraisers for the clinic, wherever it might end up being, but Toni and I quickly understood that meant anywhere but Atlanta and preferably very far away.

I thought we should just skip Birmingham, since neither of us wanted to run into Miranda, the midwife who'd brought Carmen and the others to Richmond. I had called her seven times after that fateful night, and all the calls went to voicemail. The last time I'd tried, I never even reached the voicemail, and wondered if Miranda had changed her number just to avoid us. Driving into Birmingham was going to bring all that guilt up again.

"Don't even say it," Toni said, keeping her eyes firmly glued on the cars in front of her. "We're going."

"What makes you think they'll even talk to us? We didn't call ahead. We don't know anyone here except Miranda, and she seems to have vanished."

"There's the woman from Planned Parenthood that Rabbit was talking to that night, Josie's friend. What's her name? Rita. She's the one who sent Miranda to us in the first place."

"Well I'm sure she's not going to be thrilled to see us come waltzing into her clinic."

"If we'd called, she might have told us not to come, but if we just show up, she won't turn us away. Trust me. I grew up down South."

You only grew up partly down South, I wanted to say, but I didn't.

"I guess I have no choice since you've got the wheel," I said instead.

The only trouble with Toni's plan was that the Birmingham Planned Parenthood address wasn't listed online. The number of bombings and shootings had multiplied in recent years, to the point where most clinics that had ever provided abortions no longer publicized their locations. You had to make an appointment and go through screening to get the address. It didn't eliminate targeted violence, but it cut it way down.

That meant I, who didn't enjoy talking to strangers on the phone, had to do it. I thought of taking the easy way out and saying I was bringing my daughter in for a pap smear. But I decided that getting the address under false pretenses would only make matters worse if Rita and crew really didn't want to talk to us. Might as well have it out on the phone.

"How do you even know she still works there?" I asked Toni, cradling the phone in my hand but unable to punch the buttons.

"Josie said Rita's worked at Planned Parenthood for eighteen years. She wouldn't just up and leave."

"Okay, good point."

I couldn't think of any other reason to stall. I told the receptionist I wanted to talk to Rita, and gave my name as Dr. Mary Jenkins.

When Rita came on the line, I explained who I was and braced myself for a tongue-lashing, but Rita's soft drawl told me to "come on down." She even gave helpful directions to the nondescript twelve-story office building, where we parked as directed in the underground garage. An armed security guard sat in front of the special door that led from the garage directly to the clinic. Security guards at clinics were nothing new to me; every abortion clinic in the Bay Area had had one since the seventies. And all the abortion providers I knew in the Midwest wore bullet-proof vests all the time, not just when working. A friend of mine in Racine, Wisconsin, had even had a bullet-proof bathing suit designed.

I would have liked to ask the guard if he'd ever had to use his gun, which led me to wonder if Toni had one tucked away in her shoulder bag. Someday I was going to have to deal with that taboo subject. But this was not that moment.

Rita was a gentle, as well as genteel, woman with curls that stuck out from her head in every direction like the bristles of a very old hairbrush. She kept swiping one rogue curl off of her forehead with the back of her gnarled hand. I guessed she was in her early fifties, already suffering from an advanced arthritis that left her knuckles the size and shade of small beets.

"What can I do for y'all?" she asked. Her desk was piled high with folders and medical forms. Beneath all the piles, only one picture was visible, of a much younger Rita with her arms wrapped around a grinning preadolescent girl.

"Your daughter?" I indicated the photo. Rita's face softened.

"Yeah, Felicia. She's a sophomore at Ole Miss."

I glanced at Toni and saw that she, too, was tucking that information away in case we decided to go on to Mississippi.

"What's she studying?" asked Toni.

"She's majoring in chemistry, but she's planning to be a doctor."

"Following in her mama's footsteps," I said.

"It's a tradition in my family. My great-grandfather was the first in-digenous person to graduate from medical school in Mexico."

"My great-grandmother was the first woman to graduate from med-ical school in Denmark," Toni said. I wondered if that were true, or if Toni was just trying to make Rita like her. Either way, I thought we'd had enough chitchat. Get the hardest part over with quickly.

"I was wondering if you knew anything about Carmen," I said. Ob-viously no need to specify which Carmen.

Rita propped her elbow on the desk, and her chin on her palm, the way Toni often did. I noticed little red veins in the whites of her eyes. She had clearly had a long day.

"I wish I did," she said, her "I"s sounding like "aah"s. "Miranda hasn't been back to work since that day. I think she might have taken Carmen back to Mexico."

Toni and I sat with that news for a minute. No wonder Rita wasn't mad at us. If Miranda had cut off ties to her as well, she probably felt she shared the guilt.

"I hope you know how awful we felt," Toni said. "We didn't just turn her away. We told them to come back the next day, and we were trying to think of a way to help her."

Rita didn't answer, just nodded slowly. She closed her eyes for a second and opened them again.

"It wasn't your fault any more than it was ours," she said. I didn't think she sounded completely convinced, but we silently agreed to move on. I explained how Carmen's experience had convinced me we needed to start more clinics in the South, so women didn't have to wait so long or worry about childcare and travel.

"It will be a lot harder up front," I said. "We'll need to find more providers, find them housing, pay their travel. And the medical waste will be a problem. We've been taking ours to Maryland, where they can dispose of it legally, but it's not practical to do that from here every week. But it will be safer and more comfortable for the clients. We're already starting to teach manual vacuum aspiration to a group in Richmond, and once other clinics are established, we can start training groups in every community to do early abortions in their own homes. Eventually, lay women can learn to do all the procedures, or at least all but the ones most likely to have complications."

I made sure to keep eye contact with Rita during my pitch, and wound down with a hopeful smile. Rita's mouth had been a little open when I started, and had opened wider the longer I talked. Now she pressed her lips together and moved her head from side to side with her hands.

"Y'all are loco," she said. It sounded like "laocao."

"I knew you'd say that," Toni said. Her voice was starting to twang more, the longer we were in Rita's presence. I had never been able to detect any accent in her speech, but her tongue was very malleable. I suspected that was her anthropologist's training, mirroring her informants so they would trust her. "But just think it over. We came to you first, because you know about the project and you obviously don't want to come to us anymore. This way, you all would be in control, and you could help identify women in other cities who might be able to help."

"We haven't been avoiding you," Rita said. "When someone comes to us for help, if she's American we help her go to Mexico. Your clinic was a good option for the undocumented women, but since Miranda left, they don't come to us anymore."

That made sense. I started to wonder if this whole idea was harebrained. After all, Mexico City had a dozen clinics that were safe and legal. But they only did first-trimester procedures, and many women didn't know they were pregnant that early. A Mexican clinic couldn't have helped Carmen.

"Wouldn't it be better to be able to help everyone here?" Toni said. "A flight to Mexico must cost what, two, three hundred dollars?" Rita nodded. "And then they still have to pay for the abortion, right?"

Rita gave another nod. "And a hotel."

"So you could charge each woman a hundred bucks and she'd save five hundred or more and you'd make fifty to help somebody else."

Rita's face lost some of its set negativity. She sucked in her cheeks, moved her shoulders back and forth as if she'd just noticed a kink in her neck.

"That's true," she said. "It's very dangerous, though."

"So's sending women to Mexico, isn't it?" Toni leaned forward. She knew Rita was coming their way, she just needed to reel her in.

"I guess," Rita said. "But it's hard to trace that to us. We give them the information but they make the arrangements themselves. The money is raised through NNAF, mainly up north."

I was a former board member of NNAF, the National Network of Abortion Funds. From their newsletters, I knew the funds were bleeding money since the court overturned *Roe*.

"NNAF is running out of money," I said. "It's harder to raise, and there's so much more demand now that no one can use insurance in more than half the states." I could see that Rita already knew that too.

"Just give us a chance to talk to a few women here," Toni said. "Then we'll move on and you all can get back to us if you're interested."

I held my breath while Rita argued with herself, her lips moving slightly.

"Come to my house tomorrow night," she said. She took a slip of recycled paper from a small tray on her desk, wrote down an address and handed it to Toni. Now the harder part was up to me.

"Um, I don't suppose you know a cheap place we can stay," I said. I tried to sound light but plaintive at the same time.

Rita didn't answer immediately. She twisted a ring around and around on her finger.

"I guess you could stay in Felicia's room," she said.

"We'll bring dinner. What time will you be home?" Toni asked.

We left Birmingham on Friday morning with phone numbers for two women in Mobile and one in Jackson. When I had asked about Oxford, where Rita's daughter was at Ole Miss, I got a chorus of noes.

"Nah, girl, that's redneck country," said a woman called Sharon, who worked with the national organization Black Women Stirring the Waters.

"Only good people in Oxford are the students," someone else said, "and they leave after four years."

"It would be better in terms of the waste problem," I said. "It's so much closer to Chicago."

"It's a seven hour drive at the best of times," Rita said. "And not a drive you want to be making as a colored girl late at night with a trunk full of abortions."

I had to admit that was not a welcome prospect. My experience in North Carolina as an old white woman had given me a new appreciation for the risks of interstate travel.

"Y'all go on down to Mobile," Sharon said. "They're gonna love you down there."

We hit Highway 65 with a mixture of frustration and optimism. The Birmingham women had loved the idea in principle, but had been unwilling to commit the time to the project. Like the Georgians, they were happy to raise money, and even said they could provide some practical support like transportation and supply runs, but didn't want to have primary responsibility. Mobile, they said, had a tighter community and a lower cost of living.

At Rita's suggestion, we stopped for lunch in Selma and paid homage at the Edmund Pettus Bridge, where Dr. King and John Lewis were among the hundreds beaten by police in 1965 on a march for voting rights. At Toni's insistence, we took a detour to the Old Cahawba Archaeological Park, where the ruins of a nineteenth century river town sit atop the hub of an erstwhile Native American trade route. We could have spent many hours there, but I was determined to make Mobile by dark and hustled Toni back to the car after a measly ninety minutes.

One of the Birmingham women knew a well-known artist with a large ranch just outside Mobile. Sharon had called ahead and said two of her friends were coming to town for a couple days and needed a place to stay. I liked the prospect of not having to beg for accommodations for once. I drove faster as the signs for Mobile grew closer together, taking care to avoid any encounters with highway patrol. We arrived at the ranch just as the orange sunset was shimmering off the Bay.

Devora Raskin looked like a combination of every race known to humans. Raven-black hair, dusted with salt and pepper, hung to her waist and she wore a feather behind one ear, reminding me of Buffy St. Marie. The slant of her eyes was reminiscent of Josie's, but her skin was a pale olive and her nose as long and narrow as my own. She wore black stretch pants and a t-shirt that said "My Heroes Have Always Killed Colonizers." I liked her immediately.

Devora set us up under a pagoda in the yard, and served fresh lemonade and white-chocolate-dipped shortbread. I started imagining relocating to Mobile with more enthusiasm. Our schmoozing inevitably led to lesbian geography – Devora's best friend in fifth grade had been in one of my classes at UCLA, while Toni had met one of Devora's ex-girlfriends at a rowing competition. Fortified and having established our credentials as bona fide dykes, we set out for the grand tour of the ranch. I thought it was more of an estate, since as far as I could see, it didn't have a single cow or bale of hay.

The barn was instead crammed with shelves and shelves of Devora's art, fanciful birds and trees fashioned in wood and painted bright colors, terra cotta busts of goddesses from every culture, and in the middle of the room, a huge bronze vagina, its labia studded with rhinestones so it looked like it had just had sex. Paintings were stacked five deep all along one wall, but they were all turned toward the wall. When Toni asked about them, Devora said, "Amateurish. I have no talent with a brush." Looking at the painted wooden sculptures, I couldn't concur, but held my tongue. I'm no expert on art.

By the time we had finished the tour and the lemonade, a crew of half a dozen women had arrived to meet us. Devora had only made one call, but obviously the feminist community here was adept at phone trees or text alerts or carrier pigeon or whatever communication strategy small town dykes prefer these days. And dykes they were, except for the dark-skinned transman in the tweed beret who went by Skip. Skip was the most outgoing of the group, and introduced us to Leila, a stunning Palestinian with long brown ringlets, and her girlfriend Diyala, a baby butch Syrian-Lebanese American. Leila was a speech pathologist, and Diyala was finishing a nursing degree.

"You know if you get busted, you can probably never practice nursing," I warned her.

She nodded, her huge dark eyes meeting mine squarely. "This kind of work is why I'm going into nursing," she said. "I'm not interested in being part of a system where people can't get the health care they choose."

I envied her zeal. Once I had been that sure of myself, too. But then I had faced the fact that good intentions were not bringing the revolution, and we would all need to make a living.

At the end of two days of nonstop discussion, covering every possible problem and its myriad solutions, and negotiating what support the Richmond mothership would provide her fledgling daughter, we went out for tacos to seal the deal. The sea-spiced air was warm but the breeze kept it from being sticky. We sat on the pier and ate fried fish with guacamole and salsa, and toasted with weak margaritas. Then we posed for pictures, a can-can line of women linked arm to arm, positioned like a high school cheerleading team with the shortest members squatting in front. We didn't want anyone left out, so Devora grabbed a passing stranger who good-naturedly took her phone and snapped away from a few different angles. Devora took her phone back and we were about to separate, when the good Samaritan said, "One more, if you don't mind," and pulled out his own phone.

"Wait, what's that for?" I asked.

"Posterity," he said with a smile. "It's not every day you see such a beautiful group of women." Some of the women were annoyed, but we all held still while he snapped and then he was gone and forgotten.

CHAPTER TWENTY-THREE

Obamarama

The party had been planned more than a month ago, as a birthday party for Josie. Now it was also celebrating the birth of the Mobile clinic and my escape from the unforgiving law of North Carolina. Never one to waste an opportunity to fundraise, Yvette announced that donations would go toward reimbursing Toni for the ultrasound machine.

Yvette had not only reserved the church social hall, she'd convinced a DJ to spin pro bono. Ziggy J was popular for both women's and mixed events, no help in my quest to get a bead on Yvette's sexual orientation. Ziggy played an eclectic mix of house, world, blues, Motown and indie rock. I had heard her spin at a benefit for Haiti that Nell's girlfriend Linda had helped organize.

Party guests had been instructed to "Come As Your Favorite Celebrity *(famous couples encouraged)*." Ev and Yvette had come as Barack and Michelle Obama, as had Nell and Linda, and at least two other couples I didn't know. Blackface wasn't an issue – everyone wore masks.

Josie was either Michelle Wie or Lydia Ko, the nine iron she carried the only thing giving her any resemblance to either of them. Rabbit was Tiger Woods, walking around in a paper mask inviting people to play high-stakes poker. Toni and I had decided to go retro, settling on Richard and Pat Nixon. Toni had found a Nixon mask among her ephemera from 1972. We managed to fix my hair into a reasonable facsimile of Pat's. My costume consisted of a dowdy dress with a button-on lace collar. I really didn't need to worry, since no one remembered what Pat Nixon looked like.

I saw one attempt at Joe and Jill Biden, recognizable by the sunglasses and blonde wig. The Harris-Emhoffs were visibly missing.

"Funny how no one chose the Trumps," I said to Toni, after scanning the room.

"We're all trying to forget they ever existed," she replied.

The music was just right, not too loud to talk and be heard, but giving off a compelling beat. I seldom danced, but tonight I spent much of the three hours on the dance floor. I boogied to Earl Hines and vogued to Madonna and shook my hips to Aretha and Donna Summer, sometimes with Toni, sometimes on my own or in a big group. I couldn't remember having so much fun. People kept coming up and repeating what they'd heard about my escapade, and telling me they were happy I was staying in Richmond.

I was pleasantly tipsy when Ziggy turned on the lights and began to play the Gloria Gaynor version of "Never Can Say Goodbye." I took Toni's arm and nearly stumbled in my high heels as we went to find Josie and Rabbit. We'd all come together in Rabbit's Jeep; they were the only one who didn't drink. I looked around, my eyes still adjusting to the light, and didn't see them.

"They must be outside already," I said to Toni. We were heading toward the door when one of the Barack Obamas stopped me with a hand on my arm, a little too tight for comradeship. This Barack was probably the most convincingly dressed, having gotten the dark blue suit and electric blue tie just right. I couldn't remember having noticed them during the evening. Yvette's Obama had worn a polo shirt and brown slacks. Nell had gone for the starched white shirt and gray tie with no jacket. The other Obama couples must have left early because I hadn't seen them in hours. This one, I decided, must have come late and seemed to have no Michelle.

Obama leaned toward me and said, his voice muffled by the mask, "Are you Renata Kellam?"

Don't respond, I said to myself. Don't react in any way.

I grasped Toni's hand tighter and tried to follow the crowd surging toward the exit. The hand's grip on my arm did not loosen. Obama moved with me, making an uninvited threesome with me and Toni. Two more Obamas materialized in front of us, bucking the tide of the crowd, one on my right, just in front of the one holding my arm, and the other edging Toni to get in on my left side. Now that I was sensitized, I looked at their Adam's apples and realized they were all men, and no cis men had been at the party. The Obamas closed in on me and Toni let go of my hand. I reached out frantically, wanting to scream, "Don't let go!" like Leonardo DiCaprio in Titanic, but not wanting to betray my panic. Toni felt like my lifeline, but I knew she couldn't stop whatever it was that was happening.

I looked around me and saw more Obamas. I was in a kaleidoscope of Obamas. My eyes darted around the room, trying to pick out people I knew. All I could see were Obamas, but there, with one of them, was a Michelle, and that meant it was not one of my pursuers, but a friend. I recognized Linda's hair sticking out under the Michelle Obama in back, and bent forward to catch Nell's attention.

"Nell," I said. Nothing came out. My vocal cords had been stung, my throat swelled against the pressure of trying to talk. I reached out and caught the edge of Nell's sleeve. Nell turned around, and I could tell that she was grinning under the mask. Her eyes, through the eye slits, were relaxed and jocular.

"What's up, girl?" she said. "D'ya have a good time?"

I coughed, trying to find my voice. I motioned with my head to all the Obamas escorting me. Nell's eyes clouded a bit through their slits.

"Renata's back," I managed to whisper.

My Obama guards continued to dog me until I was outside. I had no idea what it meant, or what was going to happen now, and when it did, it was the last thing I expected.

On the sidewalk in front of the church, the two men in front of me ripped off their masks in unison. One was white, the other Black. They were identical heights and both about the same build as the forty-fourth President.

"Are you Mollie O'Shay?" the Black guy said. There was no real point in denying that was my name. I'd been fingerprinted for my nursing license under that name, as well as in the North Carolina jail, which was probably how they had tracked me down. Although I still wasn't sure why they had. Who were they looking for, Renata or Mollie? The guy who had called me Renata was still holding my arm, his grip growing fiercer by the minute. I could tell there were handcuffs in my future, and I doubted they'd be any tighter.

I nodded. Toni, Evelyn, Yvette, Nell and Linda were watching, agape, behind the agents, or marshals, or whatever they were.

"What's this about?" I finally managed to say. I didn't think I sounded outraged, but at least my voice wasn't shaking. The Black ex-Obama stepped forward and pulled a folded piece of paper from his jacket's inside pocket.

"I'm Sergeant Wilson of the Richmond Police Department," he intoned. "Mollie O'Shay, I'm arresting you on suspicion of murder in that on the day of Thursday, May thirteenth of this year you did take the life of the unborn child of Caitlin Shaw, aged twenty-one, at 4628 Grove Avenue, Richmond, Virginia. You have the right to remain silent..."

I didn't listen to him tell me my rights. I was trying to focus on what he was saying, but it made no sense. Caitlin Shaw, I vaguely remembered, the twenty-one-year-old who told us she was twelve weeks pregnant and was really sixteen. I had talked to her boss, got him to give her the day off. Denny's, that's right, that's where she worked.

"Do you wish to make any statement at this time?" Sergeant Wilson asked finally.

"No, thank you," I said clearly.

"Wait a minute." It was Evelyn, who wasn't a lawyer but could definitely play one on TV, striding into the midst of the cops and their prisoner.

"Let me see that," she said to Sergeant Wilson, who relinquished the paper in his hand to her.

"Who are you?" the white guy asked.

"None of your business," Evelyn snapped. She was perusing the warrant quickly, looking, I knew, for anything she could point to to say that they couldn't take me away. She must not have found anything because she folded it up with a "humph," but she didn't give it back to Sergeant Wilson.

I didn't quite see what happened next, because I was still having trouble focusing between the alcohol I'd imbibed and the trouble I was in, but suddenly all the cops were rushing toward Toni, who was pointing a gun at the guy still holding my arm, the one who had called me Renata.

"Let her go, now," Toni said calmly. Where on earth had she gotten a gun? She was wearing a blue suit jacket like the one Nixon had worn the day he resigned the presidency. She must have shoved the gun into her pocket before we left the house. Why? Had she known something like this might happen?

And what was she thinking pointing it at a cop? Was she trying to commit suicide, a long delayed follow-up to her husband's? But was the guy holding my arm a cop? He hadn't said who he was, and the other cops were not talking to him. Maybe she thought I was being kidnapped. Maybe I was.

Sergeant Wilson and his partner rushed toward Toni, as the other women crowded around, making a wall between Toni and the advancing cops. Evelyn was yelling at them that they needed a better warrant than they had. The white cop tried to grab Evelyn, and Yvette swatted him away.

The guy holding my arm was still wearing his Obama mask, and in the second that he reached up to discard it, I saw my opportunity. I twisted away from him and ducked behind the shrubbery between the church wall and the sidewalk. I lay down among the dirt and twigs, parting the leaves just enough to see what was happening.

The cop, or agent, or whoever he was, turned in a 360 degree circle, the look on his face totally comical as he realized I was really gone. He surveyed the women piled on top of the other two cops and decided it wasn't in his interest to get involved. Instead, he pulled out his cell phone. He must not have been able to hear well enough, because he moved away from the group, facing out toward the street, and kept walking slowly away from the group, no doubt hoping to see me running. While his back was turned, I dashed into the church. Thank God, the door was still open. I didn't know the women who were cleaning up the social hall; they weren't part of the group. The organizers must have decided to splurge on a hired cleanup crew so no volunteers had to stay after the party. The workers didn't seem at all aware of what was happening outside, but were chatting about "Love & Hip Hop" while they stacked the empty trays.

I quickly climbed the steps to the main floor and walked into the chapel. It was dark except for an electric candle in one alcove, above an oil painting of the Virgin Mary cradling baby Jesus, with cupids in diapers flying around above them. I thought it might be the most hideous painting I'd ever seen in my life. I crept softly across the plush red carpeting to padded pews covered with red velvet. I sat down, fingering one of the hymnals in the book rack attached to the pew in front of me. I figured I had half an hour, at least, before the cleaners were done. The fight should be over at least by that time, but then what would the cops do when they realized I wasn't there? Would they come here looking for me, or would they assume I'd gone home or somewhere else?

Home. What was going on there? The address had been on the warrant. If the cops hadn't been there yet, they were sure to show up soon, looking for me. Kimberly had been at the party, but she'd left early, saying she was tired. I had better warn her.

I pulled out my phone, but somehow it seemed wrong to use it in a church, even one that was deader than a doornail. I got up, feeling exposed even though I was pretty sure no one was there, and crept my way down the dark carpeted hall to the bathrooms. I went into one of the stalls. Fortunately, the toilet had a cover, so I closed it and sat down. Then for some reason I couldn't explain – like some book I'd read so long ago I'd forgotten it even existed – I tucked my legs under me so my feet wouldn't show. A ridiculous precaution, since I was about to start talking. If anyone was staking out this bathroom, I'd be caught in a second. I reached into my purse and took out my phone.

The little message envelope had a red number 7 on top of it, seven new messages. I pressed the button to reveal them. All were from Kimberly.

10:13 pm "Police r here."

10:27 pm "Going through your stuff. Said it's something about a murder."

11:13 pm "Asked for key to clinic. Told them don't have."

11:39 pm "Police found keys. Raiding clinic."

12:01 am "Asking me questions. Want to know where you are."

12:22 am "More cops coming."

12:45 am "Cops taking me in. Get a lawyer."

Shit. Kimberly was busted. Probably Toni and Evelyn were busted, maybe others too, all because of me. I looked at the time on my phone. 1:06 am. Would they put Kimberly in with the others? How did I even know the others were really busted? I should try to find out.

I climbed up onto the top of the toilet basin. Standing on the very tip of my toes, I could just see out the window. That gave me a clear view of the parking lot, where the cleaners were traipsing back and forth, taking out garbage, tucking the salvaged floral centerpieces into their cars. If the cops were watching the church, would they have someone guarding the parking lot? Probably, but I couldn't really see that far. They could be watching it from across the street, or from somewhere near the building, which I couldn't see. The chapel only had stained glass windows, which were useless for looking out. If I wanted to see the front of the building, I'd need to go across the hall to the minister's office, which was probably locked.

It was, but the choir room next door was open. It was narrow and sparsely furnished, a closet really, holding nothing but a long wheeled rack of choir robes in deep purple satin with wide gold collars. I absently fondled one, enjoying the smooth feel of the satin. For no reason I could ever name, I took it off the hanger and put it on. Then I noticed the best thing about the room, which was that it had a direct entry to the choir loft via a ladder that came down from a trap door in the ceiling. The ladder was already down, or I might not have noticed it. I left my heels downstairs and climbed the loft in my stockings. When I got up there, I surveyed the church from above. I was to the left of the pulpit, which meant I was facing the front of the building, but there was no window, only a skylight at one end. I made my way over to the skylight, stood down below, and gazed up at it. I couldn't possibly reach it without a ladder, and there was none. The ladder up to the loft was fixed to the floor. But wait. If I could balance on the railing, I might, just might, be able to reach the skylight and push it open. Whether I could then get myself out through it, I didn't know.

I stood up on one of the choir seats, which were like seats in a movie theater. It rocked significantly beneath my weight, but it was bolted to the ground, so I really shouldn't be as scared as I was. From there I sat down on the high railing. That had been the easy part, and it was scary enough. I bent forward and knelt on the railing, hands flat and butt in the air, and then pressed myself up. It was just a tiny bit wider than a balance beam. I tried to take comfort from that, reminding myself I had been an okay gymnast in high school. Don't think about the fact that that was fifty-some years ago and you haven't been on a beam since, I told myself. Just think steady. My left foot wobbled, but I checked it the way I had back then, and before I could think about it too long, I stretched up until I could barely touch the lever that opened the skylight with my right hand. I pushed hard, bracing one leg on the railing, pushing off with the other, and the skylight fell open. Before I could think too hard, I followed the upward motion of the lever in my hand, trying to capitalize on the momentum, and caught the metal frame of the window with the fingertips of my left hand. Then with one hand on the frame and the other still on the lever, I hoisted myself up, careful to push upward on the lever, not down. It took three tries, but I finally managed to wedge my torso through the skylight and claw my way out onto the slanted roof.

When I tried to stand up, I had a horrible attack of vertigo. I sat back down hard. I couldn't have gotten myself up here just to be laid out by fear of heights. I sat still, head in hands, for a long five minutes. Then I steeled myself and scooched on my bottom to near the edge of the roof, keeping my hands flat on the shingles. From here I could only see the houses across the street, not the ground. I cautiously laid down on my side and then flopped over onto my belly. In that position, I grabbed onto the edge of the roof with both hands and pulled myself forward. Now I could look down and see the sidewalk directly in front of the church where the confrontation had taken place an hour ago.

The street was silent as a morgue. I saw no car lights, no one walking around. If the police were still there, they were using guerrilla tactics, fading into the night like commandos. The guys who had tried to arrest me before were definitely not that sophisticated. I lay on my stomach, trying to think about a next step that made any sense. I couldn't go home, and all my friends in town were probably in jail. Then it hit me that Josie and Rabbit had not been there when the fight started. I didn't know if they'd shown up after I left; I assumed so since they were supposed to be my ride home. I didn't want to call Josie from up here, in case someone was watching the church after all. A voice on the roof would surely catch their attention.

I curled into a fetal position and from there was able to turn myself around. Going up the slant, toward the building, I was able to stand up and walk without fear or dizziness. I took three steps, each one causing the roof to shake heartily under me. I quickened my pace. Only about two feet stood between me and the glorious solid ground of the choir loft, when a gust of wind blew and I heard the sickening sound of the skylight slamming shut.

CHAPTER TWENTY-FOUR

Whistling Past the Graveyard

I tried the window relentlessly. I should be able to push it open because it wasn't locked, but the force with which it had closed had tripped the latch. After fourteen tries, I gave up. I could break it, I supposed, but I didn't even have a shoe to do that with. The only thing I had in my purse that might do it was my cell phone, but if I blasted a hole in the glass and didn't manage to break the window, I was afraid the phone would drop through and then I'd be stuck on the roof in a choir gown and a Pat Nixon dress with no phone and police after me.

You're never gonna make it on the lam if you can't even get off this roof, I thought. That I'd been on the lam once before did not afford me much comfort. Then, I'd had a whole coast full of friends who knew a lot more about making it underground than I did. Here, I knew almost no one, and the people I did know had no experience with living on the wrong side of the law. They might not even want to talk to me again when I told them my whole story.

"Don't be silly," I said out loud. "You didn't do anything wrong."

I believed that, but I wasn't sure the others would.

I took out my phone and texted Josie, "U ok? Whats up?"

After fifteen minutes with no answer, I concluded that wasn't going to be my way out. I wasn't sure what I would have asked Josie to do anyway. Bring a ladder? Hauling a ladder up to the roof of a church in the wee hours of Sunday was not a great strategy for someone trying to avoid the cops. On the other hand, letting the sun come up on me sitting up here like a Fiddler on the Roof would not be inconspicuous either. The pastor and deacons would be here in a few hours to get ready for church, but what would I tell them?

I forced myself to stand up, ignoring the warning bells zooming around in my head.

"You're going to be fine," I said out loud. "You're going to make it."

I'd never been someone who talked to herself out loud. Now it seemed to be becoming a habit – hopefully a temporary one, but I needed to hear a comforting voice, and mine was the only one available. I mouthed encouragement to myself until I got close to the edge of the roof. Not too close. That wouldn't be brave, that would be stupid, something else I had always prided myself on not being. I peered over, looking for something, anything, that could help me get to the ground. I started with the back, not only because it would be the least visible, but it also seemed likeliest to have a fire escape or something jutting out. There was a fire escape, but it didn't come up past the second floor. I moved gingerly across the roof, checking both sides. The church was on a corner, so one side was totally exposed. The house on the other side had a chain-link fence I thought I could possibly grab onto without doing myself grievous harm if I could manage the drop. The only problem with that plan was that it was at least two body lengths over, as well as a good ways down. I didn't see being able to sail across that accurately, and if I missed, I'd be toppling right onto concrete and metal garbage cans.

I continued around to the front. There it was. The sign announcing the minister's name and when services were was bolted to a board, which was bolted to the building, leaving about an inch in between. It was just deep enough and at about the right height that I thought I could stand on it while still hanging onto the metal lip of the roof. To make it more appealing, the drainpipe was not too far over, so once I was on the sign, I thought I could reach out and grab the drainpipe to ease myself down the rest of the way.

It took me ten minutes to get up the courage to try. Every time I started, I backed off. Finally I decided I would never do it unless I convinced myself I was about to be caught. I imagined the sound of sirens in the distance, and then heard them coming closer. When I closed my eyes, I could see pulsing red lights at the corner.

"Now or never," I said to myself.

I positioned myself over the sign, flipped over onto my stomach and reached down until I felt the lip of the roof under my fingertips. Then I grabbed on and slid my feet down until they touched the sign. All I had to do then was straighten up, hanging on for dear life. I felt solid holding on with both hands, but when I tried to take one away, I felt a searing pain in the back of my calf. I gripped the roof for dear life. The pain subsided but did not go away. I felt my left leg starting to buckle. I did not have time. I wasn't going to be able to make it. I reached out with my right hand but the drainpipe was just out of reach. My right foot slipped off the sign and I started to fall.

Somehow, I'll never know how, I managed to hold onto the sign boards with my left hand, and gradually get my right hand back on. I steadied myself so I was dangling straight down. My arms ached bad. I knew I didn't have the strength to hold on for more than a few more minutes. I could feel my fatigued muscles starting to give way. I flattened myself out and let go with my right hand again, drifting rightwards so that I could touch the drainpipe, even though I couldn't grasp it. My left hand scraped against the wooden sign and wooden shingles of the building, picking up splinters, but slowing my trajectory enough that when I fell into the shrubbery, I landed without much force. I managed to land face up, so no twigs stuck in my eyes. I lay there for a minute, gasping for breath, thanking a God I didn't believe in but who must have mistaken me in my choir robe for one of His children. Then I clambered to my feet and started to run.

"Don't run," a voice said in my head. "Running attracts attention."

I couldn't stop, though, until I was at the edge of Maymont Park. Then I had to stop because I had no idea where I was going. West was the clinic and my car. At least I had my keys in my purse, but I didn't trust that my block wasn't being watched, and I had rented the car under my own name. East was downtown, the state Capitol, City Hall, the jail. I hadn't been in the city long enough to know which neighborhoods, if any, had all night businesses, or where to get a cab. I could only think of one possible plan of action, and I had no idea if it would work.

I started to walk up toward what I hoped was Meadow, which I knew would take me eventually to Cary Street. It might take an hour, but I figured as long as I was walking around here in the middle of nowhere, the chances of being caught were small, so I didn't worry when the streets started getting darker and more woody, rather than brighter and more urban. When I started seeing tombstones, however, I had to accept that I'd gone the wrong way.

I walked into the cemetery and sank onto the soft, well-watered ground, wondering what the hell I was doing. I seriously considered just getting a cab – as if I saw any cabs – to the nearest police station and asking them to page Sergeant Wilson and tell him that his murder suspect was there. The idea was seeming saner by the second when a voice behind my right shoulder said, "Got a cigarette?"

I scrambled to my feet and whirled to face a person of indeterminate gender, wearing nearly see-through camouflage pants and a ratty blanket that had once been white and covered with yellow daisies. Stringy hair that hadn't been washed in a decade hung to stooped shoulders.

"No, I don't smoke," I said.

"No problem." The person stooped to look more closely at my face. "You in trouble?"

I felt my lips parting in a slow smile, in spite of myself. "How could you tell?" I asked.

"Shows in your eyes. Nice coat." The person touched the choir robe, their fingers lingering on the satin just as mine had.

"Here, you can have it." I took the robe off and placed it around my newfound friend's shoulders. The blanket made a ridiculous looking hump underneath it, The Hunchback of Notre Dame and then some. I tried not to laugh.

"Thanks!" I'd made the vagrant really happy.

"It's nothing," I said, which couldn't have been more true. They shuffled off, eyes cast down, presumably seeking out cigarette butts that hadn't been completely smoked. I saw them squat and comb the earth with their fingers, pull up a little tan and white object, inspect it, tuck it in the wide pocket of the camouflage pants.

"Excuse me," I was the one coming up behind them this time.

The graveyard denizen swiveled on their haunches, face tilted up to mine.

"What's your name?" I asked.

"Crate," they answered, and held up a hand to me.

I made myself shake the leathery hand that had just added more soil to a buildup of many years. My gardening friends said all the microbes in soil were good for you, as long as they hadn't been exposed to pesticides. I could only hope, improbably, that this was an organic graveyard.

"Nice to meet you, Crate. I'm Mollie. Would you, by any chance, know the way to the bus station?"

Crate laughed. "Gonna take you a long time to walk there. You don't got a car?"

"Not on me." I looked around. Would I be sitting in a cemetery if I had a car to sit in? I supposed to Crate, that might not be a straightforward choice.

"Go thataway," Crate pointed, and I saw what I had done. I'd veered off onto a street that angled sharply away from downtown. If I retraced my steps, I could get back on Meadow and keep going straight. I thanked Crate and trudged off. I wondered if it had been a mistake to tell Crate my name. One of my names. No matter; if I stayed free for long, I would need a new one.

CHAPTER TWENTY-FIVE

The Man from Mobile

I detoured on Broad Street to find a convenience store with an out-door ATM. I figured it would be less likely to have a camera than a bank. In the store's side windows, I could see stacks of chips and Host-ess cakes, but sadly, the front door was chained shut. Dawn was breaking just as I made it to the Greyhound station. I ignored the people looking strangely at me. I tried to picture what they were seeing: a senior citizen with an Italian leather purse but no shoes, no luggage, wearing a summer dress in a style not seen since the 1970s. I marched up to the ticket counter and paid cash for a one-way ticket to New York City. Best place in the world to disappear. I even knew a few people there, but I doubted I'd look them up. At least not now. I wasn't a safe person to know.

"Board at four ten," the cashier said.

I looked at the clock. Three fifty. I settled in one of the chairs facing the back lot where the buses pulled in. I pulled out my iPad and saw that the battery was low. I'd better charge it as much as possible before I had to spend seven hours on a bus. I wandered around the small wait-ing room, looking for a plug. At first I didn't see any, but then I noticed that the panel where the vending machine was plugged in had another open socket. I was afraid to just leave it, so I moved to a chair near the vending machine, where I could keep an eye on my prized possession.

This seat faced the entrance, and that's why I saw the guy before he saw me. He was medium height, medium brown hair, medium brown skin, medium brown eyes. Perfect for being unnoticeable and unmemorable. He could have been Latino or Italian or light-skinned African American. He wore jeans and a gray hoodie, with the hood flopping down his back. I couldn't be completely sure, because I'd only seen him for a few seconds, maybe a minute, but I was almost positive that it was the same guy who took the pictures of me and the other women on the pier in Mobile.

He didn't come straight for me, and I managed to convince myself I had imagined it. He stood in the lobby opposite the ticket counter, as if scanning the arrival and departure board. Then he walked up to the counter and talked to the agent, but didn't buy a ticket. I thought I saw him looking toward the waiting room. I bent over, suddenly very interested in the contents of my purse.

How could he have found me? Not that this was an unlikely place to go, but there were so many possibilities. I couldn't believe they had people watching the airport, the train station, checkpoints on the highways, just for me. What was it Sarita had said? Her father tracked her through the GPS on her phone. It was probably too late, but I still fumbled in my purse for my phone and hit the off button. I had no idea if that would disable the GPS. Unlikely, but I wasn't about to leave town with no phone.

The guy did a tour around the lobby, glanced into the waiting room and walked out of the building. I couldn't see where he went after exiting. I didn't see him walk to the parking lot, but he must have, unless he got in a cab. But I didn't see a cab pull out. I must have been wrong. I felt weak with relief.

"Passengers for New York City, please board through Door Number Three. Your bus is waiting. This is an express, with stops only in Chesapeake, Maryland and Newark, New Jersey. Please look around you to make sure you have all your personal possessions before proceeding to Door Number Three."

The announcement repeated three times. I didn't have personal possessions to collect. I hoped it wouldn't be too air conditioned on the bus
and I would be able to sleep. If I was extra lucky, I could buy a jacket
or sweatshirt and some moccasins or flip-flops in Chesapeake, Maryland, although I didn't imagine it would be a megamall. I gathered my
iPad and my purse and went out to join the throng waiting to show their
tickets to the tired-looking man standing next to the bus door. He
punched my ticket with one of those hole punchers like I'd used in
fourth grade to put drawings into a three-ring binder. I grabbed a window seat and wished I had something to put on the one next to me other
than my purse. I decided to risk someone sitting there rather than lose
everything I had left to my name, at least on the east coast. I didn't want
to face out; I was still worried about the guy from Mobile or the cops
showing up before I got out of town, so I leaned my head against the
window and put my arm over my face. Then I sprawled outward, trying
to take up as much of the seat as possible as people filed past me.

It didn't work. Someone nudged my legs over and sat down heavily
next to me. I squirmed so I was more or less lying on my side, my bare
feet resting lightly on the seat in front of me.

The engine started, belching out the usual burst of carbon monoxide.
I heard the driver saying last goodbyes to the dispatcher.

"Ms. Kellam?" said the person sitting next to me.

I lay still. In thirty seconds, I'd be en route to New York. I didn't
know why on earth my pursuer had waited until this moment to make
himself known, but if he was so anxious to keep me in Richmond, he
could jolly well have done it already.

I felt a hand on my arm, pulling it down, felt the cool air on my face.
I turned to face the person who was holding my hand down by my side
with gentle pressure.

It was the Man from Mobile. He didn't have handcuffs out, and I
didn't see evidence of a gun anywhere on him. His sweatshirt was open,
and he had a folded *New York Times* in his hand, as if he was just off to
see a Broadway show.

"You are Renata Kellam?" he repeated, softly and not urgently.

I nodded. It felt good, I realized, to stop denying who I had been.

"I think you'd better come with me," he said.

The bus started beeping as the driver prepared to reverse. I sat rigid, trying to think. I could refuse, make him drag me off, if that's what he intended to do. But what would be the point? I'd been found. I wasn't some super-fugitive, Harrison Ford with a one-armed man up my sleeve. My past had caught up with me, and it was time to face the music. Mobile Man was standing in the aisle, holding up a hand to the driver, who was telling him impatiently to sit down. He held out a hand to me, the soul of gallantry. I took his help to slide out of the seat and padded down the aisle after him in my bare feet. Now, I thought, I must really make a sight – not only was I eccentrically dressed, but I was being escorted off the bus by someone out of Central Casting for a government agent.

Even out on the pavement, he didn't cuff me. He didn't seem to have any partners hanging around either.

"Why did you wait so long?" I asked.

He didn't answer. He led me through the building to the visitors' parking lot. I pulled my hand out of his and he didn't protest. I thought I could just walk away. When I veered away from him, though, he moved close and looped his arm through mine, as if we were a loving couple.

"Am I under arrest?" I asked, testily.

"We'll see about that," he said. What the hell did that mean? I was or I wasn't. Unless he was going to give me a chance to make some deal.

"Well do I have to go with you?"

"If you know what's good for you, you will." That wasn't exactly an answer, but it reminded me that he wasn't the only person looking for me. At least he didn't seem completely hostile, even if I couldn't figure out who he was or what he wanted. I might as well throw my lot in with him for now. He clicked a key fob in his hand and the tail lights of a sleek, black sedan winked on and off. It was exactly the kind of car federal agents drove on television. I waited for him to open the back door and push my head down as I settled into a seat that was separated from the front by a wire cage. Instead, he opened the front passenger's door for me and waited until I buckled myself in to close the door. I had a handle and a lock on my side. I could still get away if I decided I needed to.

He drove down Boulevard and made a right on Monument, just as I would if I were going home. Home. Funny how the little apartment above the clinic on Grove had become "home" to me in just six months. I thought fondly of how I had to blow on the front burner to get it to light, and how the morning light streamed in through my bedroom window, so I didn't need an alarm clock. I wondered if I'd ever get to go back there. A few hours ago, I had not even considered it a possibility. Now, for no good reason, I was able to hope. I wondered if Kimberly would stay there. Kimberly. I'd been so obsessed with my own predicament, I hadn't thought about Kimberly stuck in jail for hours. Since Josie hadn't answered my text, I had no idea if anyone even knew where Kimberly was. Could I ask the driver? I didn't even know who he was.

"If you don't mind, who the hell are you?" I asked.

"You'll find out soon enough."

"Why are you being so damn mysterious? This isn't a game, you know."

"I'm very well aware of that, Ms. Kellam."

"Stop calling me that. I haven't used that name in fifty years, as I'm sure you know."

"What would you like me to call you?"

"Why should I give you my name when you won't give me yours?"

"No reason."

He turned left on Malvern, swinging into the turn at the last second and nearly bashing into a semi truck with the words "Bertha's Breads" emblazoned on the side.

"Mollie. Everyone calls me Mollie," I said.

"Yes, I've noticed that they do."

Just past Cary Street, where the fashionable businesses were still slumbering, he made a left and another quick left and we were in a part of town I'd never seen before, even though it was just blocks from the clinic in one direction, and the church where I'd danced last night in the other. The houses were enormous, but the lawns were even huger, the fading flower gardens tastefully coordinated like giant wedding center-pieces. We passed a house that resembled the White House, Doric columns that could have been actual alabaster at the top of at least one hundred broad white steps. I indulged a momentary hope that whoever lived there would someday need a wheelchair to get around, but then realized it was a futile effort at class rectification – these folks would have no trouble affording an elevator and whatever retrofitting was re-quired to render it useful.

The driveway my mysterious driver finally pulled into led to a gray stone ranch house with dozens of dormer windows facing the plain ex-panse of perfectly manicured green grass. It reminded me of a Victorian sanitorium. He got out and opened the door for me as if he were a chauf-feur. Was the Colonial architecture bringing out his chivalry once again, or was he signaling that I was not really free to go where I wanted? It didn't matter, because I wasn't about to make a break for it at this point. I was too curious.

My escort rang the bell and tapped his heel impatiently as we waited. I heard heels clacking on wooden floors, and then nothing, as they pre-sumably hit a rug. The door opened a crack, and then wider. A woman near my age in a navy blue A-line skirt and white blouse stood there, beckoning us in. She had a chic black bob just to her chin line, silver hoops dangling from her ears and no makeup that I could tell. Her trans-lucent skin was remarkably unlined for a white woman of her age. I couldn't help looking down at the crows' nests that graced my hands.

"Come in, come in," the woman cried. We stepped into a dim foyer, beyond which I could make out a sun-drenched kitchen complete with a butcher-block island. Barbie's dream house come to life.

"Let me take your things," she said, although of course I had no things, just the battered Pat Nixon handbag I'd been toting around. I handed it to her.

"I'm Mollie," I said, trying to act like this was some normal house visit. "I don't believe we've met."

She slung the purse over her shoulder so she could hold my hand in both of hers. She held on, leaning in to peer into my face.

"We have," she said, "but it's been an age and a half."

I met her gaze, trying to retrieve a memory. She did not look familiar, but I'm notoriously bad at recognizing faces if other elements of the person's appearance have changed a lot. I think of myself as a context-sensitive menu.

"I'm sorry, I don't think—"

"We met in Portland," she said. "But then we were in San Francisco."

Even now that I knew who she had to be, her face didn't ring any bells. Her voice, though, had not changed a bit. I could hear it telling me about the college boy who had knocked her up and then abandoned her.

"Emily?" I didn't need the question mark. She nodded unnecessarily. Then she leaned forward and wrapped her arms around my shoulders, pulling me toward her. I didn't particularly feel like responding. I still didn't know what I was doing here, but if this entire night of hide and seek was somehow her doing, a hug was hardly what I wanted to give her.

I stiffened in her embrace, and she backed off. She looked a little hurt, turned away and busied herself hanging my purse on a hanger in a coat closet.

I had been so busy staying out of the clutches of the law, I had not focused on one detail. I'd been assuming all the men who had tried to grab me at the party had been together, one big SWAT team. But now I realized that the first Obama to accost me had called me Renata Kellam. Sergeant Wilson had said nothing about Renata. His warrant was for Mollie O'Shay, and he had mentioned Caitlin Shaw, who had had an abortion three months ago. There was no reason for a Richmond police sergeant to be interested in Emily Streeter, who had an abortion fifty years ago in San Francisco.

"Tell me what's going on," I said sternly to Emily. "Now."

"Yes, of course," she said in her melodic alto. "Come have some breakfast."

I was even hungrier than I was angry. Breakfast sounded divine. I followed Emily through the butcher-block kitchen to the formal dining room beyond. At the table, cozily set with china and sterling for five, sat Toni, nursing a cinnamon-topped latte.

CHAPTER TWENTY-SIX

Breakfast Epiphanies

Emily made me a latte, and placed a cut crystal bowl full of unseasonal fruit in the middle of the table. I ignored good manners and scarfed two bowlfuls as the smell of potatoes frying wafted from the kitchen.

Toni continued to smile at me in an infuriating Mona Lisa way, saying only, "I'm glad you're safe. Yvette's on her way. We'll explain everything when she gets here."

Now that I wasn't so hungry, I was self-conscious about my mud-caked Pat Nixon dress. Whyever Yvette was coming over, I didn't want her to find me looking like Eliza Dolittle's Before picture. I wandered into the kitchen.

"Do you think I could take a shower?" I asked Emily. "And maybe borrow some sweats and a t-shirt?"

She turned down the flame under the potatoes and led me to a bathroom that was as every bit as opulent as I had imagined. A set of clean clothes, complete with fleece-lined slippers, already sat on the vanity.

"You can just leave your dirty things in there," she pointed to a white wicker hamper in the corner. "We'll take care of them later."

I let the hot water course over me, trying to wrap my head around the events of the last twelve hours. By the time I emerged from the bathroom with damp aromatic hair, Yvette was seated between Toni and Emily, drinking her usual, mint tea, out of a glass cup.

"What are you doing here?" I asked her. "And please don't say having breakfast."

"Well, I am looking forward to breakfast, but that's not all," Yvette said. A covered pot and an oversized skillet, steam coiling from under the lids, sat on the table next to a plate of delectable pastries. I decided story hour would go better with sustenance.

"Let's eat," I said, and everyone set to, piling their plates with potatoes, eggs and fruit. I opted for a scone and more fruit with creamy Greek yogurt. Emily excused herself and disappeared, coming back a minute later with The Man from Mobile. I wondered where he had been hiding.

"Mollie, this is Steve," she said in her musical voice. "Or should we call you Renata?"

"Mollie," I said. "I've been Mollie for fifty years. Let's let Renata stay dead."

Steve sat down in front of the empty place setting, and Emily resumed her spot at the head of the table, facing me.

"Nearly a year ago," Emily began, as Steve served himself modest helpings of eggs and potatoes, "two FBI agents showed up at my office. I live in New Orleans now. This is an AirBnB," she added, seeing me looking around at the walls with their generic art. "These agents said they were part of a new squad investigating cold cases from the Vietnam War era – literally, that's what they said – and they wanted to talk to me about my kidnapping in 1971. I said there must be some mistake, I hadn't been kidnapped, it had nothing to do with Vietnam, and the person who had been accused had died. But they insisted they had an open file and they needed to get all the facts before they could close the case. They said they had reason to believe you were still alive. I told them I had no interest in digging up the past and sent them on their way. But I figured they wouldn't let it go, so I hired a private investigator to see if he could find you."

"Is that you?" I said to Steve. Surely it wasn't Yvette or Toni. I looked from one to the other. They were both eating, innocently.

His mouth was full, so he shook his head from side to side.

"The man I hired was in New Orleans," Emily said. "It didn't take him long to find out you lived in San Francisco, but by that time, you were in Mexico. He said there shouldn't be a problem as long as you were out of the country, but I told him to stay on it, and then you turned up here. He hired Steve to keep tabs on you."

"We served together in I-raq," Steve interjected through a mouthful of potatoes.

"Where do you come in?" I asked Toni. I dreaded the answer, but I needed to know.

"Steve and I had worked together as paramedics," she said. "He told me he needed someone who could blend into the group you were working with. When I found out Yvette was already involved, I got him to hire her too. So one of us could be with you most of the time."

Yvette nodded. I thought back. It was true. Nearly all the time I was working at the clinic, one of them was on duty. And then – there were the weekends. I didn't like where this was going.

"You brought a gun to the party," I said. "Did you know I was going to be arrested?"

"Steve knew the cops were looking for you," she said. "He told me to be ready."

"And you knew you could point a gun at him, and it would be okay, because he would tell the cops to let it go." Everything was starting to make an awful kind of sense. Toni nodded, sipped her coffee as if this were all normal.

"I don't feel so good," I said.

I got up from the table and wandered through the house, picking up speed as I got further from the dining room. I needed a room with a door I could close and chose the first one I found, a child's bedroom painted in circus colors. I shut myself in and curled up on the low twin bed, my back touching the wall, knees bent toward my chest. Hot tears poured down my cheeks and onto the red flannel pillowcase.

I thought I had a friend and a lover. It turned out I had bodyguards.

Every day in Richmond played like a movie behind my eyes. The first dance at the church and later at my house. The Olive Garden. The concert at the museum, the Italian restaurant, Toni's story about the end of her marriage. Was any of it even true?

Nell had known Toni for ages, I recalled. She'd officiated at her wedding, and later they'd both been involved with Hillary. Nell must have known Toni was the hired muscle assigned to keep me safe, maybe had even had a part in getting her hired. Had she told her how to win my trust?

All the satisfaction I had felt when we got back from Mobile, the new clinic a near reality, drained away. How hard had it been for Toni to touch me? Every awkward moment became a grotesque sore. She was fifteen years younger than I was. If we were both twenty years younger, it wouldn't be an issue. But seventy is a world away from fifty-five. How could I have imagined she was attracted to me?

I don't know how long I lay like that, seeing and re-seeing events on a loop, before I heard a soft knock.

"Go away," I choked out, but I heard the door creak and Toni came in anyway. She sat cross-legged next to the bed, leaning against the white dresser.

"Mollie, I know what you're thinking, but it's not like that."

"How could you know what I'm thinking? You don't know anything about me."

If she had insisted she knew a lot about me, I would have thrown her out. Instead she said, "You're right. I don't know much. I told you my story, but you never told me yours."

I turned my face from the pillow to face her. Her deep brown eyes showed compassion and concern, just as they did when she was chauffeuring scared girls to the clinic. In the bright light streaming through the picture window, I could see tiny imperfections in her skin – the beginnings of an age spot on her forehead, a zit in the corner of her nose. Her mortality emboldened me.

"It was the fall of '71," I began.

CHAPTER TWENTY-SEVEN

Fall of '71

We kept being told the war was winding down. But everywhere I looked, it seemed to be ramping up. My brother's lottery number was ninety-three. Anything under one fifty was bad. He was trying to decide what to do – go to Canada, go to jail, go to Vietnam.

"It doesn't matter which I choose, I'm doomed either way," he muttered to me as we trudged home from synagogue on Rosh Hashanah.

We were not that religious, but my father had been brought up "*frum*," observant. This was his bow to his upbringing, that we didn't ride in cars on the High Holy Days. I didn't see how getting all sweaty was supposed to bring us closer to God, but I didn't see how mouthing Hebrew prayers I couldn't understand or pronounce was supposed to do that either. It wasn't worth a fight. We would get home, eat gefilte fish and honey cake, and then my brother and I would go into his room and open the windows wide so we could smoke pot and strategize.

"The movement can help you," I said. "I know people who can hide you, or get you a new identity, or to Canada if that's what you want."

"I'm not like you." Chuck shook his head vigorously. "You put your faith in other people. I put mine in myself."

"I am a rock," I sang. "I am an ayyyyyyyyyyyayland."

"Shut up," he said. "You want to end up like your friend Allison, that's fine by me. Just leave me out of it."

"Charles Kellam, you're a horrible person."

I sped up, leaving him in my dust. I wanted to get away as fast as I could.

Allison Krause and I had been hallmates my freshman year at Kent. We'd joined the antiwar movement, and then Students for a Democratic Society, together. With her, I had joined the organizing committee for the May Day protests. I was on the security committee. We met at eleven before the noon protest, mapped out what we thought was a solid plan for protecting the crowd from the police and National Guard. I was paired with a guy named Jimmy, whom I had dated a couple times. We were assigned to the southeast side. He would keep his back to the Guard and watch the crowd for signs of agitators and infiltrators. I would face the Guard and warn people if they seemed ready to move. We tied red armbands on each other's biceps. He gave mine a little squeeze with hands rough from the carpentry work he did on the side.

Two hours later, Allison and three other students lay dead on the tarmac and my college days in Ohio were over. I limped back to Portland, enrolled in a few classes at a local community college, and served blue plate specials at the diner around the corner from my parents' house. For six months I did nothing else, even while the bombing of Cambodia escalated. I watched from afar as SDS splintered and sputtered. With equal opportunity, I shunned the Weathermen and the Worker-Student Alliance and the Revolutionary Youth Movement. But slowly, I started to make forays back into the Left, especially feminist groups. Some friends of mine had graduated and started a commune in town, and I would go over and help make cobblers for Black Panther fundraisers.

One of the women in that house, Mollie O'Shay, was my new best friend. She'd grown up in a working class Catholic family in San Francisco, where her father worked on the docks. She told me stories of walking picket lines and labor parades in The City. I wondered why she had left such an exciting place to come to sleepy Oregon. She said something about freedom to be who she really was, which I didn't understand, but I loved hanging around her. She had big loose red lips that reminded me of a marionette's, and a hearty belly laugh which carried all the way up to her wide grey eyes. I never felt sad when she was around.

Mollie was getting involved with a women's group that drove girls in trouble down to San Francisco, where abortion was legal.

"Abortion?" I said, my eyebrows shooting up toward the ceiling. "But you're Catholic."

"I used to be," said Mollie.

We were in her kitchen, making sweet potato pies in the big industrial oven. My friend Clarence would be coming by in an hour and a half to pick up the pies for the new free dinner program the Panthers were kicking off at the church across town.

"So what, you don't consider yourself Catholic anymore?" I asked Mollie, as I emptied two quarts of cream into the bowl of a standing mixer.

"You wouldn't understand," she said. She gathered up the big bowls to which flecks of orange batter still clung, and carried them to the sink. "You can be Jewish just by making potato pancakes and noodle kugel." She pronounced it "koogle." "Being Catholic is different. You can't be a cultural Catholic."

She had heard me call myself a "cultural Jew."

"Why not?" I asked.

"Because the culture is the problem," she said. She turned on the water and I started up the mixer, so I had no chance to ask what that meant. I concentrated on beating the cream to just the right stiffness so it would pipe a nice stiff collar of rosettes around the edges of each pie. Clarence's mother was going to be at the dinner, and I wanted her to be impressed. Though I wasn't sure she would ever soften toward the idea of her son with a white girl, even one who could make a mean pie.

"I'm taking a girl down to San Fran next week," Mollie said, when it was quiet enough to talk again. "Why don't you come? If we have two drivers, we can make it in one day."

"Where would we sleep? With your folks?" I liked the idea of meeting her union organizer parents. My parents were embarrassingly bourgeois – my mom a social worker, my dad teaching Classics at the U.

"No way. They'd ask what we were doing there. There's an anarchist bookstore with a room in the back."

"Sleeping in a bookstore? Cool!"

That's how I ended up driving fifteen-year-old Emily Streeter to San Francisco for a procedure that took fifteen minutes and changed my life forever.

When I got to Mollie's on that Wednesday, she answered the door in a flannel nightgown covered with tiny blue flowers. It must have been white once but had faded to a sickly yellow, and Mollie's face was the same color. She couldn't even stand up without holding onto the door jamb.

"What's the matter?" I asked. I entered and we headed toward her room. She had to stop twice for breath.

"Dunno," she said, sinking slowly onto the bed. "Some kind of flu, I guess. Fever and chills."

"Go back to bed," I ordered. I hadn't decided to be a nurse yet, but I already had the tone down. "You're in no condition to drive five hundred miles. I'll take Emily myself."

She didn't have the strength to protest more than perfunctorily. I tucked her in and let myself out.

We had arranged to pick Emily up at a gas station a few blocks from the high school. When I drove up, I saw a slender girl with a black bob and white ankle socks standing under the sign advertising gas for 4.99, biting her thumbnail. In the unbitten hand, she clutched a couple textbooks. I pulled up next to her.

I think I'm in a Mary McCarthy novel, I thought.

"Emily?" I asked, just to be sure. She nodded and hopped into the front seat.

For the first several hours, we listened to the radio and she said nothing. When we drove out of range of one station, she would fiddle with the dial until she found another playing James Taylor and Joni Mitchell. When we passed the sign "Welcome to California," I dutifully beeped my horn, and Emily released a huge sigh, as if she'd been holding her breath since we left Portland. Then she started talking.

She told me about the man who had seduced her, a sophomore at the U. He'd taken her to the movies, and then a park where they could hear other couples doing the same thing they were doing. She'd been a virgin, but she had told him she wasn't. When she found out she was pregnant, he gave her the two hundred dollars for the abortion without batting an eyelash, and helped her get in touch with Mollie's group. She had the feeling he did this all the time. The next few times she tried to call him, he didn't answer.

"Where did you meet him?" I asked.

"The library," she said and gave a half-laugh. I pictured a young man with jeans and long hair hanging around the town library, looking for lonely, bookish girls to screw. I promised myself I would get the name of this predator, and after I'd safely delivered the embryo-free Emily to her home, I would track him down and – and what? I had no idea – but I'd think of something.

In reality, I didn't deliver Emily to her home, I dropped her at the same gas station where I'd picked her up. On the way to my parents' house, I checked in on Mollie. She was better, and making brown rice and tofu in the kitchen. She wanted to know all about the trip. I told her about Modern Times Bookstore in the Castro District, where homosexuals were starting to move into an Irish working-class area that had seen better days. I had been blown away by the collection of books, on every subject you could imagine – history of the Spanish Civil War, American Indian women, Vietnam, Marxism, labor struggles, even a few about feminism. I showed her one I had bought: a big flat paperback called *Our Bodies Our Selves*.

"I've seen it," she said.

"But look," I said, opening to a page I had dogeared. "With this, we could probably learn to do abortions ourselves. It would be a lot easier than driving for two days. Someone at the clinic told me there's a group in Chicago that does it. They're called Jane. The Women's Union there started it."

"You're crazy," Mollie swiped the book away. "That's dangerous. We'd probably kill someone."

"Don't be stupid," I said. "Abortion isn't dangerous. Emily was done in fifteen minutes. We ate tacos for lunch yesterday. And she was totally fine on the drive home."

"I know, but they're trained professionals. Women die of illegal abortions every day."

"I'm not talking about using a knitting needle or feeding them quinine. We'd learn how to do it properly."

Mollie got up and went to stir the monochromatic brown glop on the stove.

"What's gotten into you?" she asked, her back to me.

"I don't know. I guess, I just saw how different things could be." I went over to stand in the corner between the sink and the stove, so I could half see her face as she added a green bell pepper to her tofu. At least it would add some color, even if it wouldn't help the taste.

"I wanted to ask you about something else," I said.

"What did you mean the other day, about being who you really are?"

"What brought that up?"

"I just want to understand you better. What couldn't you be in San Francisco?"

"All of this." She made a sweeping gesture with her hand. "Being in the movement. Living with different people. Being a vegetarian. All of it."

"There's plenty of movement work in San Francisco," I objected. "And I'm sure there's plenty of tofu too."

"Look, just because you're happy living where you grew up doesn't mean everyone wants to."

She turned away from me, messed around in the spice cabinet, threw a giant handful of cayenne pepper into her tofu. It would probably be inedible. But she hadn't invited me to stay for dinner anyway.

"Who says I'm happy here?" I said. "San Francisco seemed so alive. I was only there a couple days, but I saw all these people doing interesting things – art and politics and music right on the street."

"That's not the San Francisco I come from," Mollie said, forming the words slowly. "It's small. It's provincial. Everyone knows your business. My parents aren't like yours. They would be watching and judging everything I did."

"I'm trying to figure out what it is you don't want them to see."

"Let it go, okay?"

I knew I should let it go, but some part of me wouldn't. I reached for her right arm, and when she still didn't turn around, reached across and clasped her left. When she was finally facing me, I saw water filling her eyes, massive grey pools I could float in.

"What is it? You can tell me," I said, though I was pretty sure I knew what it was, and a week ago she would have been right not to tell me. I thought about going over to the table and grabbing *Our Bodies Our Selves*, so I could turn to the little section headed "Lesbians."

Instead, I stroked her right arm, up, down, the rhythmic insistent motion suggestive of the sex we had never talked about. She stiffened but didn't pull away, so I moved in closer. I took a deep breath, and holding her left shoulder tightly with my trembling right hand, I planted my lips on hers.

She jerked away. Her slate-colored eyes were huge with shock and – I thought – horror.

"I'm sorry." I more or less ran to the table, grabbed my book and shoved it into my backpack. "I'll go."

I was almost at the front door when she caught the back of my sweater.

"Renata. Don't go."

"I didn't mean it," I stammered.

"Yes, you did. At least … I hope you did."

I turned to face her. Her eyes didn't look horrified anymore. They were wet and open. Her red lips were slightly smiling. She reached out and took my hand. My backpack slid to the ground and I put a tentative hand on her hip. She fished my disheveled pony tail out from under my sweater, pulled off the elastic band and ran her fingers through my hair, from the tip of my scalp to the nape of my neck. My whole body tingled in response, Sleeping Beauty waking from a hundred-year nap.

She led me silently to her bedroom. I hoped she had turned off the stove. I didn't want to ask, for fear of interrupting this precious moment.

We undressed each other, sock by sock, shirt by shirt. Neither of us wore a bra, so there were no awkward hooks to mess with. When we were naked, we sat side by side, admiring each other's bodies. Mollie touched my waist lightly with her fingertips. I squealed.

"I'm ticklish," I said and we both laughed, her generous laugh seeming to come from somewhere deep within.

"What about here?" she asked, placing her cool hand solidly between my legs. "Are you ticklish there?"

We never found out if the answer would be yes. A thunderous pounding on the door made us jump up, but we had no time even to reach for our clothes before we heard shattering wood and six FBI agents in full SWAT gear were standing in front of us.

We grabbed for our underpants, managed to struggle into them – I ended up in hers, which were about two sizes too small for me, before the agents shoved us to the ground, face down. I heard the click of handcuffs being opened and then they closed tightly, much too tightly, around my wrists. They cut off circulation to my hands, and I thought I was going to faint.

"Renata Kellam?" said a voice close to my head. A hand yanked my hair and lifted up my face.

"Yeah, that's her," said the guy looking down at a clipboard. Where had they gotten a photo of me? Could only be from my high school yearbook.

"Who are you?" I heard another agent ask Mollie.

"Mollie O'Shay," she answered just as I opened my mouth to say, "Don't say anything."

"Don't have anything on her," said the guy with the clipboard.

"Maybe we should take her anyway," the first guy said.

"She doesn't know anything," I yelled. "It was just me."

I had no idea what was going on, but I assumed it had to do with Emily. There was no reason Mollie should go to jail, even if I had to. Better have her out here.

After a bit of discussion, they uncuffed Mollie and let her put my jeans on me. They led me out with no shirt, my nipples stiffening in the night wind, but at least she managed to shove my t-shirt in between my cuffed wrists so when I finally got my hands free I could put it on.

I spent two days and nights in a solitary cell in the Lane County Jail, being questioned night and day by FBI guys. I kept asking for a lawyer. They kept saying I would get one soon. At one of these sessions, a man presented me with the copy of *Our Bodies Our Selves* and opened it to the page I had dogeared.

"Why did you turn down this page?"

"How do you know that I did?"

"This book belongs to you, right?"

"I want a lawyer."

On the third day, I finally went into a courtroom, where I was greeted by a man who said he was my lawyer. He told me not to say anything, to let him do the talking. The judge read the charges. Kidnapping in the first degree, an offense punishable by death. How do you plead?

"Not guilty."

The lawyer argued that I had not known that Emily was under eighteen. The judge said that's what the trial would be for, and set a preliminary hearing for a month from now. I imagined my life slipping away. I tried to think what the electric chair would be like, or maybe the Feds used the gas chamber. I didn't know. I couldn't imagine either of them.

Around noon the next day a guard came and told me to get my things. I was being released. The lawyer had managed to get the charges reduced to second degree kidnapping, and the judge set bail of a hundred thousand dollars. Clarence and Mollie had found someone to put up their house as collateral for my freedom.

Mollie insisted on taking me out to lunch at a vegetarian restaurant near State. I couldn't eat anything. All I could think about was going to prison, years that would mirror the days I had just spent. Mollie reached across the table for my hand, which was just playing with my fork. When I didn't grasp hers back, she placed mine flat on the tablecloth and covered it with hers.

"I'm sorry," she said. "I should have gone with you." I wasn't positive if she meant to San Francisco or to jail.

"Then we'd both be in trouble," I said.

"Wouldn't that be better?" she asked. "At least whatever happened, we'd be together."

Together. I tried to imagine what that word meant to her. I'd had plenty of time in jail to relive our experiment interruptus from the other day, and I suppose she had had plenty as well, but in such a different environment. There was no way to resolve our two sets of ruminations into togetherness.

"Please don't make this into some kind of romantic tragedy," I said, more harshly than I intended. I watched her eyes fill once again with unshed tears, and somehow that fed the savage energy engulfing my heart. "I'm going to walk home," I said.

I stood, pushing the table into her as I shoved my chair out of the way. I needed to get out into the air. The muscles in my arms and legs ached, as if I were coiling into a fetal position inside my skin.

"I'll call you later," she said to my back.

When I got to my parents' house, my hands trembled so hard it took me three tries to get the key in the lock. They had gone to spend Sukkot in Israel, a long-delayed dream trip. I prayed Chuck wouldn't be home. We had not spoken since that fight on Rosh Hashanah. It occurred to me that the doomed feeling I had now must be what he felt then. It didn't make me eager to see him, but I could see how sometime, it might. Five newspapers, curled inside rubber bands, sat on the front stoop. Chuck must be staying somewhere else. Maybe he had even left for Canada. I gathered up the papers and took them into my room, where I slammed the door as a matter of habit.

I sat down on the soft twin bed and spread out the newspapers before me. The one from the day after I left for San Francisco had a picture of Emily on the front page. "Have you seen this girl?" it asked. Emily's parents had reported her missing, and because someone had seen her getting picked up at the gas station, she was believed kidnapped. An FBI spokesman was quoted saying the first twenty-four hours were critical in a kidnapping investigation. Residents were asked to keep a lookout for a blue Impala.

The paper from two days ago reported on Emily's return and my arrest, for kidnapping and endangering the welfare of a minor. Endangering, my ass. Emily's parents were quoted as saying they were relieved their daughter was alive, but that she had been horribly violated and "those responsible" must be made to pay. Emily, of course, was not quoted at all. The article mentioned that I was arrested at the home of Mollie O'Shay, with whom I appeared to be having a sexual liaison. There were pictures of both of us. Mine was that high school yearbook photo again. I wondered where Mollie's came from. In black and white, we could pass for sisters.

Thank God my parents were out of the country, but they would be back in a week. I had no idea what they would say, or what I would tell them. I didn't think they would mind me taking Emily to California. They were good liberals. My mother gave money to Planned Parenthood and my father volunteered for the ACLU. But liberalism had its limits. My parents had shaken their heads and tut-tutted over the Stonewall riots two years ago. At a dinner party, my father told one of his friends that if either of his kids were gay, he hoped we would have the grace not to tell him.

Now the whole town knew I was gay, and I wasn't even sure I was.

I lay back on the bed and covered my face with a pillow.

CHAPTER TWENTY-EIGHT

Renata Is Dead, Long Live Mollie

The phone was ringing. It had been ringing off and on for two days. Not all my parents' friends knew they were out of town. What were they calling for, I wondered? To say, "Oh, so sorry your kid is a dyke"? To offer to contribute to my legal defense? Hoping to grab some salacious detail they could drop in conversation at the next Bar Mitzvah kiddush?

I had been resolutely ignoring the phone, but I was going to have to face the music some time. It could be Clarence, or Mollie, or my lawyer, with information I needed. I ran to the kitchen and caught it after six rings. At first I heard nothing, then some heavy breathing.

"Get a life," I said.

I was about to put the phone down when I heard what sounded like a voice.

"What?" I put the receiver back to my ear.

"Please." That's all I heard. I was pretty sure the croaking voice was Mollie's, though it was so faint and muffled, I couldn't tell. But who else would it be?

"Mollie? Is that you?"

"Uh huh." At least, that's what I thought she said.

"I'll be right there," I said, and hung up. After I did, I realized my car was still at her house. I rummaged in my purse to see if I had enough cash for a cab, which I didn't. I would have to take a bus there, which could take an hour. But I had to take a shower first. I hadn't had one since the first night in jail. I still smelled like Lysol and sweat. I tried Mollie's number before leaving the house. I got a busy signal.

When I finally got there, Mollie's front door was wide open. She was lying on the living room floor, the telephone receiver still in her hand. The phone had stopped making noise and just sat there, dead. Her eyes were open and glassy. I felt her neck for a pulse, as I had seen people do in episodes of *Perry Mason*. I couldn't feel anything, but when I felt my own neck, I didn't feel a pulse either, and I was definitely alive. I looked at her chest to see if it was moving. Again, I couldn't tell. It always looked so much easier on screen.

I'd taken a first aid class once, given by the American Red Cross for eager high schoolers. They had said if you can't tell if someone's breathing, put a mirror under their mouth, to see if it clouds up. I roamed around the house but couldn't find a hand mirror. Neither Mollie nor any of her roommates were the type to have those nice wooden brush and mirror sets on their vanities.

I did find two empty pill bottles on her bed. One said it was Valium. The prescription was in the name of Kathleen O'Shay. The other didn't have a label.

On the night stand next to the bed where we had almost made love just a few days ago, several pages of cream colored note paper were scattered. I picked them up. They were covered with that perfect cursive taught at Catholic schools with the flat of a ruler. It was harder to read than it looked. The last sheet was smudged, as if someone had cried on it.

"My dear Mollie," the letter began. "Imagine my shock when I read in the newspaper that a kidnapper was arrested in your company."

At first, I was amazed that the story had made it to San Francisco. But of course, the abortion had taken place there, and Mollie was a local girl. So it made sense that the San Francisco papers picked it up.

"I cannot accept what you are," the letter concluded. "If you want to give up your sin and come home, we will welcome you. If not, we must say goodbye.

"I will pray for you hourly. Your Mother."

You had better pray harder, I thought. What would Mrs. O'Shay, Kathleen, I assumed, think if she knew that her letter had driven her daughter to suicide? Or had Mollie only intended to kill the pain, and ended up killing herself? But I didn't even know that she was dead.

I finally thought to rummage through her purse and sure enough, she did have a compact, even though she never wore makeup. When I opened it, bits of caked powder fell out onto the carpet. I held the mirror under her lips, which were blue and cold to my touch. I didn't see even a trace of condensation forming on the mirror.

I reached out to pick up the phone, dial 9-1-1. But something stopped me, like a dybbuk catching hold of my hand. If Mollie was dead – and every indication said she was – maybe she had given me a way out too. I dove back into her purse and took out her driver's license and Penney's credit card. I stared at the photo on the license. Our coloring was close, my skin was a little more olive, but in a photo this bad, you couldn't tell. Her eyes were gray and mine were hazel, but did people really know the difference?

I put her ID in my pocket, and mine in her purse. I went back to Mollie's room, put the pill bottles in my purse and made the bed. The letter I left where it was. I half-dragged, half-carried Mollie's body to the door and looked carefully up and down the block. I saw no one on the street, no one seemed to be peering out of windows. I got her into my car with difficulty, propped her up in the passenger's seat. If she was really dead, wouldn't rigor mortis have started to set in? Maybe it took a few hours. I couldn't remember, if I'd ever known.

I started driving toward the hospital. My idea was to pull into the lot and walk away. Someone would find the car and the body eventually, and assume she was who her ID said she was. But no, they would get the police involved, they would take fingerprints, and hers wouldn't match the ones they had just taken from me at the jail. They would call my parents, who of course would not answer, but eventually, they would find someone who would attest that the body in the car was not mine.

I drove back to my parents' house and threw a few pieces of clothing in a paper bag. I couldn't pack a suitcase, or that would raise too much suspicion. I found a note card in my mom's room, wrote "I'm sorry," and left it on the kitchen table, next to the other mail. I drove south, pulling over at rest stops when I couldn't stay awake anymore. I drove for two days. Mollie's body went into full rigor and then started to smell. When I got to a rest stop outside San Diego, I called Clarence. I hadn't wanted to get him involved – he had the FBI on his tail already – but I didn't know anyone else who could help me. He connected me with some white men from the Weather Underground, and they showed me a secluded wood where I could abandon the car. They moved Mollie's body into the driver's seat. By the time the cops found the car, the body was too decomposed to be identified, but it was my car and my prints were on the steering wheel. They told my parents it looked like a suicide.

CHAPTER TWENTY-NINE

She Loves Me, She Loves Me Not

"That's quite a story," Toni said when I was finally done. I had been talking for hours. The sun had moved past the windows of the circus room, and I was aware I was cold.

"It's all true," I said. "Is any of what you told me?"

"Mine's all true as well," she said. She reached out a hand to stroke my wet cheek. I batted it away before she connected with my skin. Even the touch of her hand sent a wave of longing mixed with self-doubt through my body.

"You're just a hired gun," I said. "Which explains why you carry one."

"I do security," she said. "That's not a crime. But sleeping with you wasn't part of the job."

"Why'd you do it then?" I couldn't meet her eyes, but stared past them to the Star Wars poster on the wall.

"Because I wanted to." She rose to her knees, gripping my folded arms tightly. "Don't tell me you couldn't tell."

"I don't know." I hated how my voice wobbled. Don't show weakness!

"Come on, you do."

"What's the story with Emily?" Changing the subject seemed safe, and I wanted the answer. "How can she afford all this?" I heard

222 · KATE JESSICA RAPHAEL

murmurs of the others talking in the living room. I was still hungry. I hoped they had not cleared all the food away.

"Oh," Toni said, sounding relieved to go in a less personal direction. "She started a big software company. They actually make a lot of the encryption software used by government agencies."

"She works for NSA?"

"She doesn't work for them, but they probably use her products. And so do the people trying to hide stuff from them."

"Hmmm." I wasn't a purist about how people made their money, but was a woman who sold software to the deep state someone I wanted to entrust my safety to? At the moment, though, I didn't think I had much choice in the matter.

"How did Steve end up in Mobile? Was he following us the whole time?"

"No," she said. "I called him after you got busted. After you got out, we figured it wouldn't hurt for him to shadow us for the rest of the trip."

"Did he have anything to do with that paperwork conveniently going missing?" I asked. My stomach burned. I wasn't sure which answer I wanted to hear. These people had probably saved my hide multiple times in the last month, but gratitude was not on my agenda.

"I refuse to answer on the grounds that it might incriminate me," Toni said with a grin.

"Why didn't you tell me?" I asked. "Especially after I got arrested?"

"It wasn't up to me," Toni said, scrunching up her face in a familiar signal of thinking hard. "Steve said Emily didn't want you to worry, that she was dealing with the problem. She just needed us to keep track of you for a few more months while she sorted everything out."

"Seems like she likes to play God," I said.

"A lot of those Big Tech people do," she said. "But I think her heart's in the right place."

"Well I'm glad you're so sure. So you're a security guard? I thought you taught anthropology."

"I do. I'm an adjunct. Twenty-five hundred dollars a class. Just about pays my insurance premiums. And I'm not a security guard. Steve has a security firm, and he sometimes hires me to help out with various tasks."

"Various tasks? That sounds ominous."

"It isn't ominous. Sometimes I tail people, sometimes I sweep offices for surveillance devices, sometimes I escort rich people's kids to school."

"So what were your various tasks in this case?"

"I told you. I was supposed to embed myself in the group, make sure you were as protected as you could be. I made sure there were no recording devices in the clinic or in your apartment, for instance."

"You did?" I ran through every encounter we'd had in my apartment, trying to remember furtive moments. I mostly recalled tender ones, or at least they had appeared tender to me. We had not spent much time there after our first couple dates. Usually we stayed at her place. I wanted to believe that meant she was off duty, but I couldn't.

"What else?" She was definitely holding something back. I sat up on the bed, folded my legs in front of me with my back against the wall, so I could see her face clearly. "I am sick of people playing around behind my back. I want to know everything. Now."

"Well," she swiped an invisible strand of hair out of her eyes. "That note you got? The one that looked like a ransom note?"

"Dykes go home?" I asked.

"Right. That one. I put it in your newspaper."

My lips parted slightly. I clamped them shut. I flashed on when I told her about the note, in the Winston Salem jail visiting room. I had thought her reaction seemed off.

"Why would you do that?"

"So you would tell people you were being threatened. The phone call the first night you were in town? That was Steve. We thought you'd tell someone in the group. Yvette would suggest they hire Steve to do security, saying he would give us a deep discount. That way, we could have operated openly. But you, being the tough cookie you are, kept quiet. So we had to step it up."

Suddenly, I knew where I'd seen Steve before Mobile. The night I followed Toni to Olive Garden, after I'd been sideswiped. The man who'd given me his card – Josh Good – I was just about sure he and Steve were the same person. I opened my mouth to ask, but then closed it again. I didn't want to confess to following Toni to the restaurant, if she didn't already know, even though my suspicions were justified. Maybe I just wasn't ready to hear the whole truth.

A knock on the door kept me from having to decide. Emily didn't wait for us to say "Come in." She stood on the carpet in her stocking feet.

"I have to go out for a while," she said. "Do you have everything you need?"

Her entrance tore me out of my telescopic reliving of the last six months. There were a million things I wanted to ask her, but "What are you doing about Kimberly?" was what came out.

"Who's Kimberly?" Emily asked. She hovered, glancing at her watch. I supposed she had an appointment, and my abrupt departure from her hostess-ly script had messed with her schedule.

"Kimberly's the nurse practitioner who's taken over the clinic from Mollie," Toni said. "But what should we be doing about her?"

"Getting her a lawyer? Paying her bail?" I couldn't understand why they were acting so clueless.

"Kimberly's been busted?" Toni had jumped to her feet, as if she were going to run down to the jail on the spot.

"You didn't know?" It had not occurred to me, in my feverish flight and unlikely rescue, that Kimberly had not texted anyone but me. Surely she had numbers for other OWLS in her phone by now. Toni wouldn't have been one of them, but Yvette would have heard, if anyone had. Yvette and Evelyn, but I had thought they would be arrested too.

"Yvette's not in jail?" I made it a question, even though obviously, she wasn't.

"What? Why would she be?" Emily fished in the pocket of her sweater for her phone, looked down at it to send a message to someone, presumably saying she was delayed.

"Outside the party, when the cops went after Toni, one of the cops grabbed Evelyn and Yvette hit him. I thought she'd be arrested for sure."

"Oh, that," Toni laughed a little. "That was nothing. Once they realized you were gone, they all went off to hunt for you. Evelyn was railing about a lawsuit, going around getting everyone's badge numbers. They couldn't get out of there fast enough."

"Well, Kimberly did get busted," I said. "The cops raided the clinic. I got a dozen messages from her. I thought for sure you all knew."

"Not as far as I know," Toni said. "And I'm sure Yvette doesn't know either, or she'd have told me."

"We have to get her out." I sat up, looking around the room for shoes that I of course didn't have. I got up and walked out into the hall, temporarily forgetting that I had no car, no decent clothes, and was wanted by two different authorities.

"You're not going anywhere." Toni came up behind me, put a restraining hand on my shoulder. Her pressure was gentle, but I could tell it could get intense quickly if I resisted. "We'll handle it. Just explain. Why did they arrest Kimberly?"

"I'm not sure. But the cops at the party – the Richmond cops, not the Feds – said something about Caitlin Shaw. Remember her? She's the one that didn't have an ultrasound, who ended up being so much further along than we thought."

"Oh, right," Toni said. "The one with the little kid." As if eighty percent of our clients didn't have little kids.

"Right," I said.

"So you think she ratted us out?"

"I don't know – I guess it's possible." I tried to think. Caitlin had said she'd been raped. Maybe whoever raped her had found out she aborted his child, though it was hard to imagine him caring.

"I called her boss at Denny's," I said. "He didn't want to give her the day off. I kind of threatened to call the health department on him if he didn't."

Both Emily and Toni looked more chagrined at that than I thought reasonable. The girl had a right to health care, didn't she? We were breaking about a hundred laws every day. A tiny bit of blackmail was hardly something to get moralistic about.

"Who did you say you were?" Toni asked.

"Dr. Jenkins. That's our public persona," I said.

"That could be how they found the clinic," Toni pointed out.

"True," I said. "But I never said anything to the guy about an abortion. And anyway, the warrant was for Mollie O'Shay."

"We'll figure it out," Toni said. She was trying to sound reassuring, I could tell. I wasn't buying it. "I'll call Evelyn and see about rounding up a lawyer for Kimberly. You stay here. Don't go out for any reason."

I hadn't slept since the previous morning, and I was exhausted from traipsing through the city all night. But I was wired on coffee and all the information I'd just received was spinning around in my brain. I could almost see the threads of the story come flying in from one direction, but when I tried to grab onto them, they would zoom off in another. Toni was a spy, Yvette was her henchwoman, Steve had been there when I had the accident by Olive Garden, but hadn't been driving the SUV. The Feds were looking for Renata but the Richmond PD was looking for Mollie. Both must have received records from my North Carolina arrest. But how had they connected me to an abortion in Richmond that was supposed to have been done by Dr. Mary Jenkins?

I was hungry but couldn't sit down and eat. I picked up a scone from the dining room table – Emily had thoughtfully left them on a covered cake plate – and ate it, pacing the house. I thought of someone who might be able to answer questions about one part of this puzzle. I found my purse by the door, where Emily had left it, and fished out my cell phone. Maybe I shouldn't use it; Steve wasn't the only person in town who knew how to use a GPS locator. I'd seen a landline in the kitchen. I turned on my cell, wrote down the number I wanted and quickly turned it off again. Just for good measure, I put the mobile phone in the freezer before picking up the old school phone and punching in the numbers.

"Chuck," I said, when he came on the line. "It's me, Mollie."

"Hey," he replied. "Um, this isn't a good time. I'll call you later." He hung up without waiting for a response. It had been half a year since I'd spoken to my brother, but he didn't sound surprised to hear from me. That alone told me what I needed to know, and his abrupt disconnection confirmed it. The FBI had been to see him, too.

The child's bedroom I'd been in earlier had a desktop computer. Hopefully Emily hadn't bothered to encrypt every machine in the house. Miraculously, when I turned on the screen, the Windows desktop materialized, and didn't require a password to log in. I opened the internet browser and did a search for "federal abortion law post-Hathaway." I had not kept up with every new statute enacted since the decision came down. But I quickly found what I wanted, and dreaded, to find – abortion cases that were open when *Roe* was decided could now be reopened as "felony murder" cases, at the discretion of the charging authority. I didn't really understand that, since all murder charges are felonies, right? Felony murder, I learned with a few clicks, allows a lesser crime that led to a death to be prosecuted as murder. Hence the kidnapping charge against me, whose statute of limitations would have lapsed many years ago, could now be considered a murder with no statute of limitations, even though Emily's abortion was done legally in California. The "charging authority" in this case was the federal government, and felony murder was a capital crime under federal law.

I started to tremble as if I were standing at the epicenter of an earthquake.

I made it back to the low bed, and once again curled up in a tight ball. I couldn't stop shivering, so I crawled under the white quilt with bright red and blue circles.

When I woke, the little alarm clock read 3:20. It must be afternoon, because it was still light out. I listened for any noise from any part of the house, but heard nothing. I managed to stand up. My fit of – call it death penalty-induced catatonia, a new ailment I made up on the spot – seemed to have passed. I just needed not to think about the felony murder rule for a while. That injunction, of course, put it smack in the center of my mind, but I struggled to control my reaction. A walk around the house confirmed that I was alone. I wondered if anyone had succeeded in doing anything. I dug my phone out of the freezer and turned it on.

I had messages from Josie, Evelyn and Nell, all asking what was going on, but none from Toni, Steve or Emily. And needless to say, there was nothing from Kimberly.

I didn't know if I should use the cell or not, and decided to err on the side of caution. I tried calling Josie and Nell from the landline, but neither of them answered. I had to admit, there was no reason they should. I never answered calls from numbers I didn't recognize. I thought about leaving messages, but decided there was no point, because I wasn't going to be here for long.

Toni had said not to go anywhere, but I couldn't hang around here by myself without going crazy. There weren't even any real books, only some kids' picture books. I was hardly going to sit around watching Ellen give stuff away on TV while everyone else ran around fixing the messes I'd made. I put the cell phone back into the little purse and tried to think what else I should cram in there. Maybe a snack. I shoved an orange and some crackers in and barely got the clasp to close. Next was the problem of shoes. I searched all the closets and was rewarded with a pair of flip flops that more or less fit. I took a deep breath and walked out of the house. With a pang, I let it lock behind me. I now had no choice.

I stood on the front lawn, trying to get my bearings. I remembered Steve turning left off of Cary and then taking an immediate left, but then he had driven for a few winding blocks. When I looked around, all I could see were big houses and big lawns, nothing remotely like a landmark. I didn't want to roam aimlessly; this seemed like the kind of neighborhood with private security. In the near distance I could hear a lawnmower, so I walked toward it. An older white guy with a pudgy bare torso was sweating over an old-time hand mower in front of a white ranch house with black shutters. He didn't have earbuds, so I didn't have to shout too loudly to be heard over the hum.

"I'm not from around here," I said. "I'm visiting a friend who's staying nearby. Can you tell me how to get to Cary Street?"

"Walk thataway," he pointed, not bothering to turn off the machine. "'Bout three blocks. Can't miss it."

Once I got to Cary, I saw that I was only about half a mile from the clinic and my apartment. I walked quickly, fishing my keys out of my purse as I neared Grove, only to stop short. The cops had gone there to arrest me. They had taken Kimberly instead, but they knew she wasn't me. What if they were still watching the building? I had no idea if Richmond PD was busy enough that that idea was absurd.

I turned into the alley behind the clinic, which led to the parking lot. It was deserted except for some garbage cans placed at the edge of the narrow street for pickup. I sidled along, trying not to let my flips flop, stopping every few feet to see if anything moved. I saw and heard nothing, only a few distant engines. My own breathing sounded like ocean waves in the heavy silence. When I made it to the lot behind my place, I didn't see any police cars, but who knew if they would park there? There was only one car besides mine in the lot, and it wasn't occupied. I cringed as I pressed the unlock button on my key fob; the chirp was nearly ear-splitting to me. But no one came running. I started the engine, backed out and made it through the alley before I concluded that, in fact, no one was watching for me. By the time I arrived at Denny's by Route 64, I concluded that I had overrated my importance.

I swung into the lot, got out and was halfway to the back entrance before I registered that there *were* police cars in this lot. I felt my larynx closing up, and saw spots as blood fled from my brain. I stumbled back to the car, got the door open and collapsed in the driver's seat. I banged my forehead softly against the steering wheel. How could I have been so stupid? I doubted I could even make it back to Emily's; I had no idea where it was. I should have written down the house number, at least. My only option would be to call Toni and confess what I'd done, and I'd done enough confessing for today.

Maybe I should head to the airport, hightail it to San Francisco. But that would mean presenting my Real ID to a TSA agent, who would run it through a computer and find out there was a federal warrant out for my arrest. Or there was that possibility. I wasn't sure Renata's records were cross-filed with Mollie's, but there was a good chance they were. As I sat there trying to figure out a course of action, four uniformed cops emerged from the restaurant. They were chatting and laughing as they walked to the two black and whites and climbed in. Seconds later, there were no cop cars in the lot. I released a huge shuddering breath. It felt like I'd been holding it for hours. Probably every Denny's on the map had cops in it most of the time. Like the old Carly Simon song says, I had to stop thinking everything was about me.

I collected myself and exited my car again. Inside the restaurant, I stopped by the sign saying, "Please seat yourself" and waited for a harried waitress to walk by. When one did, I caught her attention with a stammered, "Excuse me."

"What is it, hon?" she said. She could be my granddaughter, and she was calling me "hon"?

"Is Caitlin working today?" I asked. Seeing no flicker of recognition, I added, "Caitlin Shaw. Young, blonde." I pantomimed ringlets hanging to my shoulders.

"Oh, her. She should be in at five."

I looked up at the big wall clock. It was twenty of.

"Can you show me which section is hers? I'm an old friend of her family's. I'm on my way out of town, but I wanted to say hello to her before I leave."

A barely believable story, but the young woman nodded and pointed to a table. It was in between the post-church rush and blue-plate special time. Most of the booths and tables were empty. Only a few families sat loading up on burgers and fries before heading to West Virginia or Norfolk or wherever they had to be on Monday. In a corner booth, a couple leaned across the table to stroke each other's faces, their elbows perilously close to the congealing ketchup on their discarded plates. No cops were taking a Code 7 at Denny's at this particular time.

A waitress who was not Caitlin pulled a pen from behind her ear and asked, "What can I get you, hon?"

I ordered a chocolate malt, my go-to comfort food in places that use a lot of Wonder Bread and Velveeta. It's pretty hard to mess up ice cream and Hershey's syrup, and if someone does, the malt flavor usually covers a multitude of sins. I asked her to hold the whipped topping.

Since I had nothing to read, I had nothing to do except think about what I was going to say to Caitlin. That's when it hit me that I hadn't a clue. I supposed the first step would be to see if she recognized me. If not, I'd have to jog her memory – "Hi, it's me, Dr. Jenkins, the one you turned in to the police." And if she didn't scream, I would ask her why she wanted to hurt someone who helped her. As I went over it, I could not quite figure out what I was doing here. Maybe I should pay and get out before she arrived. I glanced toward the door. Some more cops were coming in, but these cops were not chatting or laughing. They were looking down at something on a clipboard. A male civilian was with them, shortish, balding, in an open-necked white button-down shirt and khakis. He was pointing toward my table. Looking around, I realized I was the only person in that section, so he must be pointing at me.

As the four officers walked to my table, I fished a ten dollar bill out of my purse and put it on the table. I wouldn't want the waitress to miss out on her tip, and I doubted the cops were going to give me a chance to pay and get change.

"Mollie O'Shay?" the only woman among the four said softly. I nodded.

"Please come with us."

I didn't protest, just followed them out. At least they didn't frisk or cuff me until we were out in the parking lot. As the woman cop gently pressed on my head to load me into the back seat of the car, I glanced at the clipboard her partner held. I saw several printouts of digital pictures. In the top one, I was mugging for the camera, my arms spread wide like a televangelist's. I recognized it instantly: it was the one Greg Patel had taken outside my apartment the day Kimberly arrived.

CHAPTER THIRTY

And Justice for All

After booking, which involved the usual humiliations, they put me in a cell with Kimberly. We were both wearing gray jumpsuits with Property of Richmond City Jail stenciled on the back. I thought a former slave state might want to rethink labeling people as property in this day and age. Kim explained that she had had a roommate last night, a strung-out hooker with two kids in foster care – "I gave her the OWLS' number," she said with a chuckle – but that woman's pimp/boyfriend had bailed her out a couple hours earlier.

"Lucky for me," I said. It really was, since I had no way to let anyone know where I was. Kim said she'd been visited a few hours ago by a lawyer, another friend of Evelyn, who must have sorority sisters in every state in the union. The lawyer, Harriet, had said Kim's bail was two hundred and fifty thousand, but she thought she could get the charges thrown out at arraignment, which was scheduled for the next day. So she advised Kim to sit tight, and Kim agreed. No one had hassled her, she said. It was just boring.

"What are you charged with?" I asked.

"Performing abortions," she said. "But Harriet said there was nothing specific. No complainant, is what she said. The cops had the code for the supply room. They confiscated everything in it."

"Even the ultrasound?" I asked. When she nodded, I groaned. We hadn't even paid it off. The party last night – just last night! – was supposed to raise the money for it. There was five grand down the toilet if we didn't get it back. Vaguely, I got that I had bigger problems than that, but I could barely contemplate those. Toni's credit card bill was a finite problem.

"I wonder where they got the code," I said.

"Not from me," she replied.

"Of course not. I didn't mean to suggest that – I'm sorry I got you into this," I said. "It's a hell of a welcome to a new town."

"It's okay," she said. I couldn't tell from her intonation if it really was. I knew Kim through nursing and union work. She and her girl-friend were progressive, but not really activists. She was more the Earth Mother type. I doubted she'd ever been arrested before. I asked.

"During the People's Park fight at Cal," she said. "Three hundred of us were arrested for occupying the administration building. They carted us off to Santa Rita Jail."

"I remember reading about that," I said. I doubted that experience, in and out, amid the adrenaline of an action, had done much to prepare her for this, but she was handling it with admirable equanimity.

"I wonder if the clinic will have to close," I thought aloud.

"I suppose it depends partly on what happens at the trial," she said, tapping her lower front teeth with a fingernail. "There will be plenty of eyes on us. The cops were at the dance, it was pretty clear who the leaders were. But Evelyn and the others are tough. It's hard to see them giving up."

"At least..." I stopped myself before saying, "There's Mobile." I didn't want to mention that here. If Richmond OWLS was history, at least Mobile was on its way.

"At least what?"

"Oh, I was just thinking that if someone had to get arrested, it's good it's just us and none of the locals. Our families won't get dragged into it."

"True," she said. She didn't sound that convinced.

Kimberly had a bad knee, so I took the top bunk. I lay there, staring at the ceiling just a few inches above my nose. Both of us were too tense to talk much. I didn't wear a watch, though I expected they would have taken it away anyway, and my phone was locked up in some police property room, so I had no way to know what time it was. I'd been arrested just before five, and booking had taken a couple hours because of shift change. I'd been given a cheese sandwich in the holding cell. I estimated it must have been close to eight when a guard came to tell Kimberly her lawyer was on the phone.

She was gone less than five minutes. She said Harriet had just called to tell her the arraignment, which had been scheduled for nine am, was pushed back to one thirty. Kimberly had told her I was here, but Harriet already knew. I wondered how, but was profoundly grateful that I was not sequestered away from civilization without a trace. I wondered if my car would be safe in the Denny's lot, or if they'd have it towed. Once again, dwelling on the nearly irrelevant. I was at least grateful not to have to face Toni's wrath for my disobedience. She knew staying out of the fray went against my nature. Hopefully by the time I saw her, she'd have made peace with that.

With Toni on my mind, I tried again to sort out our relationship. Was she my uninvited bodyguard? Unindicted co-conspirator? Guardian angel? Friend? Lover? Soulmate? Some mélange of all of the above? As I lay here, I just imagined her lithe, muscular body cradling mine. I didn't know if I had a right to that image, but its recent imprint was real. Perhaps tomorrow I would get a chance to clarify things further. I heard Kim's breathing slacken into sleep, and allowed her light snoring to lull me to dreamland as well.

Kimberly's name was called right after breakfast. The "chow hall," as I learned was its proper name, had a big wall clock, black hands on a faded white face, so I could see that we were expected to eat at the ungodly hour of five thirty in the morning. It was hard for me to eat that early, but I knew I would be famished if I didn't, so I made myself inhale the rubbery eggs and flat mix-made pancakes with some type of corn syrup colored to resemble maple. I washed it all down with extremely weak coffee laced with powdered non-dairy creamer.

Apparently the news that Kim's arraignment had been postponed to the afternoon session hadn't filtered down to the jail staff, so she would have to sit around in a holding cell in the courthouse all morning. I told her I hoped she wouldn't be back, although selfishly, I only half hoped that. A familiar face made jail a lot more tolerable. I also gave her a quick hug, which drew a disapproving head shake from the guard, and then she was shackled into the line of women heading to court.

I hoped for a visit, or at least a phone call, but none came before we were herded into the chow hall again. It was just past eleven and the offering was supposed to be enchiladas. They were covered with a gloppy brown gravy and basically inedible, though many of the other women seemed to quite enjoy the dish. There was some shredded lettuce with orange mayonnaisey dressing, which I ate reluctantly, and each tray was allocated six Doritos, one of my preferred forms of junk food.

I had just settled back onto my top bunk when I heard my name over the loudspeaker. I was apparently going to court. I was shackled to ten other women and driven three blocks or so to an underground tunnel to the courthouse, where we were crammed into a small holding cell with one wooden bench.

They kept us shackled together by chains around the waist even inside the cell, only disconnecting people when their names were called. That meant no one could sit down until we were down to a string of five. I'd seen no sign of Kimberly, and couldn't squirm around trying to see anything in the halls without annoying the others. The women who came back from court were put into a different cell, so I didn't know how things were going, which might have been for the best. If there was a hanging judge on duty, I didn't really need to know that in advance.

Naturally, I was the last one called. A cop guided me into the court-room with a hand on my back and showed me where to stand, behind a table facing the judge. A thin medium-brown woman with a shiny page-boy entered from a side door next to the judge's bench, together with a white man in his late thirties with thinning light brown hair. Their suits, gray twill, were virtual carbons of one another. The Black woman smiled at the guy as they separated, he walking to the prosecutor's table and she toward me. I tried not to hold that smile against her, knowing that good will from the prosecutor is a defendant's best hope.

"You're representing this defendant, Ms. Robbins?" the judge said. She was a generic white woman, probably late fifties. Hair no-nonsense, like Linda Hunt's in The Year of Living Dangerously.

"Yes, Your Honor." The lawyer turned to me. "Harriet Robbins," she said, sticking out her hand. She barely gave me time to shake it before popping open her briefcase and rummaging for my file.

"Donald Green for the People," said the guy at the other table.

"Call the case," the judge said to her bailiff, and the uniformed man read, "People of the State of Virginia versus Mollie O'Shay, also known as Renata Kellam. Charges are murder in the second degree, practicing medicine without a license, reckless endangerment, conspiracy to com-mit murder, attempted murder in the second degree, possessing tools of abortion, corruption of a minor, failure to obey a lawful order by a peace officer, resisting arrest, escape."

My body suddenly felt like cement while my legs were foam rubber. I would have sat down, but there was no chair behind me, so I gripped the edge of the table so hard my knuckles whitened. I knew about over-charging, but this was a virtual smorgasbord of crimes. I expected the murder charge, and I guess I should be relieved it wasn't first degree, but escape? Didn't you have to be in custody in order to escape? And with murder and attempted murder, they had to go adding resisting ar-rest? What about corruption of a minor? Caitlin was twenty-one. Conspiracy was bad, because that could mean they were looking for other members of the network. That would explain why no one from

OWLS was here. And here I was facing all this with a lawyer I'd never met before.

"Your Honor, we move to strike the name Renata Kellam from the indictment. I have an affidavit here from an FBI agent stating that my client's DNA and fingerprints do not match those on file for Renata Kellam."

Harriet approached the bench, waving a sheaf of papers held together with a giant paperclip. The judge took them, rifled through and then gestured to the bailiff to show them to the D.A. He was silent for five minutes or more as he read carefully. Then he took out an iPad and punched some buttons and handed the documents back to the bailiff.

"The people amend the indictment to remove the alias, Renata Kellam." That was anticlimactic. I don't know what I expected. It was a big revelation to me that my DNA and fingerprints no longer matched...themselves? It seemed worthy of more than a few words being stricken from an indictment that still contained "murder" and "conspiracy."

"Ms. O'Shay, you have heard the charges against you?"

Harriet looked at me and nodded and I answered, "Yes, Your Honor."

"And how do you plead?"

"Not guilty." I didn't need a lawyer's advice for that one.

"Do you waive time for trial?"

I shook my head, but Harriet didn't even look my way.

"Not at this time, Your Honor." I was glad we were on the same wavelength. The more time the state had to put its case together, the more danger to OWLS. We could only hope that they had acted hastily, and didn't know much more than they had already revealed.

If the judge was surprised, she didn't show it. Mr. Green looked unhappy but didn't object, maybe because there was no reasonable objection he could make.

"Preliminary hearing is set for next Friday at one thirty p.m.," the judge said. The bailiff wrote something on a calendar. The prosecutor took out his iPad. A cop materialized at my elbow and prodded me toward the door I'd entered through, even as Harriet was mouthing, "I'll see you soon."

They hustled me straight into the transport bay, where five other women were already shackled up and ready to go. I was connected to the chain gang and we shuffled into the waiting paddy wagon. Our line just fit on one bench. Kimberly was in the group already seated on the opposite side. By happy coincidence, I ended up across from her.

"What happened?" she whispered. I wasn't sure why she was whispering. Had they been told not to talk, or did she not trust our fellow prisoners? If the latter, I wasn't sure whispering was going to help. If I could hear her, so could they. But I followed her lead. I leaned halfway across and she did the same.

"Second degree murder, and a bunch of other stuff," I whispered into her left ear. "What about you?"

"Harriet got them to drop the charges," she whispered into my right. "She said they had no probable cause to believe I gave anyone an abortion. The tools were not in the apartment. She said I was just here visiting you."

I sat back against the wagon wall, just as it started to rumble out of the lot. Kimberly was not smiling, but I could see she was relieved. I was too. Worrying about my own future was enough weight. I didn't need to feel guilty about getting her in trouble.

"That's great," I mouthed. She did smile then. I wondered what she would do, stick around to see what happened, or hop on a plane to abortion-loving California as soon as she was able? I wouldn't blame her too much if she chose the latter.

CHAPTER THIRTY-ONE

An Old Flame to Light the Dark

It was not until late the next afternoon that Harriet arrived to tell me what was going on.

"Your bail is set at two hundred and fifty thousand," she said. "Toni wants to put up her house as collateral."

"No," I said. I took a breath, meaning to go into all the reasons I didn't want that, but she was nodding, so I stayed quiet.

"I agree," she said. "If you get out on bail, they have three months to try you, and the D.A. can easily get extensions by claiming he has conflicts. As long as you're in custody, they have to bring you to trial within thirty days, or at least, they are supposed to. There are always exceptions, but we don't want to give them a lot of time to dig around."

"I'm glad you got Kimberly out," I said. "Is she staying in town?"

"I've advised her not to, but she hasn't decided yet. As of now, she is still here."

I desperately wanted to ask about the clinic, but I didn't trust the state not to be illegally bugging lawyers' consultations.

"Is she working?" I asked. I figured that was nonspecific enough to mean anything.

"She's meeting with some folks," she said. "Let's get back to your case."

I assumed that meant the safe house was still functioning, for whatever good that could do. I imagined they were trying to get more meds, and appointments in Maryland or Delaware for women who needed later procedures.

"What was all that about Renata Kellam?" I asked.

"Some FBI database identified you as the defendant in an old kidnapping case," she said. "They'd used a combination of facial recognition and fingerprint comparisons. When you were arrested in North Carolina, they compared the fingerprints and came back with a match. But the field office here did a finer analysis and ran your DNA. They came back no match. So the Feds are not looking at you anymore."

"Where did they get a DNA sample?" I asked. My understanding – strictly from television – was that DNA tests had to be run on swabs taken from cheeks or noses or hairs pulled out at the root. I was pretty sure I had never provided any of those, either in 1971 or this year.

"They found some hairs at the clinic," Harriet said. I had an image of myself, threading the hair through the keypad on the supply closet. "I don't know where they got DNA from that Renata person – but they don't match."

However that had happened, at least right now I was not facing a federal death penalty. Something to be grateful for.

"So what's our strategy?" I asked.

"We really can't build one until we see what they have," she said. "That's next Friday, at the prelim. We do have the police report though."

She pulled a thick stack of pages from her briefcase.

"Caitlin Shaw, she's the young woman who says you gave her an abortion on May thirteenth. She says she came to your office by bus, is that right?"

"No!" I started to protest. Then I thought about it. I held out my hand for the report and Harriet gave it to me. I quickly read through Caitlin's statement. She said someone gave her the number for a Dr. Jenkins, she couldn't remember who. She made the appointment on the phone and took the bus to the address. Afterwards, Dr. Jenkins drove her home, she contended. No mention of the safe house. No mention of Jeremy or

Sylvia. Whatever Caitlin was doing, she was trying to minimize the harm.

"I don't know," I told Harriet. "Maybe she did."

"But you drove her home? Is that typical?"

"It happens," I said. Harriet nodded and made a note in her file. She reached out for the police report and I handed it back. She flipped to a page near the back, scanned it.

"Who is Greg Patel?" she asked, without looking up.

"Who? Oh, the father of a girl that Josie and I – that came to a self-help workshop I led. He found out she was there and came to my house to get her. A few days later, he showed up taking pictures."

"But what does he have to do with this?" I asked.

"He says you made advances on his daughter, Sarita."

"I did not!"

"Sarita agrees with you. She says she and her friends were practicing dance moves in your apartment."

"I thought it was supposed to be Bible study." I, who'd lied every day for fifty years, was suddenly having trouble keeping all the lies straight.

"He didn't believe that and confronted her. So she confessed it was really a dance group. Greg's an evangelical Christian. He doesn't believe in explicit dancing." Hadn't Hillary said Greg Patel went to her church? What would an open lesbian be doing in a fundamentalist church? I put that aside for later.

"Okay. I guess we were dancing then." It was hard to see my seventy-year-old self as a dance coach, but I would let Sarita explain that if the time came. It was her story. Hopefully I'd never have to testify.

"And what about Paul Manning?" Harriet asked.

"That's Caitlin's boss. I called him and convinced him to give her the day off."

"He says you threatened him."

"I threatened to call the health department on his restaurant."

"He says you threatened him physically."

"What? I never even saw him."

Harriet made more furious notes.

"I think he might have raped her," I said. That got her to look up from her papers.

"What makes you say that?"

"She said she was raped." I said. "I asked if she wanted to talk about it and she said she couldn't. But she sounded afraid of him. She kept saying she'd get fired. I had the feeling he'd made threats like that before."

"That's not much to go on," Harriet said, but she wrote it down, or at least I assumed that's what her pen was scratching out on the lined yellow pad in front of her.

"I have one other thing I'd like you to look at," she said. I barely noticed her tuck something into the stack of pages before she thrust them toward me. I took them carefully, opened to the page where a stiff card was wedged between the sheets.

"Thanks for being you," it said on the cover, above a picture of a cartoon tiger clutching a bunch of balloons. I quickly moved it to my lap and opened it. "Sorry we can't visit. We love you," I read, recognizing Josie's precise handwriting. It was signed by most of the active OWLS, Josie, Evelyn, Yvette, Sylvia, Nell, Marie, Sandy, Maureen, Rabbit. But not Toni.

I brushed it with my fingers. It felt good, even as I felt sad knowing I wouldn't see friends while I was here. It made sense though. No doubt, the cops would be watching to see who came to visit me. It wasn't worth compromising the whole project just to cheer me up briefly. I'd just have to do that for myself.

As I replaced the card under the clip, I felt that the page under it was a different size and weight of paper than the rest. I looked down at it. It was just a thin sheet of paper ripped from a spiral notebook, but I knew the handwriting. I quickly folded it tiny and thrust it into my shoe. Then I passed the report back to Harriet, who stashed it in her briefcase.

"Try to stay cool," she said. "See you next Friday in court."

"We'll get you out. Love you madly. T"

That was all she'd written, except for a P.S. *"Can't you ever do as you're told?"*

I kept that scrap of paper under my pillow and looked at it many times every day. Other than that, I had nothing to read or look at until Saturday, when the library cart came around. Then we were only allowed three books, so I chose not necessarily the most interesting but the thickest ones. Somehow they had acquired a copy of *Sacred Games*, and not surprisingly, a seven hundred page Indian police procedural was not snatched up before the cart got to my cell. I also took Jane Fonda's *My Life So Far*, which was also pretty hefty even without the last twenty years. Margaret Atwood's *The Testament* was not what I was looking for, but there was a book called *Uptown Thief*, which despite its trashy cover, was about a collectively run women's clinic supported by some underground activities. I thought I might learn something useful from it – like how not to get caught – and it sounded like a good time.

I decided to start with *Uptown Thief*, and before too long, I was chasing through the streets of New York and Puerto Rico with a shit-kicking ex-hooker running both a women's health center and a racket to divest billionaires of some ill-gotten loot, all while carrying on a romance with a disillusioned New York cop. I was almost disappointed when a guard appeared to tell me that I had a visitor.

I couldn't imagine who it could be. Everyone I knew in Richmond had something to do with OWLS, and it was clear that they had all been told to stay away. Harriet had also made it plain she would not be back before the hearing. Maybe Toni had decided love trumped fear. On that hopeful supposition, I quickly checked the tiny tin square over the sink that functioned as a wavy, blurry mirror. I had no comb or brush, but I fluffed my hair with my hands and confirmed that I had no obvious schmutz on my face or collar. I squared my shoulders and followed the guard to the visiting hall, a row of glass booths with video screens. They showed me into one of them and told me to sit down and not touch anything.

After a minute of staring at a blank wall, I saw the lower half of a man's torso and then his face came into the frame as he sat. He had aged of course, since I had last seen him in San Francisco, and even more since I had tried to win his affection with pies. But his dark brown eyes betrayed the same humor and compassion, and his full lips made the same slow smile, revealing the same ultrawhite teeth that he'd somehow kept intact through years of hard living.

"Clarence," I said. "It's great to see you."

"You too," he said, "but I wish it weren't like this. How're you holding up?"

"You know," I said. "You do what you have to do. What are you doing here?"

"I owe you," he said.

"You don't." In the early years after 9/11, the government used new antiterrorism money to retry former Black Panthers on cases they'd never been able to make in the seventies. Clarence, in his early sixties then, had been arrested at the college where he taught in Pennsylvania and flown in shackles to San Francisco, where he sat in a solitary cell for five years. Every Sunday during those five years, I'd dragged myself out of bed at seven in the morning to get to the jail for visiting hours. But those five years had not come close to repaying my debt to Clarence.

"How did you know I was here?" I asked.

"Your brother called."

I started to ask how Chuck knew. Then I remembered I had called him from the landline at Emily's, and it was clear the FBI had been in touch. Maybe he had called back and talked to Emily, or else he just tracked the area code and got the rest from the press. One way or the other, he'd done a giant mitzvah. I hoped and prayed I'd get a chance to thank him in person.

After I escaped from Oregon, Clarence had connected Chuck to a network that helped draft resisters get to Canada. Chuck spent the rest of the war years working in canneries in Alberta, and came back under President Carter's amnesty, working in a halfway house for his community service and transitioning to social work school when he was done. He'd become a high school guidance counselor, and eventually a principal in upstate New York. I had had no idea how to find him until the internet came along. He was long married by then, with a son and daughter nearly done with college. I'd seen him intermittently since then. We didn't have that much in common, but with our parents dead, he and his children were my only known relatives, and I was glad to have them back in my life.

"How's Ginger?" I asked Clarence. She was his third wife, a college instructor almost forty years his junior.

"She's pregnant," he said, grinning broadly.

"You're going to be a dad again?"

"Yeah, you know how I love kids," he said.

He had five kids from his first two marriages, scattered around the country, some doing great and others struggling with the demons of everyday racism along with the specifics of being brought up in tumultuous political collectives.

"I hope Ginger knows what she's doing," I couldn't help saying. As competent as Ginger was, I wondered if she'd thought about what a handful an aged husband and a small child could be.

"She does." That sealed that subject. I looked around for another safe one.

"Where are you staying?" I asked. "And for how long?"

"At the Holiday Inn," he said. "Harriet's cousin got us a deal. She and I, we go way back. I'll be here at least for your hearing on Friday. Then we'll see."

"Well it's great to see you," I said again.

"Same here," he said. Something beeped and my screen went dark. A deputy appeared and impatiently gestured for me to follow her back to the cellblock.

CHAPTER THIRTY-TWO

Law & Order

The next days passed much more quickly than the previous ones. I had my books to whisk me away from my cell. I would normally be allowed only one visitor per week, but that didn't include legal visits or religious advisors. Harriet managed to send Clarence as her legal assistant, and Nell paid a visit as a chaplain. She said many of the OWLS planned to attend Friday's hearing.

"The local press covered you," she said. She'd even snuck in a copy of an article. It was salacious, but at least it didn't name Caitlin, referring to her throughout as "the victim." It talked about accusations that I'd had inappropriate relations with teenage girls, alongside a photo of me with Sidney at a Gay Pride march decades ago. The only upside was that it was a pretty nice photo and reminded me of a time when I was blissfully ignorant of my coming tribulations.

The media coverage had generated some outrage and, according to Nell, students from the VCU Women's Union had reached out to Planned Parenthood to organize a protest. PP wouldn't participate officially – as always, maintaining their deniability and fund base – but said they would put it out to their members, and suggested the VCU students talk to NOW. Evelyn, as president of NOW, said that sure, she might just be able to convince her board to stand up for the right of women to seek the health care they wanted and for young girls to learn about their bodies from knowledgeable professionals. India and her friends were eager to help spread the word. So there would be a tame picket and press conference outside the courthouse before the hearing.

When I was escorted into the courtroom, I saw dozens of familiar faces. Evelyn and Yvette, Sandy and Maureen, Rabbit and Josie. Clarence, in the second row, half lifted a power fist. Nell had warned me she couldn't come; if the jail people suspected we had a personal relationship, it could jeopardize her access to the inmates. Hillary wasn't there, but I didn't really expect her to be. I identified a few journalists in the front row, notepads and phones at the ready. No cameras were allowed in the courtroom, Harriet had told me. I didn't see a sketch artist at least. I wasn't high profile enough for that, I supposed.

The same judge who presided over the arraignment was seated behind the bench, severe in standard black robes, her black bowl cut freshly trimmed. The nameplate in front of her said Hon. Penelope Hunter.

The person I most wanted to see wasn't in the room. I searched twice, sure I had missed her, but Toni was not there.

Emily slid into the back row just as the first witness, Sergeant Wilson, took the stand. He testified about arresting me at the party, the fight that broke out and how I disappeared.

"Why were you looking for Ms. O'Shay?" asked D.A. Green.

"We believed she had performed an abortion on the complainant, Caitlin Shaw, on May thirteenth of this year."

"Will Ms. Shaw be testifying?" the judge inquired.

"Yes, Your Honor," said Mr. Green. "She's scheduled for tomorrow. Sergeant Wilson, Ms. Shaw told you a Dr. Jenkins performed her surgery, is that correct?"

"Yes."

"And the medical office at 4628 Grove Avenue where Ms. Shaw's surgery was performed is rented to a Dr. Mary Jenkins, is that correct?"

"Yes."

"Who is Dr. Mary Jenkins?"

"A Dr. Mary Jenkins had an office in that building at one time. She is a retired psychologist and no longer lives in Richmond."

"So how did you determine that it was Ms. O'Shay who performed the operation on Ms. Shaw?"

"We obtained a warrant to search the premises. In the course of that search, we took fingerprint evidence which led to Ms. O'Shay. We also recovered a hair which contained Ms. O'Shay's DNA."

"How did you have fingerprint and DNA evidence to compare to those you recovered from the crime scene?"

I stiffened at hearing my home and work place referred to as a crime scene. Harriet laid a gentle hand on my wrist and I settled back in my chair.

"In August, Ms. O'Shay was arrested in North Carolina," Sergeant Wilson said. "They collected fingerprint and DNA evidence."

Once again, I thought about where they might have gotten DNA evidence. There were plenty of opportunities, I supposed, with all the invasive searches. Then I remembered that odd jailhouse medical exam, just before I was released. Maybe it was a ruse, or a dual-purpose exam, but swabs had been placed into specimen bags. Not surprisingly, no one had ever contacted me about the results of a pap smear.

"So you had the hair and fingerprints you collected at the office of Dr. Jenkins compared to the DNA and prints taken from Ms. O'Shay in North Carolina and they came back a match?"

"Yes."

"Were they a perfect match or a partial match?"

"A perfect match."

The district attorney produced an affidavit from fingerprint and DNA experts attesting to the perfect match. The judge marked them People's One.

"Now Sergeant Wilson, after Ms. O'Shay escaped from custody, how did you reapprehend her?" Green asked.

"We received information that she was in the Denny's on Highway 64, where Ms. Shaw works," the sergeant replied.

"Who provided that information?"

"The restaurant manager, Paul Manning."

"And what is Mr. Manning's role in this case?"

"He filed the original complaint, saying that he suspected Dr. Jenkins had performed an abortion on his employee, Ms. Shaw."

"Did he say how he knew?"

"Objection, hearsay." Harriet was on her feet.

"Sustained," said the judge.

"That's fine, Your Honor," Green said. "Mr. Manning will be testifying this afternoon. No further questions for this witness at this time. We reserve the right to recall."

Harriet stood up.

"Sergeant Wilson," she said, "you seized a quantity of equipment from the office on Grove Avenue, didn't you?"

"Yes," he responded. I could see he was well trained, not to volunteer anything.

"Can you tell us what equipment you took?"

Good for Harriet, making the cops sound like robbers.

"May I consult my notes?" Wilson said in the direction of the judge.

"Go ahead," she said. Sergeant Wilson withdrew a small spiral notebook from the breast pocket of his grey sport coat and flipped through it.

"We seized twenty boxes of 5 millimeter cannulas, twenty boxes of ten millimeter cannulas, fourteen boxes of 4 millimeter dilators, forty packages of Dilapan-S, sixteen biohazardous waste receptacles, twenty-five boxes of gauze, four hundred and thirty-six bottles of misoprostol, four hundred and thirty-six bottles of mifepristone, two hundred thirty-four boxes of Tylenol packets –"

"I think you can just tell us the names of the items, without the quantities," Harriet said.

"No objection," said Green. I detected relief in the faces of the reporters, who had been scribbling furiously to keep up.

"You have the quantities in the police report?" the judge asked Green.

"Yes, Your Honor."

"That's fine then," the judge said. Wilson went back to reading from his list. Alcohol wipes, syringes, sanitary napkins, adult diapers, infant diapers – I cringed, thinking about what the reporters might make of infant diapers in an abortion clinic. We kept a small stash in case a woman needed to bring a small child with her, but those who wanted to believe the sinister might conjure images of us delivering babies, diapering them and then killing them. Wilson concluded his enormous list of supplies with the ultrasound machine, giving the make and model. I wondered if they had tried to trace its purchase, which would lead them to Toni. It wasn't illegal to buy an ultrasound. They could be used for a lot of things besides pregnancy care. But the person who had bought this particular ultrasound could easily be implicated. Was that why Toni wasn't here?

"Where did you find these items?" Harriet asked. She propped her glasses on top of her head, so her dark brown eyes could peer straight into Sergeant Wilson's medium brown ones. She leaned toward him slightly.

"In a supply room," he said.

"Was the supply room unlocked?"

"No."

"Did you have a key?"

"It had a combination lock."

"The padlock kind that you use for a gym locker? That you can buy at the dime store?"

I smiled at that phrase. It had been decades since anything you could buy there cost a dime, but Richmonders still liked those old-school names for things. No one in California ever talked about dime stores.

"No. The type with an electronic keypad."

"Did you drill through it?"

"No."

"Then you had the code?"

"Yes."

"Who gave you the code?"

For the first time, Wilson did not look cool and confident. He inclined his head slightly, lips slightly parted, and looked at Green.

"Objection, relevance," Green said. I could see he didn't expect that to work, and it didn't.

"Approach, Your Honor?"

Judge Hunter motioned to Harriet and Green to come forward. They huddled for more than five minutes, and then the judge said into the microphone, "Ten minute recess," and the two lawyers followed her through the interior door that I presumed led to her chambers.

I wondered what was going on, but took the opportunity to turn around and face the audience. Josie waved enthusiastically and started to get up.

"Please remain seated," the bailiff ordered. I was afraid if I tried to speak to anyone, they would take me away or clear the courtroom, so I just watched people chat among themselves. I didn't think anything that had happened so far was very good or very bad for us. For *me*, I guessed I should think. There really was no "us" right now, and it was my responsibility to try to keep it that way. Seeing everyone here had lightened my feeling of burden, but that was an illusion. If I had to go down for murder, please let me go down alone, I prayed to the God I didn't believe in.

The swinging doors at the back opened and Toni entered the courtroom. Her face was ashen and she looked like she had been crying. What could have happened? Could she have heard something from or about one of her daughters? I blew her a kiss, and she blew a half-hearted one back. Emily moved over so Toni could sit in the aisle seat next to her.

A moment later, the judge and the lawyers returned.

"They have a confidential informant," Harriet said to me, keeping her voice very low. "Green argued they should get to keep her identity secret, maybe have her speak from another room and disguise her voice. But the judge didn't go for it. She'll be up next."

She asked Wilson a few more questions about the search of the clinic, Kimberly's arrest, and my arrest at the diner.

"No more questions for this witness at this time," she said. Green declined to redirect.

"Call your next witness," the judge said.

"Again, for the record, the People request to shield this witness's identity," Green said.

"For the record, that request is denied," Judge Hunter said. I was warming up to her. She was the right age to have benefitted from the relative freedom of the few post-*Roe* years before the anti-abortion backlash swung into full gear. I suspected she might do us a favor or two, maybe was doing one right now.

"Hillary Cooper," District Attorney Green said, and Hillary walked up the center aisle to the witness chair. Her face was as white as Toni's, and she had obviously been crying too.

CHAPTER THIRTY-THREE

Who Your Friends Are

I didn't feel much when Hillary sat facing me, telling her tale of betrayal. She had once been in love with Toni and Nell, and so had I, so I had thought that made us lover-outlaws or some such Second Wave bullshit. But I'd never felt like I could really trust her, never wanted to open up to her, even when we played tennis and she'd tried to pump me for information. I suppose some thin silver lining in all of this was the confirmation of my instincts. Too bad that hadn't come along in time to do any of us any good.

Any of us. My breath caught in my throat and I started to cough. The room grew silent, waiting for me to stop coughing. Every time I thought I had it under control, it started again. Harriet poured a glass of water from a pitcher at her left elbow, which I hadn't even noticed before. I sipped at it, knowing that drinking much would make the gag reaction worse. Finally it subsided.

If Hillary was a mole, every person in the group was in danger of exposure. Hillary wasn't at any meetings, but she'd been at the dances, she knew Nell was involved, she knew Toni was involved. She'd seen Yvette in the clinic. She could have given names even of people who weren't in the group, like Linda. Yet here I was, the only one charged. Was that because she had half a conscience? Or had she given the police other names but they had, for some reason, only decided to come after me?

"How did you meet Ms. O'Shay?" Green was asking.

"I met her at a party."

Her first lie, first of many. According to her, we had first met at the dance at Our God the Father Methodist Church. Her years with Nell eclipsed.

"When did you next encounter Ms. O'Shay?"

"At a softball game, at Thomas Jefferson High School. She invited me to play tennis." As I recalled, she had made the invitation. But no matter. The only thing that concerned me was why. Why was she lying? Who was she trying to protect or harm? What had I done to incur her enmity? And more to the point, what could I do about it now? A big fat nothing was the obvious answer, but that didn't stop me from obsessing over it.

"When did you first visit Ms. O'Shay at the office at 4628 Grove Avenue?"

She named a date in mid-August. "I went to pick her up to go play tennis, but she wasn't ready. She told me to wait in the clinic while she went upstairs to change."

Another lie. I had distinctly tried to get her out of the clinic.

"And what did you see while you were in the clinic?"

"Bins full of pieces of aborted babies."

What the hell was this? I felt like this totally normal person I'd known had been possessed by an alien or a demon. Maybe I should get a note to Evelyn to go scare up an exorcist from somewhere.

"She's totally lying!" I said to Harriet in a stage whisper. In my days as a rape counselor, I had accompanied numerous survivors to court. I knew the importance of keeping your cool and not allowing yourself outbursts. But then, my clients were never on trial for murder, listening to people invent ghoulish stories about them. No, just listening to people impugn their moral character and say they were asking to be raped, I reminded myself. We all have our moments when we have to rise above.

"It's okay," Harriet whispered, stroking my wrist lightly. "We'll have our shot at her soon."

It wasn't okay. No matter what Harriet said or did to impeach her, it wasn't going to erase the memory of those words. At least there was no jury, but there were media, which was even worse. They would report all this to the future jury.

Hillary finished answering the D.A.'s questions. She insisted that she had not gotten the key code furtively, that I had been proudly showing her around the clinic and had told her the code, which was Jane Tiller in numeric equivalents. Jane, for the Chicago underground, and Tiller for the murdered Kansas abortion doctor. According to her, I had bragged that I was carrying on their legacy. That almost made me wonder if the conversation had actually taken place, because I would have said that, except that I would have said, "We" not "I." And I would not have been bragging.

"When did you decide to help the police frame your friend Mollie?" was Harriet's first question.

Hillary was gratifyingly rattled. "I didn't. I mean – I – it wasn't my idea. They came to me. I mean, they didn't frame her."

"You say that you saw bins full of body parts, is that correct?"

"Yes."

"Can you describe what they looked like?"

"They were big. Big blue barrels, like trash cans, lined with black garbage bags."

"What did the body parts look like?"

"I don't know – they were gross – I didn't look carefully. I was upset."

"Well, if you didn't look carefully, how could you tell they were body parts?" I wished Harriet would stop saying "body parts." Every time she did, I saw those reporters' pens fly, even though they were all recording on their phones anyway. I felt like I should give them each a scorecard, so they could mark every utterance of the phrase. Or maybe they could do jello shots for each one.

Harriet was laying out a series of photographs on the witness stand. I couldn't see what they were. Please, not aborted fetus tissue, I thought. Even though if it were, it would clearly show that Hillary could not have seen what she was claiming. Harriet moved down the line of photos, labeling each with a large black number on a square of white paper.

"Your Honor, please mark these Defense one through twelve," she said.

"Ms. Cooper, I'd like you to look at the pictures. What do you see in this one?"

"Um, a bed."

"And in this one?"

"A chair."

They went on like that. Clearly, these were photos of every room in the clinic, from various angles, closeups and wide-shots.

"In any of these pictures, do you see the blue barrels that you just described?"

"No."

"Can you show us where, in any of these rooms, you saw these barrels? You can just make a little x with this pencil."

Harriet handed Hillary a red pencil, the kind grade school teachers use to mark up student tests. I felt like my life was about to be graded, and I was going to get an F.

When Hillary took the pencil, her hand shook visibly. She hovered it over each picture, glancing at D.A. Green, who was no help. Finally, she made a mark or two, barely even looking at the picture as she did.

Harriet didn't respond, didn't say, "Aha, you just put that mark on a picture of my kitchen," like they would on Law & Order. She just gathered up the pictures and handed them to the judge, then to the D.A., then put them back in her own briefcase. I assumed whatever the exercise had revealed would be addressed later. Probably much later, while I sat rotting in jail. Harriet walked to the judge's bench and they exchanged a few sentences. Then the bailiff left through the back door and returned carrying a red Sharps container.

"Do you know what this is?" Harriet asked Hillary. Hillary shook her head.

"Please answer out loud," Harriet said, her voice even.

"No."

"Let the record reflect that this is a biomedical waste container removed by Richmond police from the office at 4628 Grove Avenue," Harriet said. "Let the record further reflect that no other style or color of waste container was found there."

"So noted," the judge said.

Harriet removed a thick file from her briefcase, set it on the table and flipped through it, adjusting her glasses once to peer at something. Then she closed the file and snapped the briefcase shut with an audible click. Hillary half stood, assuming she was through.

"One more thing," Harriet said. She walked a few steps closer to the witness stand.

"You said the police approached you to testify against Mollie." Mollie, not Ms. O'Shay. Harriet didn't say anything without a plan. Was she humanizing me to the judge and the reporters? Or trying to remind Hillary that I had been her friend?

"That's right." Hillary's answer was barely audible.

"How did they know that you were friends?"

"Greg Patel, a member of my church." Hillary looked around, trying to spot Greg, who was not in the courtroom. He hadn't testified yet, if he was going to. "He saw me with her at the tennis courts. He said she was messing with his daughter."

"Did you believe that?"

"Um – I didn't know what to believe."

Great, thanks. Hillary was the closest thing to a friend of mine the judge would hear from.

"They said if I didn't help them, I could be prosecuted for helping her," she said finally. Green did not look happy.

"And were you helping her?" Harriet managed to make her questions sound totally innocent, like she was just curious.

"No! I didn't know anything about what she was doing. I hardly even know her."

"Nothing further at this time," Harriet said.

Paul Manning was called right after the lunch break, which I spent eating a peanut butter sandwich in a holding cell in the basement of the courthouse. I couldn't help thinking of the dank row of cells as a dungeon.

Manning was a small rooster-like white man, greasy brown hair slicked back and the marks of teenage acne still visible on his middle-aged face. I recognized him as the one who had identified me to the cops in Denny's, though I had no idea how since I'd never set eyes on him before. He settled into the witness chair on an uncomfortable angle, as if resting most of his weight on his right hip. That meant he was always looking at the prosecution table, and I saw his face only in profile.

He testified about the threats I had made on the phone, amplifying what I had actually said almost to the point of incredibility. That, he said, made him wonder what kind of doctor I was. He mentioned it to a friend from church, Greg Patel, who said he had found his daughter at the home of a Dr. Jenkins, and he thought they were doing something sketchy.

Harriet objected to the statement about what Patel thought as hearsay, and the judge sustained the objection.

"How did you learn that your employee, Caitlin Shaw, had had an abortion?" the D.A. asked.

"She told me."

"Objection, hearsay."

"Overruled."

Why was this one overruled? I wondered.

"When she came to work the next day, I asked her how she was feeling. She started crying. I took her in my office, gave her some tea.

She was real upset, and finally she said she'd gone to this doctor because she wasn't feeling good, and the doctor killed her baby."

"Were those her exact words?"

"Objection, hearsay."

"Overruled."

"She said the doctor gave her an abortion." The D.A. didn't ask again if those were Caitlin's exact words. He just stood and looked at Manning, who buttoned and then unbuttoned his ill-fitting brown sports jacket. "She said she had an abortion."

"Your witness," the D.A. said to Harriet.

"Caitlin told you she went to a doctor, who gave her an abortion?" Harriet asked.

"Yes."

"Are you aware that my client, Ms. O'Shay, is not a doctor, but a licensed nurse-midwife?"

"No. Why is that important?"

A good question, from where I sat. It sure didn't seem likely to help my case.

"Did Caitlin ever tell you the name of the person who did her procedure? If, in fact, she had any procedure?"

"No."

"And the person who called you, to encourage you not to retaliate against Caitlin for taking a sick day, said her name was Dr. Jenkins, right?"

"Right."

Point to Harriet. Manning had talked to Dr. Jenkins, not Mollie O'Shay. Even if I worked in the office rented to Dr. Jenkins, and my fingerprints and DNA were on the equipment, that didn't mean I was the person who made that phone call or performed Caitlin's surgery. Only Caitlin could tell. She would be up soon, to do just that.

Just as she had with Hillary, Harriet gathered up her files and turned away from the witness stand, only to turn around and say, "One more question." She was Columbo in heels.

"Are you a rapist?" Did I hear gasps from the audience, or was it just my own sharp intake of breath ringing in my ears?

"Objection, foundation and relevance." The D.A. was very quick on his feet. Did that suggest he wasn't totally taken off guard by the question?

"Withdrawn," Harriet said. "Nothing further."

Clever woman. I had been terrified she was going to repeat what I had told her about Caitlin's disclosure to me and my suspicions. But Harriet had had no intention of doing that, and she didn't need to. She knew Manning would not be allowed to answer the question. Which left it hanging there.

Manning got that too. "No," he shouted as he was excused from the witness stand. "No, I'm not a rapist."

He was much less clever than Harriet.

CHAPTER THIRTY-FOUR

With Prejudice

Caitlin was escorted in by a bailiff. None of the others had been, which made me wonder if she was hesitant about testifying. Maybe I just wanted to think that. As she faced me, I looked for signs of apology in her delicate features. I couldn't keep my lips from forming a small smile. She fingered the ends of her softly curled blonde hair, then flipped it behind her neck. She bent forward and it slipped back.

"State your name for the record."

"Caitlin Shaw."

She gave her address, date of birth, and responded to the D.A.'s questions about her job at Denny's, the age of her son, Jeremy, and the fact that she was unmarried.

An old-fashioned clock with big Arabic numerals hung on the wall behind the witness stand. Its two hands were perfectly aligned on three.

"Counsel, my granddaughter has a piano recital at five o'clock," Judge Hunter said, "and I need to get home and shower first. You have no idea how sweaty it is under these robes." She smiled, and the two lawyers obliged her with faux-sympathetic chuckles.

"We'll recess and continue at nine o'clock tomorrow morning." She turned toward Caitlin. "Miss, I'm sorry, but you will have to come back tomorrow morning. Will that be a problem for you?"

I wasn't sure what she would do if Caitlin said no, but Caitlin met the D.A.'s gaze and then shook her head.

Judge Hunter banged the gavel, and a buzz filled the courtroom as everyone stood and started chattering at once. I turned and searched out Toni, just able to give her a smile and a fist pump before the bailiff caught my arm and cuffed my wrists in front, fastened shackles to my ankles and connected both sets of restraints to a chain around my waist, for the short walk from the defense table to the holding cell. There I waited an hour before being shackled to a string of women, half of them in tears, and half beaming with the news that makeable bail had been set or that their charges were dismissed.

Dinner was a remotely edible facsimile of manicotti, with a side of spinach, canned peaches and an apple crumb cake for dessert. I was reasonably content by the time I was locked into my cell for the night. I pondered Hillary's motivations for a while, then gave up. Was she genuinely religious, trying to get back at Nell through me, or was it really just self-preservation that got her to lie like that? I was madder at myself than at her. I had known I should not allow her to see inside the clinic. I had jeopardized the whole project – maybe ruined it – because I hadn't wanted to be rude to a friend.

My contentment started to wane.

I slept fitfully, haunted by restless dream encounters with Hillary, Toni, Harriet, Nell, Evelyn, Josie and Clarence. At one point they were all yelling "Renata" at me while I punched a tetherball that failed to reach any of them. I woke, sweating, which made me think of Judge Hunter and wonder if the anecdote about her granddaughter's recital had been some signal of sympathy toward me, or if she was just a chatty person.

Unlike Judge Hunter, I couldn't take a shower just because I needed one. We only got them twice a week, and this wasn't one of those days. I couldn't even wash my underwear or jumpsuit, since I had no others to put on. I would just have to be smelly in court.

I tried not to think about that as I was shackled into the van and driven to the courthouse, led into the dungeon and then to the elevator, and finally unchained just outside the courtroom door. I asked the bailiff why they took the shackles off before ushering me into court, but put them back on before taking me out.

"That's the rules," he said.

Today, Sergeant Wilson sat next to D.A. Green at the prosecution table.

Caitlin was reminded that she was still under oath. She looked just as miserable as she had the previous day. I could see faint puffy circles under her eyes and remembered how she'd fallen asleep on the examination table, while I was threatening Paul Manning to get her the time off to have an abortion. An abortion that had brought us to this moment.

She confirmed her name and address for the record. She said she had looked online to find out how to get an abortion, found a number to call and made the appointment by phone. None of that was true. OWLS did not make appointments by phone except to talk in a public place. Their advertisements on social media only said they provided pregnancy options counseling. But Caitlin stuck to her story through D.A. Green's rigorous questioning. Bless her heart.

"So you went to this address on Grove Avenue, and what did you do when you got there?"

"I rang the bell."

"Who answered it?"

"A Black woman." Presumably she meant Yvette, who had been on reception duty that day. So she was telling the truth, except for everything else about how she got to the clinic. I steeled myself for what that would mean.

"What was her name?"

"She never told me."

"Do you see her in the room today?"

Caitlin didn't look at anyone in the room. "No."

"Are you sure?"

"Yes."

"Objection, asked and answered." Harriet on her feet.

"Move on, Mr. Green," said the judge.

"Sorry, Your Honor." I didn't think Green was sorry at all. "Ms. Shaw, what happened next?"

"I went into a room and took off my clothes and put on a paper dress. The doctor came in and told me to lie down on the table and she put something inside my vagina."

Caitlin's voice had sunk to a near whisper, so that the word "vagina" was barely intelligible.

"Ms. Shaw, I need you to speak up," Judge Hunter said. "I know this is hard to talk about in court like this."

"Yes, Your Honor." Caitlin sounded ready to cry.

"Do you know what this doctor put inside you?" D.A. Green asked.

"She said it was something to dilate my cervix faster, so she could suck out the baby," Caitlin said. I sat on my hands to keep from kneading my knuckles, a habit when I'm agitated. I definitely did not like the sound of "sucking out the baby," even though technically that is what I did all day. Though in Caitlin's case I actually scraped out the baby, which would sound worse, so I should be grateful to her.

"Did the doctor tell you her name?" Green asked after a few more details about this baby-sucking process.

"She said it was Dr. Jenkins." Caitlin was looking straight at me. I looked coolly back.

"Do you see Dr. Jenkins in the courtroom today?" Green looked at me, as if Caitlin might not otherwise know who to identify. Or maybe just anticipating her answer.

"No," she said. Once again, her voice was so soft I almost doubted what I'd heard.

"Please speak up," the judge said.

"No," Caitlin repeated.

"No, what?" That was Green.

"No, I don't see her."

"This is not Dr. Jenkins?" Green pointed to me with his right hand, pivoting his body so he was half facing me, half facing the courtroom.

I could see him scanning the people seated, wondering if all along, he had been played, if this illusive Dr. Jenkins might be someone else.

"No." Caitlin lifted her chin and looked straight at Donald Green, not at me. Her blue eyes were wide open, and I detected a little fear in them.

"Your Honor, I move to dismiss the case against my client, Mollie O'Shay," Harriet jumped out of her chair, waving the now-worthless police report.

"Ms. Shaw, you know you are obligated to tell the truth here, right?" Judge Hunter said, leaning over slightly to create a more menacing presence.

"Yes," Caitlin said. "I'm telling the truth. That's not her."

"Mr. Green, how did you determine that Dr. Jenkins and Mollie O'Shay were the same individual, other than through fingerprints and DNA?" the judge asked.

"We showed Ms. Shaw a picture of Ms. O'Shay. She identified her as the person who had performed the abortion procedure."

"May I see that photo?"

Green rummaged through his files. Sergeant Wilson pointed to a page, and Green approached the bench, holding out a full-page color image. Harriet didn't wait for anyone to show it to her, but walked up and looked at the picture as well.

"Ms. Shaw," Judge Hunter said, "have you seen this picture before?"

"I might have," Caitlin responded.

"You might have or you have?"

"I'm not sure – I think I did."

"When I showed you this picture, in Mr. Manning's office at the restaurant where you work, you told me this was the woman who performed your abortion, isn't that right?" said Green. His voice was somewhere between hostile and scared.

"I guess so, but I was wrong."

"You were wrong? You mean you lied?"

"I knew you wanted me to say it was her. I was scared so I told you what you wanted me to say." Caitlin's volume was rising. That wasn't good for Green.

"Why were you scared?" Judge Hunter asked.

"The police told me if I didn't cooperate with them, I could be prosecuted for killing my baby," Caitlin said.

"Is that true?" Judge Hunter asked Green.

"I don't know, Your Honor. I certainly never heard that." The Virginia law only penalized the person who performed an abortion, not the woman seeking it. That meant women who went to an illegal provider were not guilty of a crime, but those who self-aborted could be prosecuted.

Green walked back to his table and whispered with Sergeant Wilson. When Harriet returned to her chair, she didn't smile at me, but she made a high sign behind the table.

"I'm inclined to grant defense motion to dismiss," the judge said.

"The People request leave to refile with new evidence," Green said.

"Your Honor, this is the second witness who has testified that the police threatened her to get her to identify my client," Harriet said. "I submit that the police are carrying out a vendetta against Ms. O'Shay."

"I don't know about a vendetta," Judge Hunter said. "But I'm concerned about the police behavior in this case. I am dismissing these charges with prejudice. If you have another complaint against Ms. O'Shay, you can file a new case."

She rapped her gavel and stood up. Harriet turned to me with her arms out and I fell into them, tears springing to my eyes.

"I can't thank you enough," I said.

"Don't thank *me*," she said. I had no chance, at that moment, to ask her what she meant by that. A bailiff tapped me on the shoulder, handcuffs and shackles at the ready. Just because I was no longer a defendant didn't mean I was no longer a prisoner. I left the courtroom in chains.

CHAPTER THIRTY-FIVE

Inlaws and Outlaws

The jail staff were in no rush to process me out. To most cops, being charged with a crime means you're a criminal, and if you beat the rap, that just proves you're crooked. My case was dismissed at ten am, and it was after seven when I was finally strip-searched one last time and released with an admonition to keep my nose clean from here on out.

Fat chance.

Toni, Evelyn and Clarence were waiting to whisk me off to Sweet Sally's, where Josie, Rabbit and Yvette were already deep in fries and beers. A clean-shaven young man in a pistachio-colored polo shirt sat next to Yvette. He jumped up when he saw us and pecked Evelyn on the cheek, then pulled out a chair for her.

"This is my grandson, Malik," Evelyn said to me. "India's brother."

"Nice to meet you, Malik." I held out my hand, looking way, way up to meet his eyes. He had the natural grace of a basketball player. He sat down next to Clarence and they went through a complicated routine of fist bumps and hand slaps.

I ordered a Veggie Luther Burger I made up on the spot: garden burger, avocado and American cheese – "it's plastic!" I assured the vegan Josie – on a Krispy Kreme donut, with a side of curly fries and a local amber microbrew.

"This is heaven," I said, sipping my beer and munching on a spicy, crisp fry. "I was so sure I would be spending my life picking the baloney off slices of Wonder bread."

"We wouldn't have let that happen," Clarence said. He waited a few seconds. "We would've smuggled in some tofu."

Everyone laughed. I looked around, filled with love for all these people who had put themselves at risk for me, as well as for the women of their city. I studied Evelyn and Yvette, sitting next to one another, chatting. I still wasn't sure what their relationship was. I guessed if I stayed here another couple years, they might trust me enough to let me know, but that didn't seem likely now. There was nothing I could do in this town anymore.

"So how do you all know each other?" I swept my hand across Evelyn, Clarence, Malik and Yvette.

"The Movement," Evelyn said. "Clarence was in Atlanta when I was at Spelman. He helped me organize a teach-in on the role of Black colleges in the movement to end the Vietnam War. Then we met up again organizing a fundraiser for the Museum." I knew Evelyn had been part of the team that finally got the African American History Museum built in Washington. I'd had no idea Clarence was part of that organizing as well. His activities had gotten a lot more respectable since I'd known him in Portland.

"Clarence is the reason you're sitting here with us now," Yvette said. "He and Malik."

"What do you mean?" Toni and I asked simultaneously.

"Jinx," we said, again simultaneously. I figured it was time to stop talking then.

"After court yesterday," Clarence said, "I just happened to hear Caitlin tell the police she needed to get to work. So around dinner time, Malik and I got a craving for some good old Denny's food."

I laughed, trying to imagine what on a Denny's menu one could legitimately crave.

"Ms. Caitlin heard Clarence call me Jeremy," Malik said.

"What? Is Jeremy your... oh." I blushed, realizing how dense I seemed. "Sorry. Ten days in the slammer dulls your brain."

"Naturally, she said that was her son's name, so we started talking about him, and then we got on to some stuff about me and she asked if Clarence was my granddad. I said he was my uncle, but he'd raised me after my mom died. Died trying to give herself an abortion, because she was too far along to get one where she lived. I said I was worried more kids would be without moms, now that they're prosecuting people for helping women who don't want to be pregnant."

"Wow, you should get a Tony," I said. Toni stuck out her hand and squeezed mine.

"Well, I should get a Toni," I said, "but you should get another strawberry lemonade."

I started to hold up my hand for the waiter, but Malik shook his head.

"One's my limit," he said.

"How about a brownie sundae then?" I pleaded. I hate having debts, though I realized I couldn't buy my way out of this one with a diner dessert.

Malik shook his head. "I'm stuffed."

"Rain check," I said and he nodded.

"What about that Hillary?" Clarence deftly changed subjects. "She's a piece of work."

Somber nods went around the table.

"I'm sure she was really scared," I said.

"That's no excuse," Yvette snapped. "We're all scared. There are some things you don't do."

"Well, but she's not an activist," I objected. "We all knew the risks we were taking."

"Why are you standing up for her?" Josie demanded. "You could have gone to prison for the rest of your life, you know that, right? I mean, really."

"I do know that," I said. Why *was* I defending the villainess? Was it just my usual perversity, or did taking all the blame make me feel more in control? "But she did try to limit the harm. At least she didn't implicate any of you."

"True," said Rabbit. Josie glared at them; no quarter for traitors.

Next to me, I felt Toni tense. When I looked at her, she was looking down at the remains of her tuna melt, but I saw a telltale twitch in her lips.

"What?" I asked her.

"She threatened to give other names," Toni replied.

"When?" I asked, but then realized I knew the answer. "Were you talking to her in the hall, just before she testified? You knew what she was going to do?" I wasn't sure why that infuriated me. If Toni could have stopped Hillary, she would have.

"I saw her with the police. I didn't know until then," Toni said. "I asked her what was going on and she said they were making her testify. I argued with her, but it only made her double down. She said unless I helped her get Nell back, she'd rat on all of us."

"Bitch!" Josie practically shrieked. I couldn't help half-laughing. Josie, the radical gender scholar, could have given a ten-minute exegesis on why that patriarchal slur should be retired. "Sorry," she said, obviously following my thoughts.

"I don't think you're the one who should apologize," I said. "What do we do about her, though?"

"She better be on her way out of town right now," Yvette said and Evelyn nodded. No doubt, someone had delivered that message in the hours between court and this moment. I kind of forgot that the world had not stood still for a day. I wondered who had done the deed, and how they had made it clear it wasn't a request.

"Where will she go?" I wondered aloud. "She's lived her whole life here. They're not going to put her in witness protection with no case pending."

"Not our problem," Evelyn said. "She should've thought of that before she got up on that stand."

I could tell no one wanted to hear any more defenses so I let it go. But for some reason, I couldn't feel anger at Hillary. I had friends who were sure they would always be able to resist intimidation and even torture. I had never been that confident. I tended to think none of us knew what compromises we would make until we were asked to give up something important to us.

I insisted on paying the check for everyone, and then we split up into our various cars. I couldn't wait to get to Toni's house, take a hot shower and then curl up next to her for a week.

We didn't get a week, but we did have a lovely weekend. The leaves were just starting to turn, each wide city boulevard a riotous corridor of flame. On Sunday we drove out of the late October heat into the Shenandoah Valley, where the colors were so bright they almost hurt my eyes. We hiked to Jones River Falls, an easy two-hour walk at a leisurely pace, picnicking on deviled eggs and goat cheese puffs with a half-bottle of Merlot to give us a pleasant buzz as we made our way back up the mountainside.

"I don't get what happened to the federal case," I said, as we strolled hand-in-hand on the wide trail. "How did my prints and DNA come back no match?"

Instinctively, I looked around, to be sure no FBI agents were lurking behind us, masquerading as bird watchers. We were deep enough into the woods, I saw no one.

"Emily," Toni said. "She made the security software they're using, remember? She hacked into their system through a back door and changed Renata's DNA profile and fingerprint records."

"Wow." I mused on that for a few minutes, looking down at a lizard slinking its way across the trail. It vanished into the thick carpet of soft, dry leaves.

"Why did they think I – Renata, that is – was still alive?" I asked. It was weird, how I didn't really think of myself as Renata now, after fifty years as Mollie. It was like I had frozen Renata at twenty-one and lived

Mollie's life instead from then on. I didn't like thinking about what Mollie could have done, been, if she had lived. I swiped at my eyes and looked back up at Toni.

"Clarence said you visited him in San Francisco jail," she said.

"I did, yeah. Oh!" It had never occurred to me, when I was going to the jail every week, presenting my driver's license and signing in on the register, that anyone might be looking at those logs besides the bored sheriffs who ran the chaotic visiting hours. And even if I had, I wouldn't have thought I was in any danger. After *Roe*, charges against abortion providers had been dropped all over the country. I assumed no one would have any interest in pursuing mine, especially since they thought I was dead. But Mollie's name would have still been in the case file, and facial recognition software was all the rage these days.

Hopefully Emily's hack meant I was out of danger now, but how could I be sure?

By the time we got back to Richmond in twilight, the jail felt far behind me; but as we parked at Toni's house, I felt a little clutch in my stomach, reminding me this was not quite the safe little community that met the eye.

Toni had no classes on Monday, and apparently wasn't working any security gigs these days. Or was she? I wondered if she'd been instructed, by Steve, or Evelyn, or whoever, to stay close to me. I didn't want to ask. We hung around the house, reading, and worked in her garden in the late afternoon. Just before six, she took her keys and said she'd be back in a couple hours.

"There's some leftover pasta if you're hungry," was all she offered.

"Hot date?" I tried to keep my voice light. It wasn't her Mah Jongg night – that was Thursday – and she wasn't playing racquetball with Lee because she wasn't taking any gear with her. She had a perfect right to have dates with her friends, and it wasn't her fault that my only friend outside of OWLS turned out to be a weasel. Still, I wished she would have told me she was going out, so I could have made plans with Yvette or someone. Clarence had headed back to Ginger and his responsibilities in Hartford. Maybe I could call Kimberly, who hadn't had time to make many friends.

"It's kind of a meeting," Toni said and made her exit before I could ask any more questions. I stood at the window, forlornly watching her back her car out of the driveway. My mind flashed back to another time when I had watched her get into her car, the first day she worked at the clinic. That had been a Monday too, I realized, and she had scooted out the door right around the same time.

Miraculously, my car had not been towed from the Denny's parking lot after I was arrested. Toni and Yvette had retrieved it, and I could see it now, parked at the curb in front of the house. The lure was too great. I tried to talk myself out of it, but my worst demons were in charge.

Remember what happened the last time, I told myself, thinking of the sideswipe and the encounter with Josh Good who turned out to be the enigmatic Steve. I still wasn't positive that was a random accident. No matter, my car keys were in my hand and Google Maps told me I would be at Olive Garden in fifteen minutes.

The lot was nearly full, as it had been the other time I had been there. I spied Toni's Mini Cooper and parked a discrete distance away. Brazenly, telling myself I was a total idiot, I walked in and scanned the front room, then barged past the hostess and made my way to the back room. The balding man was feeding bites of breadstick to the baby, who had graduated from a highchair to a booster seat. Toni's long pianist's hands were deftly folding a cloth napkin, while the little girl's curly blonde head was bent over her own napkin, trying to copy Toni's motions. From the doorway, I watched the little girl get frustrated and ball her napkin up. Toni took the cloth, smoothed it out and put it back in front of the child. Then she unfolded her own napkin and started again; one fold – see? – and waited until the little girl made the same fold, then they moved on to the next. After five minutes, they both tied the two flaps in a knot, flared out the sides, and set two perfect swans beak to beak in front of the man.

"Papa, look!" the child said, and the man looked at her and beamed. The little girl unfolded her napkin and began folding it again, following the creases from before. When Toni started to pick up her own, the child slapped her hand away.

"I want to do it by myself!" she said loudly.

The waitress appeared and they placed their orders. It all looked quite ordinary and innocent. I should just turn around and go back to the parking lot, get in my car and go home. Instead, I walked over to the table.

"Hi," I said at Toni's elbow.

Confusion, and then something between annoyance and anger filled her eyes. I recognized the set of her chin as something you didn't want to see.

"Mollie," she said evenly. "This is my son-in-law, Daryl. This one here is Ella," setting a light hand on her granddaughter's head, "and that's her brother, Leo."

"Nice to meet you, Daryl," I said. I could feel the heat in my face. "That's a great swan, Ella." She had finished folding it and set it on the edge of the table, facing me.

"Grandma taught me how to do it," Ella said.

"Grandma is very smart," I said. "I didn't mean to interrupt your dinner. Just wanted to say hi."

"Hi," Ella said obligingly.

"Bye," I said. I prayed for a trap door in the floor to swallow me up, but none did, so I had to walk back through the crowded front dining room past the harried hostess and out to the parking lot, like Orpheus afraid to look behind me.

CHAPTER THIRTY-SIX

Mobile Home

It was after nine when I heard Toni's key in the lock. I was on my third episode of the British crime series, *Scott & Bailey*; a new season had recently become available for streaming. I switched off the TV and listened as her soft footfalls made their way to the den, where I curled into a ball in the corner of the couch, as if I could will myself small enough to disappear.

She stood in the doorway, purse slung over her shoulder, keys still in her right hand, as if she might take off again if she didn't like my answers.

"I can explain." That sounded pathetic, even to me. What could I explain: that I wanted to be sure she wasn't feeding information about me to the FBI or the police?

"How did you know where to find me?" she asked. Her voice, to my ears, sounded a lower pitch than usual, one step above a growl.

"Remember the first day you worked in the clinic?" I said.

She nodded, and moved slightly into the room, perching on the arm of the loveseat nearest the door. Maybe she would work her way toward me based on my answers, a high-stakes game of Twenty Questions.

"You were acting totally weird," I said. "You told me you'd switched shifts with Josie because she had to work, but she said she was sick. Then you put the moves on me, and I could tell you were packing heat."

Where on earth had I picked up the phrase "packing heat"? I sounded like I was in one of the trashy mysteries I liked to read.

"I was sweeping the clinic for bugs and cameras," she said. "You came downstairs and surprised me. I said the first thing that came into my mind."

"So you said you were hot for me?" This was worse than I had imagined. "Were you ever really interested in me?"

"Mollie! Don't go there!" I stared at her. She was mad at me? When she had just confessed that the basis of our whole relationship was because she couldn't think of a better lie?

She crossed the room, but still couldn't bring herself to touch me. She sat on the other end of the sofa opposite the corner I was trying to shrink even further into.

"That's not what I meant," she said. "We'd already been together, remember? Saturday night, Sunday?"

"True, but …."

"But nothing. If I didn't want to have sex with you, believe me, I would have found another way to hang around."

"I guess." I studied her wide-set eyes, strong cheekbones and tapered jaw, looking for signs of truthfulness or deceit. I didn't have a good track record of being able to tell who was trustworthy. A physiognomist, I wasn't.

"You said you had to leave, but then you got in your car and didn't leave right away," I said. "And you were snooping around my trash."

"That was part of my job. Steve told me to make sure you weren't leaving anything incriminating around," she said.

"Well I didn't know what you were doing, and it seemed fishy, so when you left, I followed you. You went to Olive Garden and I saw you give someone – Daryl, as it turns out – an envelope, and then walk away. I didn't know who he was. I thought maybe you were spying on me, which you were."

"I wasn't spying on you, I was protecting you. And Emily didn't want you to know. She just wanted us to make sure you were okay until she could get in and fix the records."

"What about Daryl?" I asked. "You told me you weren't in touch with either of your daughters."

"I'm not." Her face went slack, her left eyelid quivered. "Caroline moved back here to do her residency at MCV. She never told me. I found out from an old friend, whose daughter went to high school with her. I read in the paper that she set up a primary care clinic there, serving low-income and homeless folks."

I thought back to the night Carmen ODed, how Toni had refused to come to MCV with me to look for her. She'd waited in the car as I tore around the hospital.

"Eventually, I got in touch with Daryl, and he agreed to let me see the kids," she continued. "He didn't even know I still lived here. On Monday nights when Caroline has clinic hours, he takes the kids to Olive Garden, and I meet them for dinner. I give him some money for them so they can have something extra – Ella's started to take piano lessons. I don't know what he tells Caroline about where he gets the money, but that's between them."

"What about the kids?" I thought out loud. "Ella's too young to keep a secret like that for long."

"That's why we have to go to Olive Garden. They go there with their other grandma."

That won't work forever, I thought. I was surprised it had worked at all. Maybe Caroline knew and was pretending she didn't.

"But that night, you didn't stay. How come?"

"There were a few times the clinic was closed and he said she was coming to join them, so I could only stay for a few minutes. That must have been one of those nights." I recalled the red-haired woman who left with him. I'd seen Toni's daughter. I wondered if she had.

"Do you ever spy on her?" I couldn't help asking.

I felt her stiffen, then relax. She moved a hair closer to me on the couch. At this rate, we would be touching in forty-eight hours.

"At first, I found opportunities to see her when she wouldn't notice me. I went to an event where she was getting an award, sat in the back. But it just made me feel worse, so I stopped."

Her face was taut, but I could tell she wanted to cry.

"Come here," I said finally. I sat lengthwise, my back against the sofa arm, stretched out my legs, and she nestled against my tummy. I put my arms around her chest and felt it heave as she sobbed. It wasn't a comfortable position, but I was afraid to budge, lest she get up and never come back into my arms.

"I'm sorry," I whispered into her hair. Her wracking sobs abated into occasional tremors and then stillness.

The OWLS met the next night, at the safe house. It had not been compromised, as far as we knew, and they were still meeting clients there for counseling and help finding the services they needed. They had even taken over dispensing abortion medications; a new shipment had just come in from New York to replace what had been confiscated.

"There's no way we can get the prescription meds back," Evelyn reported, "but Harriet's working on seeing if we can get the ultrasound and everything else released, since there's no open case."

"Not holding my breath on that," Josie said with an eyeroll.

"Don't sell Harriet short," I said. "If she said she could get us a plane, I'd sign up for flying lessons." Evelyn gave me a little smile.

"It doesn't make sense to open a new clinic," Shawn said. "How long will it be until someone turns us in again? We should concentrate on getting meds, and helping women who are too late for that get to states where abortion's legal."

"I don't agree," Josie said, her volume climbing. "Every experiment needs refinement. We can learn from our mistakes, put better security measures in place."

"Don't have a practitioner who's an idiot," I said. If I said it, no one else would.

"Don't say that," Maureen said. She swept her kind, nunly eyes over my face. "Anyone could have made the same mistakes. No one blames you."

I wasn't sure about that, but I loved her for making the effort. Some of the others were bobbing their heads. I took note of who wasn't.

"Don't play tennis with a police informer," Rabbit said, and everyone laughed.

"I'll second that motion," Josie said.

"The ayes have it," Evelyn drawled. I could tell she was impatient to move on, but willing to let me have a Mollie Mollification Moment.

"I think we can continue," Yvette surprised me by saying. I would have bet she and Evelyn would be for cutting their losses. "We already found a space in Jackson Ward."

"Jackson Ward?" I couldn't tell if that was skepticism or fear in Shawn's voice. Maybe a combination of both. "There's more cops there than you can throw a stick at."

I wanted to suggest that throwing sticks at cops was not a good way to stay under the radar, but I ordered myself to keep quiet.

"Yes, but no one talks to them," Yvette said.

"And the white church people will be afraid to go there," Evelyn added.

Jackson Ward was a rapidly gentrifying but still majority Black neighborhood in the East End of the city.

"Are we keeping this space?" Rabbit asked. "It would be pretty far to drive back and forth."

I wanted to laugh at that idea of far. In normal traffic, you could drive from where we sat, on the edge of the Fan, to deep inside Jackson Ward in fifteen minutes. From here to the old clinic took ten. The bigger distance was psychological.

"We could," Evelyn said. "But I think we should get a new safe house, something in Church Hill. White and Black women would feel comfortable going there, and we don't know for sure Caitlin didn't give the cops this address."

"We have a lease for this place," Josie said. "But it comes up in March. I'll talk to the landlord, see if he'd let us out a few months early if we could find someone to take it over."

"Kimberly, what are you thinking?" Evelyn turned to Kim, who'd been sitting silently across from me. "We'd certainly understand if you don't want to hang around here. You didn't get a very good welcome."

"Well, I don't hold you all responsible for that," Kim said. "I'm in if you want to keep the clinic going."

"You sure?" I said. "We don't know you're not being surveilled."

"I'll keep an eye on her," Yvette said. "Watch for anyone suspicious."

"Get a new phone," I said. "That's how they found me."

"What do you mean?" Yvette asked.

"That's how the police found me, right? By tracking my phone?"

"No." Yvette shook her head vigorously. "Paul Manning recognized you from Greg Patel's photo and called them." She must have been able to *see* me wondering how she knew that, adding, "It was in the police report." How had Yvette seen the police report and I hadn't? Harriet, presumably, had enlisted her to help plot my defense. I couldn't hold it against her. I was otherwise occupied at the time.

"Well, I didn't know that. But Steve found me at the bus station because of my phone."

"No, he didn't." Yvette was a Wikipedia of information. "He saw a guy in the park wearing a choir robe and asked him if he'd seen you. The guy told him you asked for directions to the bus station."

"Moving on," Evelyn said, "we need to raise a ton of money. The new clinic is more expensive than the old one, and we need a new ultrasound. And obviously, some better security measures."

I wasn't sure there were security measures they could buy that would prevent what had happened. To me, it all seemed like human error, but

I wasn't going to call attention to that fact, since all the errors were mine.

"I'm wiped out," I whispered to Josie, and slipped out the back door. There was no point helping to plan fundraisers I wouldn't be here for.

Toni was watching a British mystery series when I got back. I settled onto the couch next to her, entwining my legs with hers on the ottoman. Soon our lips and hands got involved, and I never found out who killed the Bosnian prostitute by feeding her poisonous herbs. I was past the days when I could manage couch sex. We made our way to the bedroom, and after hours of pleasure fell into sated sleep.

The next day, she helped me reclaim my meager possessions from Kimberly's apartment and pack them into the Volvo.

"I wish you were staying" she said.

"I wish you were coming," I said.

"I can't right now. I have to keep seeing the kids."

"I know."

"I asked Daryl to talk to Caroline about meeting with me. He said he'd think about it."

"That's good," I said, reaching up. We held each other for a long time, our lips melding.

"Come visit soon," I said. "Devora and the others built a whole little cottage for me on her ranch. It's even got a hot tub."

I climbed into the car and plugged my phone into the radio. As the engine came to life, I queued up the playlist Devora had sent me for the road. Avril Lavigne's Mobile – everything's changing. Dylan's Stuck Inside of Mobile. Blind Boys of Alabama. 39 Miles from Mobile. Johnny Cash singing about Mobile Bay. Magnolia blossoms, cool summer nights, warm rollin' seas.

By the time I hit Mobile, I'd know the words to all of them.

Acknowledgments

Creating a book truly takes a village. I'm so grateful for mine!

Steve Masover of Salted Rose Press has been a stalwart friend and confidant throughout the agonizing process of producing and publishing this book. Your thoroughness and command of the complexities of publishing never cease to astonish. Mikaela Barad, thank you for a masterful proofread on a tight timeline.

Susan Greene, artist extraordinaire, bless you for stepping up to produce amazing cover art. You define solidarity.

Thanks to everyone who read drafts in whole or in part, for your loving and perceptive feedback: Alicia Smith, Amanda Bloom, Blue Murov, Barbara Ridley, Cameron Cowan, Elana Levy, Fern Feldman, Ingrid Rojas-Contreras and the other participants in her workshop at the awesome Mendocino Coast Writers' Conference, Jean Tepperman, Joan Annsfire, Jody Sokolower, Julie Starobin, Linda Hatton, Marjorie Larney, Matt Duffy, Paula Zaby, Phillippe Diderich and Sasha Wright.

Thanks to Tory Becker for inspiring me to dream up new career paths for retired nurse practitioners, Gretchen Virkler for supplying a critical tidbit of nursing wisdom, and Vern Nuanez, who probably doesn't remember coming up with the emotional support goose.

The very very best thing about being an "author" is being welcomed into a circle of brilliant and generous writers. I will forever cherish the relationships I've been privileged to develop with, among many, Allison Green, Aya de Leon, Barbara Ridley, Benjamin Heim Shepard, Carolina de Robertis, Carla Schick, Celine Keating, Charlotte Allen, Elaine Beale, Elana Dykewomon, Ellen Meeropol, Fida Jiryis, James Tracy, Jennifer Dwight, Jimin Han, Laura Petracek, Leslie Batson, Lisa Weil, Lucy Jane Bledsoe, Max Elbaum, MB Austin, Moazzam Sheikh, Nancy Au, Nina Serrano, Radhika Sainath, Renate Stendahl, Sarah

Lazare, Sasha Wright, Starhawk, and Yang Huang. You've all inspired and improved me in more ways than you know. I'm also extremely grateful to be part of the sisterhood of She Writes Press (Brooke Warner, you are a national treasure) and the Goddard MFAW community.

Thanks to Chris Baty for inventing National Novel Writing Month (NaNoWriMo), an incredible tool for cranking out a BFD (bad first draft). This book would not exist without you.

To all the abortion providers, clinic defenders, self-help educators, herbal wisdom purveyors, abortion fund donors, shouters, resisters, freedom fighters, current and former political prisoners, civil rights campaigners, movement lawyers, loud out queers and truly radical feminists in my life, every one of you is a gift to the world.

Adelante.

Call to Action

This book is fiction, but the threat to our freedom is not.

Abortion rights are all our rights, whether or not we have uteri, are of childbearing age, or have to worry about unplanned pregnancies. And despite all the ground we have lost over the last fifty years, we still have many rights to protect and many more to win. We can do it, and we must do it.

For more info and to get involved:

National Network of Abortion Funds, https://abortionfunds.org/, The National Network of Abortion Funds builds power with members to remove financial and logistical barriers to abortion access by centering people who have abortions and organizing at the intersections of racial, economic, and reproductive justice.

Abortion AF, https://www.aafront.org/, We are a coven of hilarious badass feminists who use humor and pop culture to expose the haters fighting against reproductive rights.

Sistersong, https://www.sistersong.net/, SisterSong's mission is to strengthen and amplify the collective voices of indigenous women and women of color to achieve reproductive justice by eradicating reproductive oppression and securing human rights.

Handbook for a Post-Roe America, by Robin Marty, https://postroehandbook.com/. What you need to do before and after Roe v Wade is overturned, including information on how to manage your own abortion if you need to.

ABOUT THE AUTHOR

Photo: Ingrid Martin

Kate Jessica Raphael is a Seattle-based writer, activist and radio producer. She is the author of the IPPY award-winning *Murder Under the Bridge: A Palestine Mystery* and its sequel, *Murder Under the Fig Tree*, a Foreword INDIES Book of the Year and Lambda Literary Award finalist. Her writing has appeared in Sinister Wisdom, Reclaiming Quarterly and Truthout. Kate received a 2011 Hedgebrook residency. She is a former board member and volunteer of ACCESS Women's Health Justice and San Francisco Women Against Rape.

Connect with her at www.kateraphael.com or https://www.facebook.com/kate.j.raphael.